Dead Man Running

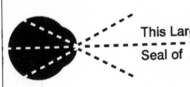

This Large Print Book carries the
Seal of Approval of N.A.V.H.

Dead Man Running

Rett MacPherson

Thorndike Press • Waterville, Maine

Published in 2006 by arrangement with St. Martin's Press, LLC Inc.

Thorndike Press® Large Print Mystery.

The tree indicium is a trademark of Thorndike Press.

L P
MacPherson

The text of this Large Print edition is unabridged.
Other aspects of the book may vary from the original edition.

Set in 16 pt. Plantin.

Printed in the United States on permanent paper.

Library of Congress Cataloging-in-Publication Data

MacPherson, Rett.
    Dead man running / by Rett Macpherson.
        p. cm. — (Thorndike Press large print mystery)
    ISBN 0-7862-8763-2 (lg. print : hc : alk. paper)
    1. O'Shea, Torie (Fictitious character) — Fiction.
2. Mayors — Election — Fiction. 3. Women genealogists
— Fiction. 4. Organized crime — Fiction. 5. Missouri —
Fiction. I. Title. II. Series: Thorndike Press large print
mystery series.
PS3563.A3257D43 2006b
  813'.54—dc22   2006012303

FOR MY COUSIN, SUZIE,
without whom life will never quite be the
same. Peace.

AND FOR KELLEY RAGLAND AND
MERRILEE HEIFETZ,
two classy ladies

Acknowledgments

The author wishes to acknowledge the following people for helping bring this book to light. Thank you to my editor in chief, Kelley Ragland, and her assistant, Ryan Quinn, for all of their hard work, especially so on this book. And the copy editors for putting in a nice finishing touch (and figuring out my time-line issues). My agent, Merrilee Heifetz, for her unwavering support.

I'd also like to thank all of those kick-butt women I know, who have held me up under some pretty tough times. My nickname among a certain group of friends is Spunk, because of my talent for "bouncing back," but I don't think they realize just how impossible it would be to bounce back and stay afloat without them: Laurell K. Hamilton (my fairy godmother), Darla Cook (my guardian angel), Sharon Shinn, Debbie Millitello, Martha Kneib, Jean Erickson, and

Regina Hensley. What a great group of strong-willed women. You all make it look easy.

The guys in my writers' group, as well, Mark Sumner and Tom Drennan.

As usual, to my husband, who is close to sainthood by now. And my kids.

Oh, and special thank you to Darla for all of the work on the Web site! Visit me at www.RettMacpherson.com.

One

I have come to the conclusion that boys are different from girls. Case in point: My son never stops moving. He's almost three, and I don't think he's stopped moving since last March, not even in his sleep. He has a lot more spit than my daughters ever had. Everything comes with sound effects, even if it's just milk being poured into a glass. With Matthew, nothing is ever what it is. A ball isn't a ball. It's a spaceship ball flying through space at a zillion miles an hour. A dog isn't a dog. It's a secret agent dog. Not that he can comprehend exactly what a secret agent is, but he and our wiener dog, Fritz, have their own secret code that only they can speak. He's constantly telling me what Fritz is thinking. The worst part is, I'm beginning to think he really does understand what Fritz is thinking.

Then there was that lovely week when

after having seen *Finding Nemo* my son spoke nothing but whale. Every single sentence was in whale. By the end of the week I was getting pretty good at deciphering whale, although I'm not sure which dialect it was — but that's beside the point. There's a reason people say things like "boys will be boys." I never knew that ball bearings and a stick shift could make that much difference in the sexes.

My husband, Rudy, is a perfect example of a male. When he's driving down the road he isn't thinking of what bills to pay or what to have for dinner or . . . or where pomegranates actually come from. No, he's thinking of . . . nothing, and he thinks of nothing like nobody else I've ever seen. I mean he's really good at thinking of nothing. Men do that so much better than women. If I'm looking at the Mississippi River, I'm thinking of how pretty it is or how polluted it is or *Gee, I wonder just how many gallons of water are in that sucker?* Not Rudy. No, he's looking out there going, *River. Water. Mmmm.*

My father, another male. He insists on wearing white gym socks with dress pants, because nylon socks, especially colored ones, are for sissies. And only a man would go off into the woods and fish without any sunblock or bug spray, no cell phone, no

10

weapons, nothing. Just worms and a pole. He'll suck the poison right out of snakebite — I've seen him do it, twice. I stopped camping with him, by the way, after the second time. Yuck! But that same man squeals like a baby if he has to get a shot and freaks out when food is left in a can. My father firmly believes he will drop dead of botulism if he eats anything that has sat in an open can for more than ten minutes.

Last but not least, my stepfather. The sheriff, Colin Woodrow Brooke. He's not happy with being sheriff. No, he has to be mayor. So the whole town of New Kassel, Missouri, is plastered with his big ol' signs that read BROOKE IS BETTER. In response, the current mayor, Castlereagh, put up bigger signs that read NEW KASSEL IS IN GOOD HANDS WITH KASSELREAGH! At which time my esteemed stepfather put up even bigger signs that read BROOKE FOR MAYOR. AT LEAST HE CAN SPELL. The signs just keep getting bigger and bigger, because, you know, it's that whole bigger, faster, farther thing with men. The only thing left is a billboard.

Now my wonderful, cozy tourist town of New Kassel looks as if a carnival has taken up permanent residence. If I, Torie O'Shea, were running for mayor, I would do it with a bit more aplomb. Just the fact that I can use

11

the word "aplomb" shows that I would be better at the job than either one of them. If I ran against my stepfather and lost, though, there'd be no living with him, and if I ran against him and won, there'd be no living with my mother. Since I firmly believe I would win, I'm not running. My mother's wrath is far worse than my stepfather's.

So, on a glorious Tuesday afternoon in autumn, this is what I was thinking about in my office at the Gaheimer House on River Pointe Road. I was sitting there, pulling my hair out, strand by strand, clicking my ballpoint pen nervously, wondering just what it would be like to have New Kassel testosterone free for one week, and hoping like hell that none of the men in the town were smart enough to think "billboard" next.

Having said all of that, with the exception of my stepfather, I couldn't live without any of the men in my life. Even if it means dealing with spit, secret agent dogs, whale speak, empty minds, white gym socks, and botulism. It was just bugging me today for some reason. Maybe that's because I felt totally helpless to do anything about the complete insanity that had taken over my town.

I should probably think about the other things at hand. My daughter Rachel's marching band season, my daughter Mary's volleyball season, the Octoberfest coming up, which I am managing, and the possibility that my son might need counseling if he didn't start speaking English as well as he could speak whale.

"Earth to Torie," somebody said from the doorway. I looked up to see Helen Wickland, one of my good friends and the owner of the Lick-a-Pot Candy Shoppe, which was across the road. She's usually good stress relief and almost always comes bearing things good for the soul, like chocolate. She's known throughout the county for her fudge, but it's those chocolate-covered cherries that I can't stop thinking about. I find myself daydreaming about them. At any rate, she's also the vice president of the historical society, of which I am the president. It's nice when your vice president is a chocolatier. I couldn't have planned that better if I had to.

"Sorry, Helen," I said. "What's up?"

Helen is almost fifty. I know this because she's ten years or so older than me, with a generous dash of gray in her hair, and I'm almost forty. I don't have a dash of gray in my hair — I look as if somebody tripped and spilled the whole damn salt shaker on my head. If it weren't for Clairol, I would have looked like the Bride of Frankenstein years ago. The other day, Mary got a good look at my gray hair, because it's in bad need of coloring. She screeched and said, "Mother, you're dying! All the color has faded from your hair." It took me three days to convince her that just being gray did not mean that I would kick the bucket any time soon. She still looks at me with big puppy-dog eyes, as if she's expecting me to expire at her feet.

Kids are supposed to keep you humble. If Mary continues at this rate, I'll be more humble than Gandhi.

"I've been calling your name for like ten minutes," Helen said. "What is going on in that head of yours?"

"Oh, come on. Don't you want to guess?" I asked.

"The mayor's race?"

I nodded my head.

"It'll be over soon," she said in a comforting way.

"Good, because I think I may be bald if it goes on much longer," I said. I wouldn't need to worry about having anything to color.

"Well, I just came by on business," she said. She handed me a white bag, and I knew what was inside. I peeked: chocolate-covered cherries. I nearly kissed her right then and there. "The bands are a go."

That's the great thing about a small town.

People actually come by, rather than using the phone. It's quicker and easier for Helen to run across the street and tell me something than to pick up the phone, dial, and wait for me to answer. "The only thing I'm having trouble with is getting Bill to sign off on the parade," she added.

Bill Castlereagh. The current mayor. The man who hates me the most. The man who will be the A-number-one suspect in my murder, if it ever happens. I find it important to know who your enemies are, just in case you ever turn up mysteriously dead. "Why won't he sign off on it?" I asked, and sank my teeth into chocolaty, gooey, creamy, fruity goodness.

"Says it will cause discord in the town," she said. "You know, he's just a stick-in-the-mud. He can't stand change of any kind. We've never had a parade for the Octoberfest, well, actually for anything, so of course, he's going to fight it. It must be painful to be that . . ."

"Big of an ass?" I said.

"Unbendable," she said.

"Oh, of course," I said. "That's what I meant to say."

"And his wife doesn't want us to release balloons. She says they do something bad to the ozone."

"I'm surprised Mrs. Castlereagh even knows what the ozone is."

Helen laughed and took one of the chocolate-covered cherries and plopped it into her mouth. "My," she said in between chews. "You're feeling . . ."

"Irritated."

"That's a good adjective, too. That would have been my second choice."

"Sorry," I said. "It's just that, well, Rudy and I started building on the new house a few weeks ago, and . . ."

"And? I thought you were excited about building a new house." She licked her fingers, one by one. Can I just say that I find it extremely unfair that Helen owns a candy shop, she's a chocolatier, and she's not the least bit overweight? All I have to do is work across the street from her shop and I gain ten pounds from the fumes.

"I am," I said. "And you know I've always wanted some acreage. For the chickens. Maybe get a horse or two. It's just that I won't be *in* town any more."

"No offense, Torie, but we'll survive with you living a mile and a half outside of town," she said.

"It's almost two miles," I said. "I know New Kassel will survive, but I might not. And talk about stressful. Do you know how

16

many questions I have to answer every day? Like, how many plug-ins do I want in the master bedroom? How the heck should I know? I just assumed there was a standard number of plug-ins."

She laughed.

"Plus, the sheriff and the mayor are driving me insane. Rachel has a boyfriend. I'm drowning in testosterone, and I need to color my hair."

"Rachel has a boyfriend?"

I nodded. Rachel is my oldest child. I'm not sure why people have children if they're not prepared for them to become grown-ups, but, boy, was it hard to get through this midteen thing.

"She's dating a trumpet player," I said.

"You say that as if a trumpet player is the worst thing in the world," she said and laughed. She eyed the bag of chocolate-covered cherries. If she ate another one, I would chop her hand off.

"In marching bands, it is a well-known fact that the trumpet players are the playboys."

"Really? I thought it was the drummers."

"Well, in New Kassel it's the trumpet players. Remember Tommy Whitmore?"

"A little after my time, but yes . . . I remember him," she said. "I think he was personally responsible for eight virgins biting the dust."

"He was like a plague in our town," I said. "Whitmore was a trumpet player."

"Oh," she said. "I'm sure everything will be fine. I'm sure Rachel's boyfriend is nothing like his predecessors."

I rolled my eyes, grateful for her vote of confidence but not believing it for one minute. "Well, I'll talk to Bill about the parade," I said.

"You think that's a wise thing to do? The mayor hates you."

"I realize that I am his least favorite person in this town — well, probably period," I said. "But maybe I could appeal to his more sensible nature."

"He has a sensible nature? Huh," she said, and smacked her lips. She was eyeing my chocolate. "Guess I missed it."

"Yeah. I'll use the mayor's race against him."

"Blackmail."

"Of course," I said.

"Are you gonna eat that last cherry?" she asked.

"I'll kill you if you touch that bag."

I walked down River Pointe Road, which is the main road in town, to city hall and the mayor's office. New Kassel is a tiny town in the shape of a square, made up of about ten streets crossing each other. Of course, there are farms and outlying subdivisions that are considered part of New Kassel, so the town actually covers several square miles, but "downtown" New Kassel is completely accessible by foot, which I love. The mayor's office is the ugliest building on River Pointe Road. Of course, I could be biased. It might be because I know the mayor is in the building that I think it's so ugly. It could also be because it's the color of vomit, perfectly rectangular, with a flat roof. It looks like a giant brown brick. The fact that it stands next to the Murdoch Inn doesn't help matters, since the Murdoch — as it's known by the locals — is a gorgeous white Victorian building with porches and turrets and shutters.

Rose Gunther is the mayor's secretary. In fact, she's been the secretary for every mayor since 1954. I think she's over seventy, but probably not by much. As I entered the office, her face blanched. Usually I only enter the mayor's office when I've come to yell at him over something. Well, maybe not always, but regardless of my intentions, yelling and cursing usually happen before I leave the building. Sometimes it's him yelling at me. I'm not always the troublemaker. He would never publicly admit that he hates me. Publicly he says that he hates my chickens, which I keep in a coop in the backyard. In reality, my chickens are just the excuse. He despises me with every fiber of his being.

Rose Gunther is a tiny thing, about five feet even, with narrow shoulders and bright, youthful blue eyes. It was almost as if I were looking at a twenty-year-old trapped in a seventy-year-old body. She was in mourning because the NHL was in a lockout. She's a die-hard hockey fan and drives a little red Mazda with vanity plates that read BLUSFAN.

"Torie," she said. "What can I do for you?"

"I need to speak to Bill," I said.

"Well," she said pretending to glance at a date book, "he's full up this afternoon. Has an interview with one of the local news stations."

I crossed my arms. "Why don't you just buzz him and see if he wants me to come to his house this evening or if he'd rather talk to me now." I was betting he would rather talk to me now. There were witnesses all around, in case things got ugly. There wouldn't be any at his house.

She smiled and buzzed the mayor. Sure enough, he'd rather talk to me now. "Hang on just a second, Torie," Rose said as a man walked into the building and up to the desk. Rose smiled at him. He was about fifty, with dark, slicked-back hair, and he was at least six-foot-four and three hundred pounds. I counted no fewer than four gold rings on various fingers.

"Hi," he said, and winked at Rose. "I'm Tiny Tim Julep."

"Oh, yes, the new shop owner," Rose said.

"You're opening a new shop?" I asked, and turned to him.

"Why, yes," he said. He extended his hand to me.

Something told me that Tiny Tim Julep wasn't his real name. I smiled and shook his hand all the same. "I'm Torie," I said. "I run the historical society. What sort of shop are you opening?"

"Tiny Tim's Tobacco," he said. "Pipes and cigars. No Cubans, though."

"Oh, yes," I said. "I heard we were getting a tobacco shop. How exciting."

There was a buzz behind the desk, and Ruth smiled at me. "Go on back," she said.

"You know, Rose, don't take this the wrong way, but you are way too nice to be working for Bill," I said.

"That's why I'm hoping, come November, I'll be working for your stepfather."

I contemplated that as I headed back to

Bill's office. I was used to having Colin as the sheriff. Life in this town would be so different, not because he would be mayor, but because he wouldn't be sheriff any longer.

I wasn't so sure it would be for the best. Although I would never tell him that. And to think, none of this would even be possible if he didn't have a dual citizenship and own an antique shop here in town.

Besides, then who would be sheriff?

I knocked once, heard Bill say, "Enter," and went in. "Hello, Bill."

"Torie," he said. "What can I do for you?"

"About this parade," I said.

He held a hand up. Bill reminds me of a bowling ball. Bowling is his favorite thing on earth, but he's also round like a bowling ball — and shiny. All he needs is three holes drilled in his head.

I didn't really mean that.

"I've already said no," Bill said. "You think I'm going to say yes to you when I've already said no to Helen?"

"Well, yes," I said.

"Why?" he said and smiled from his lofty position of mayorhood.

"The parade is the perfect way to advertise, Bill. Just think. A whole float dedicated to your worthiness for office," I said.

I could see him mulling it over in his

22

mind. Then he realized that Colin would have just as big a chance to put a float out there with his name on it. The idea was dead in the water. Well, nobody could say that I hadn't tried to play fair first.

"See ya, Torie. Nice try."

"All right," I said. "*Everybody* will be so interested to hear how afraid you were that your float wouldn't be as good as Colin's, and that's the real reason you nixed the parade."

"You wouldn't," he said.

"I'm on my way to Eleanore's right now," I said, and headed for his door. Eleanore, the town's ink slinger and gossip monger and the owner of the Murdoch Inn, would have a field day with this, and he knew it. "We all know that the real reason you don't want a parade is because Colin's float will be bigger and better and make you look like a ninny."

"You were switched at birth," he said. "I've met your parents. There's no way you came from either one of them."

"I am the demon seed," I conceded, bowing my head.

"Even your mother-in-law is good," he said.

"Hey," I snapped. "Don't you bring my mother-in-law into this."

He sighed heavily. One of two things was

going to happen. Either he'd stick to his guns, just to spite me, because he'd go to any length to make sure my plans were foiled. Or he'd realize that Eleanore's mouth could do more damage than a thousand Monica Lewinskis.

"Fine, you get your damn parade," he said. "But if there's any property damage, the historical society will pay for it."

"Great," I said. "Most people have their floats made already. So you better get on the stick."

With that, I left. It was true. Most people had made their floats over the summer, in case we would get to have the parade. A parade was something I had always wanted, but when Sylvia was alive, there was never any chance of one. Sylvia, the president of the historical society for decades, had been a dear friend of mine and had also been my boss. When she died, she left me everything, including the Gaheimer House, which was home to the historical society and all of its holdings. Sylvia used to be in charge of everything and she hated parades, so we never got one.

It had taken me a while to get used to the fact that I no longer had to worry about money and that I was the owner of the Gaheimer house, but one day I woke up and

24

realized that I was finally in charge. It's not like I'm some sort of dictator; we do things democratically at the historical society. We vote on everything, but what fun it's been to suggest something and have it voted on, rather than having one person decide the fate of all. The historical society had voted back in July that we wanted a parade this year. All we had to do was get past the mayor — and I'd just done that.

I waved to Rose on the way out, stepped out into the street, and ran smack dab into my stepfather. Colin, who is a really big guy — like Bubba big, but not as big as Tiny Tim — tried to stop himself before barreling into me, but there is such a thing as inertia, and he couldn't quite get stopped all the way. I ended up on the sidewalk.

"Oh, sorry, Torie," he said. "I tried to stop."

"That's all right," I said and stood up and brushed off my butt. He was well over six feet tall, pushing fifty, and . . . an okay guy. He's twelve years younger than my mother. People used to think the whole age thing bothered me. If my mother had married George Clooney, I wouldn't have cared about the age difference. My problem with my mother marrying Colin stemmed from the fact that Colin wasn't George Clooney,

25

and he had actually arrested me once. Okay, he'd arrested me twice now, but at the time she decided to marry him it had been only once, and I was convinced that she was deserting me for the enemy. I'm over all of that now. "Hey, I was just going to call you."

He glanced at city hall, where I'd just been, and then back to me. He was worried. He always thought I was getting into trouble. Even when I wasn't. It was a little annoying, and now I knew how my daughter Mary always felt.

"Why?" he asked.

"The parade is a go. Do you have your float ready?"

"You mean it?" he asked, beaming. "How'd you do it?"

"I just told the mayor in no uncertain terms that we had the interest of the town at heart. By depriving us of the parade, he was depriving us of much-needed revenue and county-wide exposure. Besides, our children's hearts would be broken if they didn't get a chance to have a parade at least once in their lives."

"You threatened him with Eleanore, didn't you?"

"Yup," I said. "Go get your float ready! We're parading on Saturday."

Two

"Mom, can you give Riley a ride home?" Rachel asked. There she stood, my little baby girl. I'd spent sixteen hours in labor — shedding all notions of propriety and innocence — to bring her into this world. She stood smiling and expectant at the door of the car, big doe eyes and pink cheeks, asking me to give that trumpet player a ride home when he only lived two blocks away and both of his legs worked perfectly. It'd be one thing if he were on crutches.

I just smiled and said, "Sure." After all, she was my baby, and I kept thinking that at any point now her genes would kick in and she'd realize she was too smart for Riley.

Riley Graham. Good Scots-Irish stock, Rudy would say — and he was, as far as I could tell. I was a genealogist, for crying out loud; it was my job to know these things. For the record, it didn't matter to me what sort of "stock" he was, as long as his hands were slow and his intentions pure, but I knew the first time I met Riley that there was no hope for Rachel. He was lean and lanky, with gorgeous green eyes and black eyelashes, ruddy cheeks, and curly brown hair that just touched his shoulders. He could have come off the cover of *Teen Beat*, but the main thing was, he was gaga over Rachel. Rachel had never had anybody be gaga over her, much less a *Teen Beat* stud muffin.

Rachel and Riley got in the car with their instruments, and I drove to his house. Rachel sat in the backseat. I can remember a time when she would have drawn blood on her sister to get the front seat. Not since the discovery of Riley the Great. No, she wants to be wherever he is. One inch away is too far, so you can imagine how horrible a whole front seat away would be! I remember being like that, so infatuated with a person that it almost physically hurt. Riley whispered something in her ear, and she giggled. I don't know, maybe it's all those band camp jokes going around, but I was in the front seat nearly having a stroke. He whispered in her ear! My daughter's ear! Didn't he realize that her ear wasn't on the open market yet?

Two blocks went by slowly. Riley opened the door when I finally stopped in front of his cozy ranch house. "Thanks, Mrs. O'Shea."

"You're welcome," I said, but he didn't hear me. At that moment I glanced down and saw him squeeze Rachel's hand. She squeezed back.

Absolutely not! There would be no squeezing of any kind going on in my backseat! He just . . . *they* just squeezed! He got out of the car before I came to my senses and threw something at him.

I drove away, contemplating whether I should call his mother about all of this squeezing and gazing stuff they were doing. I knew Cyndi Graham because she served on the Council of Charitable Organizations and we'd combined forces for a few events in the past. Very nice lady. That didn't mean she didn't have a rogue son.

Rachel was quiet. "So, how was band practice?" I asked, trying to keep my voice even.

"Good."

One-word answer, coming from the girl who had ad-libbed to the Pledge of Allegiance since she was three.

"Just good?"

"Yeah," she said, and sighed.

"So . . . Riley plays the trumpet," I said.

"Yup," she said. "You know that."

"Yeah," I said. "Has he ever thought of

playing a different instrument?"

I checked the mirror. Rachel rolled her eyes. "You've got something against trumpet players, don't you?"

"No, no, no, I don't," I said. *Can't disapprove of Riley or she'll like him all the more.* This was a girl, a teenaged girl, after all. "Just curious if he played any other instruments. You know, your grandpa will be interested. Since he's a musician."

My father wouldn't have much use for a brass section, though. Dad plays mostly honky-tonk from the sixties, some bluegrass, and, every now and then, some really old stuff from the Sun Studio sessions. Still, it would give him something to talk about with the kid. I made a left and a right and then was a few hundred yards from our house. My mood picked up considerably as I realized that when we moved into the new house, it would put more distance between Riley and Rachel. Almost two whole miles.

We got out of the car, and I took a deep breath. The smell of autumn was heavy on the air, the blue sky so deep it almost seemed as if I were standing on the bottom of the ocean looking up. Brilliant red and orange leaves flittered against the sky, and I realized with some satisfaction that my favorite stretch of the year was just beginning.

From October to June is my favorite time, especially any months in there that contain snow. I'm pretty miserable from July to September — in the St. Louis area those months are hot, humid, and more hot — but October is usually so grand that Mother Nature seems to be apologizing for any insult she dealt during the summer.

We were walking into the house just as Rudy pulled up. He'd picked up Mary and Matthew from my mother's house. As soon as we were inside, everybody went his or her own way, and I started dinner. "Mary!" I called. "You need to feed the chickens!"

"All right," she said. She ran through the kitchen, out onto the back porch, and into the yard. I watched as she jumped from rock to rock along our pathway to the chicken coop. Mary is at that stage where she can't just walk anywhere. No, she has to run, skip, jump, and walk backward, what have you, as long as it isn't just plain old one foot in front of the other. Matthew had turned on the television and was watching cartoons. I took a casserole out of the freezer and turned on the oven. The phone rang. It was for Rachel.

Mary came traipsing in, cheeks rosy from the chilly air, and grabbed a cookie out of the cookie jar. "There's some weird guy in the mayor's yard," she said.

Mary is quite a little jewel in her own right. She still has a preteen sparkle to her. At the same time, she's far too smart and knowledgeable for her own good. She's the middle child, not always a good place to be. Actually, she'd been the baby for years, then been displaced, quite unexpectedly, by her brother. Matthew had not been planned and had come as quite a surprise to all of us. I think Mary felt we'd dealt her some unjust punishment in the way of a brother, and she's been making us pay for it ever since.

"Mary," I said, "there's a big fence out back. The only way to see the mayor's yard is to stand on a ladder or get up on top of the chicken house. Which did you do?"

"Which one will I get in the least trouble for?" she asked.

"Give me that cookie," I said and snatched it from her. As she turned to leave the room, I added, "What kind of weird guy?"

"I don't know," she said, shrugging. "He was hiding behind a bush."

"He what?" I asked.

"He was hiding behind a bush," she said. "Since you're not going to let me have that cookie, can I go now?"

"Yeah," I said.

"Mom?"

"What?"

"Are you ever going to color your hair?"

"Eventually."

"How far off is eventually?"

"Go to your room," I said.

I put the casserole in the oven, snapped the ends off of a pile of fresh green beans, and then got the biscuits ready. I wondered why there was somebody hiding behind a bush in the mayor's backyard. Was it Colin? Was it somebody Colin had hired? I mean, this race was getting so nasty, I wouldn't put it past Colin to try to dig up some sort of dirt on the mayor or his family, but I found it really hard to believe he'd stoop to spying. That would be something I would do.

I wiped my hands on a dish towel and then headed out into the backyard to the chicken coop. I opened the gate, and half of the chickens immediately scattered and the remaining brave ones came up to see if I had come bearing food. Bob, the rooster, pecked my toe, which is what he usually does. I tried peeking through the privacy fence to see into the backyard next door, but all I could see was a sliver of green. Well, I was just going to have to follow Mary's lead.

I put my foot in the window of the chicken house, grabbed the top of the fence, and pulled myself up onto the roof. I know that's how it's done because I've seen Mary do it in the past. I swear — any time I've ever spied on the mayor, I've used a ladder, but I didn't feel like hauling it out of the garage and carrying it back here, just to check to see if there was a guy hiding in the mayor's bushes. I peered into the yard and didn't see anything unusual. Then my chickens started squawking and making a ruckus, and I saw something move in the bush behind the big oak tree. There really was somebody sitting there watching the mayor's house. Mary hadn't been lying. Not that I don't trust Mary, but she has a really active imagination, and if there's a way for her to get attention from her sister, she will. So sometimes she sort of stretches the truth. A lot. In fact, in some circles it would be considered lying.

I was more stumped than worried by the man's presence. Who would be watching the mayor's house? And why? About that time the board I was standing on snapped. The last thing I saw was the man looking up quickly, just as I came crashing down into the chicken house.

Somehow I ended up with my head on the floor and my butt wedged into a nest, with my feet up in the air. I groaned and rolled over and realized I had egg yolk on my backside.

Of course, there was no way that I could

have made it to my house without anybody seeing me with egg on my butt and straw in my hair. No, Rudy stepped outside the back door just as I was coming out of the chicken house. He took one look at the hole in the roof and one look at me and shook his head and went back inside. He didn't even ask me if I'd broken anything.

"Hey," I said five minutes later, standing in the kitchen. "I could have broken something. Don't you care?"

"I figured if you had, you would have said something."

"Rudy!"

"I decided a long time ago to stop asking what it is you're up to. I figure it's the only way to keep my sanity," he said and poured himself a glass of cranberry juice.

"Rudy!" I said.

He walked into the living room and sat down to watch cartoons with Matthew. I followed him.

"Hey," I said. "If Lenny Kravitz comes knocking on the door, I'm outta here. I bet he'd ask me if I broke something."

"Right," Rudy said. "You have egg on your butt."

"I can't believe you're just going to sit there. I think I bruised my tailbone."

"Grown woman standing on a chicken

house . . . I figure you deserve it."

I stalked off and picked up the phone. Rachel was talking to Riley on the extension. I came in just as he said something sweet and she giggled. "Get off the phone," I said. "I need it." Rachel made a whiny noise and told Riley she'd call him back later. I dialed, and after two rings Colin picked up his cell phone.

"Hello?" he said.

"Call off your dogs."

"What?"

"The guys you've got spying on the mayor," I said. "Call them off. Really, Colin, this race isn't that important."

"I don't know what you're talking about," he said.

"Don't play dumb with me, Colin. Because of you, I think I just broke my tailbone." I slammed the phone down and then hobbled off up the stairs to change my clothes. I murmured under my breath about my husband's lack of concern, but really, anybody who knows me knows that I have put my husband through . . . some trials. Okay, I've put my husband through hell sometimes — but never without a really good reason.

I pulled my shirt over my head and glanced out my bedroom window. I saw the man who had been in Bill's backyard run along the side of our house and cut across our yard. He got into a dark-colored four-door car and, glancing over his shoulder at my house, sped away. He was in a serious hurry. He kicked up gravel, and the back end of the car shimmied all over the street.

What the hell?

The phone rang, and I picked it up. "Torie," Colin said, "I'm not sure, in the name of all that is sacred, what I have to do with your tailbone, but I'd just as soon not know. And I don't have anybody watching the mayor. Does he have somebody trespassing on his property? Should I send over a squad car?"

Small towns. Gotta love them.

"Oh, I get it," I said. "You come to the rescue and save the mayor. This way, when the people go to the polls, they'll remember that you, the sheriff, are the protector and caretaker, and that the mayor needs saving. That's brilliant, Colin. And you did this knowing that I'd be nosy enough to catch the guy and call it in. You're a piece of work, I'll tell you that."

I hung up the phone, pulled on some clean clothes, and ran a brush through my hair. The phone rang again, and I picked it up.

"Hello?"

I heard Rachel's voice on the other end saying, "Hello?"

"I got it, Rache."

"God," she said. "I have got to get my own line." She slammed the phone down, and then I heard a crackly old voice.

"It's your grandmother," my grandmother said.

"Oh, hi, Gert. Whatcha need?"

"I was wondering if you could go to Sears and Roebuck for me. I need a new blender."

I didn't bother to explain to her that our local Sears no longer had "Roebuck" in its name. I simply said that I would go and get her a new blender.

"Oh, great," she said. "New dentures are making it hard to chew."

"Okay," I said. "I'll grab it for you tomorrow."

The phone rang again as soon it dropped into the cradle. I picked it up before it even finished its first ring. "Hello?"

"Torie, I swear to you, I don't know what you're talking about," Colin said.

"Really?" I asked.

"Yes."

"Oh, great," I said.

"What?"

"Then I need to go over and talk to Mrs. Castlereagh." I hung up on my stepfather for the third time, shoved my feet into my shoes, and headed over to the mayor's house.

The few times I have ever knocked on the mayor's front door have been either to tell him something dreadful — like smoke was coming from his roof — or to take my kids trick-or-treating. Halloween was still a few weeks off, so when Mrs. Castlereagh answered the door, it was understandable that she had a worried expression on her face.

"Torie?" she said.

"Hi," I said. "I hate to bother you — I know it's the dinner hour and all — but, um, Mary was just out back feeding the chickens and, well, you know how kids are. She was climbing on the chicken house and saw a man hiding in your backyard."

Mrs. Castlereagh smiled. She has a generous smile, one that spreads easily across her face, causing adorable wrinkles to form on the bridge of her nose. If she hadn't been married to the mayor, I would have liked her. Well, I still like her, but I don't go out of my way to be cozy with her. Conflict of interest.

"I know that sounds weird," I said, "but I was wondering if you happened to see the guy."

"It was probably just one of the neighborhood kids," she said. "Sometimes they use our backyard as a shortcut to the river."

The neighborhood kids couldn't use our yard as a shortcut because we had a big privacy fence. Not that I wanted the privacy fence. That was one of the things I was looking forward to about the new house: I wouldn't have the blasted fence. We had to put it up because the mayor made such a huge fuss over being able to see the chickens from his back door. Now, honestly, there is nothing legal he could have done to us. He had tried passing a city ordinance against any "kept animal" in the backyard, but then his buddy, Alderman Tony Rivera, would have had to find a new home for his two pit-bull guard dogs. Alderman Rivera asked me politely to please put up a damn privacy fence, and so I did.

"Well, Mrs. Castlereagh," I said, "I'd like to think it was just a bunch of kids, but then I myself saw the guy get into a car and speed away."

A confused expression crossed her face. "I don't understand. What did he look like?"

"Well, he was just sort of average looking. It all happened so fast. Dark suit, shiny shoes, black hair. He got into a dark car. I mean, it looked like he was spying on you guys. You think this has something to do with the mayor's race? Maybe a reporter?" I asked.

Mrs. Castlereagh stared at me blankly.

"Mrs. Castlereagh?"

"A . . . mistake," she said. "Has to be."

It looked as though she had turned into a black-and-white photograph right before my eyes. All the color drained from her face, and it was an unsettling thing to witness. It was as if she didn't even see me. "Mrs. Castlereagh?" I said, a little louder.

"Um, thanks, Torie."

"Hey, wait. Do you want me to call Colin?"

"No!" she said. "I mean, no, thank you."

"Is Bill home?" I asked.

"Not yet. Thank you again, Torie."

With that, she slammed the door in my face. I stood there for a second, scratching my head and trying to figure out what all that was about. Mrs. Castlereagh had looked downright distraught. Of course, being married to Bill was enough to make her permanently distraught, but this was different.

I shrugged and headed back to my house. I glanced out at the massive Mississippi River. My house was located across the road and a set of railroad tracks from the river. I would miss it when I moved. It was so soothing to be able to stand on my front porch and watch the tugboats and barges creeping up and down the water. Late at night, if I

41

couldn't sleep, the lights from the tugboats would dance through my window and across the walls. It was oddly comforting.

No more lights. No more moaning from the boats. Change was really hard to get used to.

Just as I was about to go in the house, Colin pulled up in his squad car. He jumped out but left the engine running. "Well?" he asked. "Did you talk to Mrs. Castlereagh?"

"Yeah," I said. He took the front steps two at a time — not so much because he was in a hurry as because it was nearly anatomically impossible for him to take them any other way. "She seemed a little freaked out by it but thought it was probably just somebody using the yard as a shortcut to the river."

"What do you think?" he asked.

"I dunno. Man in a dark suit gets into a dark car and stares up at my house because he saw me seeing him. I'd say that doesn't sound like somebody using a backyard as a shortcut to the river. I mean, the guy never even looked at the river."

"Well, we do get some city people who come down just to look at the boats and such," he said.

"Right," I said, "but like I just said, this guy never looked at the river. He was too busy staring at my house."

Colin looked anxious. "You think this has something to do with the mayor's race?"

"I dunno. I think he could have been a reporter or something, but if he was, he wasn't from around here."

"Well, I guess I'll go on over and talk to Mrs. Castlereagh," he said. "You didn't happen to get plate numbers, did you?"

"No," I said. "Sorry."

Colin got back in his car and turned it off, then walked over to the mayor's house. I stood and watched as Mrs. Castlereagh answered the front door. Then I went back in the house and realized that nobody had been watching the food that I'd gone off and left in the oven. I saw Rudy waving a towel around the smoke-filled kitchen and looking about frantically for a pot holder.

We'd be eating out tonight.

Three

The next day I was hard at work in my office when the phone rang. I picked it up without taking my eyes away from the two-hundred-year-old baptismal records that I'd been poring over. My half sister, Stephanie, was on the line. "Hey," she said.

"How are you feeling?" I asked. Stephanie had just had her second child, a boy, about six weeks ago. My nephew, Jimmy, had managed to steal my heart within the first five seconds I'd seen him.

"I feel good," she said. "I'm ready to come back to work."

"Well, good," I said. "When do you start teaching?"

"No," she said, "I mean with you."

Stephanie is the secretary for the historical society, but that's never been what you'd call a real job. She had helped me go through all of Sylvia's things after she had died. I had no idea she wanted to come to work for me full-time. I tried to think fast; I couldn't hesitate too long, because I didn't want her to think I didn't want her. After all, we'd only been sisters for a few years. She was the child of an affair that my father had in his younger days. I never knew she existed until she waltzed into my office and declared her lineage. You have to give her credit for being spunky. We get along great, and I'm extremely happy that she's now a part of my life, but we're still in that sort of "polite" phase. I couldn't be as blunt with her as I was with other people, because I was worried she'd think I didn't want her around anymore. Which was completely untrue.

"Here?" I asked. "At the Gaheimer House?"

"Well, I wasn't sure if you had room for me on the payroll, but I could help give the tours and free up your time for the other stuff. Whatever that is exactly."

Nobody really knew what my job entailed. Not even me, most of the time.

"Well, sure," I said. Sylvia had left me a fortune, so of course I had room on the payroll. I couldn't really say no. "You can help do the tours, and I need somebody to clean the silver and the chandeliers on a regular basis. I can lose two days a month just doing that."

"That's great," she said. "Can I bring Jimmy?"

Jimmy was probably the reason she most wanted to work for me. How many other jobs would allow you to bring your baby with you? I used to bring Matthew with me all the time and still do on occasion.

"Of course," I said. "But are you sure you want to give up teaching for this?"

"I'm positive," she said.

"Okay, well, come on in tomorrow."

"I will," she said.

"Great. In fact, I've already got a job in mind for you," I said.

"What's that?" she asked cautiously.

"I want you to contact a few insurance agents and have somebody come out and tell me what we have to do to the tunnel so we can give tours in it," I said. Last year, right after Sylvia died, I discovered a tunnel that had been part of the Underground Railroad that ran beneath the Gaheimer House. I'd been trying to figure out a way to be able to give a tour of it without our insurance going through the roof.

"Sounds great. I'll get right on it," she said.

We hung up, and I began entering the church records for Santa Lucia Catholic Church in the computer. The records were on loan to me from Father Bingham. I would type them into a readable format and then give them back to him. Later, I'd publish them on a small print run and distribute them through some local libraries. The best part was, I'd have them in the computer so I could run a word search on them. I planned on doing this for all the Granite County churches eventually, not just the ones in New Kassel. I figured once I got the Catholic churches out of the way, the others would be a breeze, because nobody kept records like the Catholics. Except the Mormons.

The phone rang again. "Hello?"

"Have you seen his Web page?" Colin asked.

"Good morning to you, too."

"Oh, yeah. Good morning."

"How's my mother?" I asked.

"Wants you to come for dinner tonight. So act surprised when she calls."

"All right," I said.

"Have you seen Bill's Web page?"

"No," I said. "I haven't. When did it go up?"

"Last month! That weasel has had a Web page for a whole month."

"Is he a weasel because he has a Web page or because you didn't think of it?" I asked.

"People can't seriously think he's better for the job of mayor than I am, can they?"

"I don't discuss politics," I said.

"Why not?"

"Fastest way to lose a friend or gain an enemy. And with you, things are too precarious to begin with."

"Oh, like you care."

"Is that all you wanted, to tell me about the Web page?"

"Yeah," he said.

"Okay, I'll check it out. Oh, hey, what did Mrs. Castlereagh have to say?"

"Same thing she said to you, but she looked worried," he said.

"Yeah, that's what I thought, too," I said. "I need to go, Colin. I have to go by and check on the float for the historical society before lunch. I've got some other appointments later in the day, and I won't be able to get by the warehouse any other time."

"Right. See you tonight."

No sooner had I hung up the phone than my mother called. I was never going to get those records transcribed at this rate. "Hello?"

"It's your mother."

"Hey, I'm on my way out the door. Whatcha need?" I asked.

"I just wanted to know if you and Rudy and the kids would like to come for dinner tonight."

A vision came to me of Rudy dancing around a smoky kitchen looking for a pot holder and waving a towel around. "We'd love to," I said.

I heard the front door open and shut, and I put my hand over the receiver. "I'm in the office!" I called out. Mom was droning on about what she was fixing for dinner. Little did she know, I didn't really care what it was that she was cooking, only that she was cooking. My mother is the greatest cook in three counties and I . . . am not. That's all I'll say on the subject.

"Hey, Elmer," I said as our fire chief came into my office. He's also the treasurer of the historical society and sometimes provides security for the Gaheimer House during festival weekends.

"All right, Mom. I've gotta go. I'll see you tonight."

"Six o'clock," she said.

"We'll be there."

I hung up the phone, and Elmer took the chair across from me. "Hiya, Torie. I was wondering if you could do me a favor."

"Sure," I said. I have no idea why the word "sure" just flies out of my mouth before I even think about what I'm agreeing to, but it does.

"Sam Hill over at the *Gazette* wants to know if you'll do family trees on the two candidates for mayor." Elmer is older than dirt. Well, there is some dirt older than Elmer, but he's older than most of it. He's been claiming he's going to retire every year for more years than I even want to think about, but when it comes right down to it, since there is rarely a need for the fire department in New Kassel, he says his job is too easy to quit.

"Why?" I asked.

"He wants to do a historical piece on the two candidates. A biographical sketch, but he wants to do it with the angle of whose family has been the most influential in the town," he said.

"Well, hands down, Elmer, Bill's family would have to be. I think his father was born here, and Colin was born and raised in Wisteria," I said.

"Wisteria's only five miles down the road. I think he's trying to get a feel for what their forefathers brought to the community," he said. "Can you get him a family tree on both of them or not?"

"Sure. Bill's is on file. I'll have to ask Colin about his. I mean, I know part of it. His family married into Sylvia's years ago, but he wasn't actually related to her. You know what, though? I'm not real comfortable with this, Elmer."

"Why not?" he asked.

"Because the son of horse thieves and whores can still be a better man than the son of kings," I said. "I don't really think their family trees have anything to do with which one would be better as mayor. Now, if he wants me to go through the newspapers and find articles that show who's done the most for the community, based on their proven records, I'd be happy to do that."

"Torie," he said, "I just need to know if you can get me a copy of the family trees or not."

"It's public access," I said. "Of course. That's why we collected the family trees in the first place."

"Good," he said. "I'll tell him. Did you get a new cell phone yet?"

"Yes," I said. "I did." The last cell phone I had sort of got thrown away by a deranged deputy who was trying to kill me. Not too many people could make that statement and be telling the truth. I wrote down the number and handed it to Elmer.

He left my office, and I pulled up Bill's family tree on the computer and printed it out. I could stop by Sam's office and give it to him on my way over to the warehouse to check on the float — and let Sam know that I didn't like what he was doing with this information. I shut off the computer, grabbed the papers from the printer, and locked up the Gaheimer House.

I had to drive my car, instead of walking, because the warehouse was located a little south of town, in the "industrial" section, next to the river. I stopped by the office of the *New Kassel Gazette* and went inside. The receptionist was new. I didn't recognize her, so she was probably new to the area as well. It's pretty rare that I don't recognize somebody local. Her nameplate read KAREN FRANKE.

"Can I help you?" she said.

"Hi. Can I see Sam Hill?"

"Sure," she said. She buzzed him and told him he had a visitor. Then she actually drew directions to his office on a notepad.

"Are you new?"

"Uh-huh," she said and smiled and handed me the map.

"Are you from around here?" I can't tell you how ridiculous the map was, since the *Gazette* has one editor and three on-staff writers. Most of the rest of the columns are written by the townsfolk.

"Sorta. I'm from Meyersville," she said.

"Welcome," I said. I followed her little map back to Sam's office. Sam was on the phone when I knocked, but he waved me in anyway. I went in as he threw a wadded piece of paper at the trash can and missed. He leaned back and put his feet up on his desk.

His office has one wall of windows, looking out on the town and the river, which is barely visible in the distance through the buildings. One wall holds copies of articles he'd written. The other wall is covered in pictures of his kids, mostly pictures of them playing their various sports. He's convinced he has a future NBA star on his hands; his fifteen-year-old is already six-foot-three and wears a size thirteen shoe.

"I don't care if Ruby Markham had mono or not, I'm not printing a column about it. No, no, I don't think there's an epidemic. Yes, yes, I'll keep that in mind. Thank you," he said, and hung up the phone. He sighed heavily and smiled at me.

"An outbreak, eh?"

"Rosie at the bank is convinced it's as bad as Ebola," he said. "She just skipped right over meningitis and went right to Ebola."

"Well, let's hope not," I said.

Sam got up and picked up the piece of paper he'd thrown at the trash can. He sat back down and tried throwing it again. He missed. Sam and I had gone to school together. He graduated a year after me, married his high school sweetheart, and had four kids — and unless he's hitting the Grecian Formula, he doesn't have near the gray hair that I do. He also has a fairly athletic body and a healthy tan.

"Here's the family tree on the mayor," I said.

"Thanks."

"You know, Sam, I don't really agree with this," I said.

"What do you mean?"

"Bill's family tree has nothing to do with his ability to be mayor," I said.

Sam looked a bit surprised. I guess what I'd just said could be misconstrued as sticking up for the mayor, and the whole town knew our history. Really, though, I would say this no matter what. Because I really believed it.

"Look, I'm not going to compare ancestor to ancestor, Torie. I just want to get an idea of where each man came from," he said. "You know, something like 'Colin is a fourth-generation American whose father was a farmer over in the next county.' No biggie."

"Oh," I said. "Elmer didn't make it sound quite like that."

Sam smiled. "Oh, well, we still love him."

"True," I said and smiled. I felt much better now that Sam had made it a little more clear what he was going to use the genealogical tables for.

"Besides," Sam said, "I don't really know that much about the mayor's family. I mean, I know about his kids and that sort of thing, but beyond that . . . I don't remember ever even meeting his father."

"I understand," I said. "Well, I'll try to get some info from Colin tonight for you. I have one side of his family tree on file but not the other. I'll bring it by as soon as I can."

Sam got up and picked up the piece of paper, sat back down, and tossed it into the trash can, finally succeeding on the third try. "Aha! Two points," he said and made a fist.

"I'll see you later," I said and went out to my car.

I drove south about two miles until I came to a small industrial park that was located right on the river. I pulled in, made a left, and followed the street down to the very end where the warehouse was. I was surprised to find that there wasn't anybody there. This was where most of the floats were being stored, and with only three days to go until the parade, I figured people would be here doing last-minute touch-ups. I glanced at my watch. It was straight up noon, so I guessed everybody had gone to lunch.

I got out of my car and pulled on the door. It was locked. I stuck my fingers down in the potted plant next to the door and pulled out the key. It helps when you know the owner.

The lights were still on, so I knew somebody had just been here. I walked down aisles lined with floats of all kinds, listening to that weird sound that shoes make in a building with forty-foot ceilings, and finally came to the float belonging to the historical society. We had paid about fifteen teenagers in Mr. Holbrook's shop class to build a small version of the Gaheimer House on the float. The officers of the historical society were going to dress in period costumes and stand on the float next to the house. We had also found a reproduction of a spinning wheel, which we put on the float, and Helen had taken a class down in Progress, Missouri, to learn how to use it. She'd be spinning the whole time we marched. Of course, there were banners with the name of the historical society, and the sides of the float were covered in roses. Except I immediately saw that none of the roses were on the float yet.

I took out my cell phone and called the woman in charge of the flowers. "Betty? It's

Torie. How's it coming with the roses on the float?" I asked.

"I've got all of the roses here at the shop," she said. "I'm separating them by color. I should start putting them on tomorrow."

"Is that enough time?"

"I don't want to put them on too early, because they'll wilt."

"All right," I said. "Give me a call when you finish with them."

"Sure will." She hung up.

I walked around the float to see if anything needed touch-up painting. I had just found a spot on one of the window shutters when I heard a noise. I jumped just because I always jump when I hear sudden noises, but I didn't think too much of it, since I figured there'd be lots of people coming back to work. Then I didn't hear anything else — which made me think whoever had made the noise didn't want to be heard.

Goose bumps danced down my arms. I bent my head, listening for another sound. Total silence. Maybe it was just a stray dog. I did the stupid thing. I called out. "Hello?"

Nothing.

I glanced around the warehouse, which was full of floats. There were twenty-foot clowns, and a twelve-foot dog for the Granite County humane society. Floats were kind of creepy, now that I thought about it. At least when I was alone in a warehouse with them. A big tall riverboat with a paddle wheel was by the entrance. I wasn't sure whose float that was, but it was really detailed.

At that point, I saw somebody run past the giant clowns and out the door. Whoever it was wore a dark suit and shiny shoes. Seemed to be a lot of that going around. This guy was blond, though.

Why would somebody run through the warehouse? All of us working on floats were allowed in it. It didn't make sense, unless it was somebody who didn't have any business being here. So the fact that this person took off running made me think he was up to no good.

I decided right then and there that I could check on my float when there were other people around — or when I came accompanied by a small army. Of course, now I didn't want to leave, because I thought whoever it was might be waiting for me outside.

I called Colin from my cell phone and told him to meet me at the warehouse. I was fairly certain that if the prowler was up to no good, he'd flee when he saw the sheriff's vehicle.

Colin showed up about twenty minutes later, and right behind him were some other people who'd come to work on their floats.

He looked irritated, but I didn't care. That's our relationship in a nutshell. He's irritated. I don't care.

"What's up?" he asked.

"There was a prowler in here," I said.

"You called me all the way out here for that? Torie, it coulda been anybody working on a float."

"I know," I said, "but he took off running fast, like he wasn't supposed to be here."

"How do you know he didn't get a call from his wife saying she'd gone into labor or something?"

"I didn't hear a phone ring, for one thing."

He sighed.

"Can you just check around the warehouse?" I asked. "Make sure everything looks . . ."

"Looks . . . what?"

"In order?"

"You called me out here all because somebody ran through the warehouse," he stated, and blinked his eyes. When he said it that way, he made it sound ridiculous.

"Well, no, actually I called you because I was afraid to leave the warehouse. I was afraid whoever it was would be outside waiting for me."

"I am not your personal bodyguard," he said.

"Come on, Colin. After that weird incident with the guy in the mayor's yard, I'm jumpy," I said. "Look, it wouldn't hurt for you to check it out."

"Fine."

He walked around the warehouse and checked things out, just as I'd asked. More and more people came in to work on their floats, and I waved and said hello to the ones I knew. A few people asked me if there was something wrong, even though they knew Colin had a float in the warehouse. I assured them everything was fine.

In a few minutes, I *knew* everything was fine, because Colin came back to my float looking as ticked off as a rattlesnake. "Nothing," he said. "Happy?"

"Better safe than sorry," I said sheepishly.

"Ever heard of the girl who cried wolf?"

"I wasn't crying wolf," I said. Colin and I walked out of the warehouse together. "Somebody ran like his butt was on fire. That just screams guilt like nothing else, Colin. You know it."

"Maybe his lunch didn't set well with him. Thank God, you're not a cop," he said.

"Speaking of which," I said, "who's taking your place if you become mayor?"

"I should know by tonight," he said as we made it out into the bright sunlight.

"I'll see you in a few hours," I said.

"Right," he said.

The New Kassel Gazette
The News You Might Miss
By Eleanore Murdoch

It is that time again! Pumpkins and squash, goblins and ghosts! Tickets for next Friday's horse-drawn hayrides will go on sale Thursday afternoon, and the tickets for the tractor-drawn hayrides will be sold at the time of the event. Our illustrious mayor has finally agreed to let us have some fun and have a parade in this town! What the heck took him so long?

Our soon-to-be mayor, Colin Brooke, wants me to remind you all to wear some reflective clothing on Saturday night, if possible. Reflective stickers that you can put on your jackets are available at the Smells Good Café, the Lick-a-Pot Candy Shoppe, the sheriff's office, and city hall.

On a more personal note, Virgie Burgermeister is asking for help this year with making jams and jellies for the Strawberry Festival in June. She needs somebody to agree to help by the end of

May. I think she'll have plenty of time.

Last but not least, I'm putting together a New Kassel recipe book, called *The Tastes and Smells of New Kassel.* Please donate your recipes. I plan to have them for sale by the Strawberry Festival. All proceeds will go to Clean Our County.

Until next time,
Eleanore

Four

My mother and the sheriff live in a cozy two-bedroom house in Wisteria, about five miles west of New Kassel. Wisteria is actually a much bigger town than New Kassel, much more spread out, with a Wal-Mart and every fast-food restaurant you could ever imagine. The population is fifteen thousand, and the town is home to the only hospital in the county.

Large oak trees shade each side of my mother's yard, and the leaves were all changing, making her entire yard glow orange and red. I knocked on their front door and then entered without waiting to be invited. Before I could get my foot in the door, Matthew squeezed between my leg and the door jamb and took off running for his grandma. My mother, who has been in a wheelchair since she contracted polio at the age of ten, was waiting in the archway to the kitchen to kiss him. He stretched on his tippytoes, and she leaned over as far as she could and kissed him on the cheek. We don't do a lot of lip kissing in my family because I am a germaphobe. I realize that she's his grandmother, but grandmothers can still give grandkids the flu.

We don't eat or drink after each other in my family, either. Backwash is the most disgusting thing on the planet.

"Hope you're hungry," she said.

"Always," Rudy said and rubbed his stomach. I wasn't exactly sure what he meant by that remark. Was he always hungry just because he's Rudy and he's always hungry? Or was he alluding to the fact that he was always hungry because I'm a terrible cook?

The girls made their way to hug and kiss my mother and Colin. Weird, to see the sheriff playing the role of grandfather. My kids call him Grandpa Badge or Grandpa With the Badge, because that's what Matthew started out calling him. I must admit, Colin plays grandpa well — and really, can children have too many people to love them?

The spread of food on the kitchen table was impressive by my standards. For my mother, it was average. She'd made fried chicken, mashed potatoes, homemade bread, those little candied carrots, sliced tomatoes, snow peas, and blackberry pie. I could make all of that food, too. Every bit of it. Nothing except maybe the sliced tomatoes would taste anything like my mother's, though. Her fried chicken should win an award. Part of the reason her chicken is so good is that she cooks in thirty-year-old cast-iron skillets, like the ones used back in her home state of West Virginia. They aren't just any cast-iron skillets, either. They're seasoned. It makes a difference. I'm not lying.

We all sat down to eat. I put Matthew next to me so I could intercept any of his food that might end up on the floor or go flying across the room. I'm not sure why he throws his food. It's not like he's ever seen the rest of us doing it. The girls took TV trays and ate in the living room. It's not like they were banished from the kitchen. It just seems to be a tradition at Grandma's house to eat in the living room. My mother had a small Coca-Cola glass that Mary insisted on drinking out of when she was over. Guess that glass was seasoned just right, too.

Rudy and Colin are fishing buddies, so, of course, my mother and I had to sit through about ten minutes of fish stories and testimonials on fishing products. That's all right, I suppose. They have to listen to me talk about dead people all the time. Anyway, I'd rather hear them talk about fishing than bowling. They are respectable as fishermen. As bowlers, they just plain old stink.

"So," I said. "Colin, you mentioned that you might have an idea of who is going to replace you as sheriff if you should win this election."

"Don't they vote on that?" my mother asked.

"Of course," I said, "but nobody has come forward to run. I guess the whole county is convinced you're going to lose to Bill, or else they're all frightened that you'll win and they'd lose you. I have to admit, I'm sort of in that crowd that's afraid you'll win myself."

Colin's expression owed as much to surprise as it did pride.

"God, it's not like I said you were the greatest man on earth. I'm simply saying that I want Bill out of office, but I'm not sure I'm willing to get a new sheriff in order for him to get the boot."

There was silence at the table.

I swallowed a snow pea. "What?"

"Honey, have you just admitted that Colin is good at his job?" Rudy asked.

"Probably because I don't really have anybody to compare him to," I said.

"Well, thanks, Torie. For that near compliment," Colin said.

"So who's running for sheriff?" Rudy said.

Colin has never even so much as had to campaign for his job before. Granite County isn't exactly a big county, or even one with a large population. It's mostly farms and the occasional small town. When the county seat only has a population of fifteen thousand, that tells you something. I'm not sure if nobody has ever felt worthy enough to run against Colin or if everybody just figured there was no point. Before Colin decided to run for mayor, it never occurred to me that there would be a time that he wouldn't be sheriff.

"Mort Joachim just called me yesterday to say he's running," Colin said.

"I've never heard of him," I said.

"And Lou Counts."

"Never heard of him, either," I said.

"Louise Counts," Colin said. "Lou is a she."

"Oh," I said. Well, that would certainly be interesting, to have a woman in the office.

"In fact, she's coming by after dinner to talk with me. I'm thinking of endorsing her," Colin said.

Whoever Colin endorsed would pretty much be guaranteed the office. It really bugs me that somebody who irritates me as much as Colin does is so beloved by everybody else.

I took a slice of bread and shoveled it through my mashed potatoes. I firmly believe that there is no point in eating mashed potatoes if you don't have any bread to pile them on. "Well, I can't wait to meet her," I said.

A woman. Somebody who will understand woman things. Like intuition. She'd probably understand why I was so freaked over the guy running out of the warehouse earlier. There had been no logical reason for me to feel that way, but something about the person's body language told me he didn't want to be seen, and if you don't want to be seen, there has to be a reason. And that reason would be? See, Lou Counts would understand that because she's a woman. I was warming to the idea. Maybe it would be a good thing to have Colin as mayor after all.

We finished dinner. Rachel helped me do the dishes and take the leaf out of the table. Matthew found his stash of toys that my mother keeps in the spare bedroom. Mary had taken a plate of food over to the elderly neighbor next door. Ms. Rhodes is almost ninety and has broken her hip three times, so my mother feeds her whenever she has the chance. Mary, who has never met a stranger, didn't come back on her own, so I had to go over and fetch her. About fifteen minutes after that there was a knock at the door. Colin answered it and stepped aside to let in Lou Counts.

"Good evening, folks," she said.

Lou was about five feet tall, maybe a little older than I was, with hair so short it was nearly a flattop. She wore jeans, a T-shirt with one of those quilted camouflage vests over it, and army-issue combat boots — and a gun secured to her hip.

I suppose my gaping mouth was a sign to Colin that he needed to explain, because he immediately started speaking. "Deputy Counts, this is my family. Um, everybody, this is Lou Counts. Lou has been a deputy over in Deutsch County for about ten years. She just bought a house outside of Meyersville. If I don't win the election, I'm going to hire her to replace Deputy Duran."

"Nice to meet you," Rudy and my mother said.

I cleared my throat. "Yes, nice to meet you. Can I get you something to drink?"

"No, thank you, ma'am," she said. "I find it's best not to fraternize with civilians."

"Lou was in the army for twelve years," Colin explained.

Nobody said anything. Colin excused himself to go get some paperwork for her. While he was gone, a terrible silence hung in the air like a poisonous fog. Finally I thought, *What the hell? Can't hurt to be neighborly.* "I'm Torie O'Shea," I said. "I run the historical society in New Kassel."

"Yes, ma'am."

"Have you ever taken a tour of the Gaheimer House?" I asked.

"No," she said. She spoke in clipped sentences with a gruffness that had to be practiced. Nobody could naturally be like that.

"You should come over," I said. "I'll give you a tour for free."

"I don't indulge in such frivolities, Mrs. O'Shea."

Frivolities?

"Well . . ." I glanced at my mother, who was trying hard to communicate with only a shift of her eyes. She was saying, *Tread lightly.* Rudy stood and stretched and declared he was taking Matthew out back to play on the swing set. Even though it was dark.

"Have you been to any of our festivals?" I asked.

"No, ma'am."

"You should come by sometime. We're having the Octoberfest all this month. It kicks off this weekend. We're having a parade and hayrides. A pumpkin-carving contest. Live music, too. All sorts of things."

"Why would I do that?" she asked.

"It's fun," I said. "The Boy Scouts built a huge haunted house out by the pier."

"Uh-huh," she said and rocked on her heels.

"Won't you have a seat?" my mother asked her.

"No, thank you, ma'am. I'd rather stand."

"So, what sort of hobbies do you have?" I asked.

"None. Hobbies are a waste of time. Make you soft," she said.

Soft. Well, she certainly couldn't be accused of that.

Before I could say anything, she spoke again. "Mrs. O'Shea, I know who you are."

"What's that supposed to mean?" I asked. My mother closed her eyes and shook her head.

"We're not going to be best friends, and we're not going to be working together. You can stop the fake small-town friendliness."

I was shocked beyond comprehension. This was a case where somebody came into a situation expecting me to behave a certain way, so no matter what I did — even if I was being genuinely friendly — she'd read it as just what she expected. Well, she had taken the gloves off first . . .

"Hmmm, votes don't concern you?" I

71

asked. "Because running for an elected office is as much about schmoozing as it is ability. You'd be wise to know who the influential people are in this county — and not alienate them."

Her gaze flicked down to her boots.

"By the way, it really is small-town friendliness. It's not fake. So, are you from around here originally?" I asked, trying to start over. I'd give her the option of having an epiphany in front of me and coming to her senses. It's hard to know when to be confrontational, when to be passive, and when to kill somebody with kindness. I'm still working on it, but I think I'm getting better.

She nodded her head. Yes, she was from around here.

"Oh," I said. "Counts. Are you related to old Bram Counts, used to own a farm out on Junction H?"

She shrugged her shoulders. "Not that I know of."

"Well, was your grandfather born in this county?"

"I wouldn't know that, ma'am. Not too concerned with the past."

I jumped off the couch. "I'll be right back," I said to my mother. I ran through the kitchen and down the basement steps to Colin's office. "Colin!" I called as I descended the stairs two at a time. "Colin, Colin, Colin, Colin!"

"What?" he called out.

"Oh, my God, Colin," I said as I came running around the corner and barreled right into him, sending the papers flying.

"What is the matter with you?" He bent over and started picking up the papers.

"That woman cannot be our next sheriff!" I said.

"What are you talking about? Why not?" he said.

"Aside from the fact that she makes a zombie look warm and fuzzy?"

"Personality does not catch bad guys, Torie."

"Listen to me, you cannot endorse this woman. She has no hobbies, she's never been to any of our festivals, and fun is a four-letter word to her, without one of the letters! And she's rude!"

"Torie," he began.

"No, no, no. I'm serious, here. Colin," I said, and took a deep breath. I spoke my next sentence clearly and slowly. "She has no concern for the past."

He stood up and stared at me, horrified. "Are you serious?"

"Yes!"

Then I saw the corners of his mouth

twitch, and I knew he was making fun of me. "Oh, my Lord, Torie. She doesn't care about the past. The world will tilt on its axis and kill us all! The sky is falling!"

I put my hands on my hips. "I'll have you know, Colin, that history is what makes New Kassel. It is what pays everybody's bills. It is the only thing that attracts tourists other than deer hunting and fishing in this entire county. We have no industry here. The only reasons this county has any revenue are that little old historical town known as New Kassel and excess animals that can be shot or punctured. So I think at least a deep appreciation of the past is needed in all public officials."

"You are being so . . ."

"So what?"

"Well, normal for you," he said.

"Colin! Mort Jackman has to be a better candidate."

"Joachim."

"Whatever."

"Torie, look. Voters aren't concerned about her hobbies, her personality, or her lack of respect for the past. They are concerned about leadership, arrests, convictions, and a clean record. She has all of them," he said.

I stared at him long and hard. "Colin, she

is so clean, she probably shampoos her nose hairs!"

"You're being ridiculous."

"She is wearing a gun! Off duty."

"I always have my gun with me." He shrugged.

"Not strapped to your leg, for God's sake! Think about how off-putting that is."

"Stop shouting," he said. "I was thinking how it might make people feel safe in this time of terrorism."

"Terrorism. In New Kassel. I'll bet you the terrorists couldn't even *find* New Kassel."

"You're being silly," he said.

I sighed heavily. "I will pay you a thousand dollars to drop out of the mayor's race."

"What?" he said, laughing. "You're nuts."

"Maybe."

"I have way more cash than that just tied up in that damn float!" he exclaimed.

"Fine. Name your price. I'm wealthy now. I've got more money than I'll ever use even if all three of my kids decide to go to Harvard six times apiece," I said. "I'll pay you anything, just please, please do not let that woman be our next sheriff."

"You know what?" he said and smiled. "I think she'll make a perfect sheriff."

With that, he swept by me, turned off the lights, and left me standing in the dark.

The drive home was quiet. Well, at least on my part. The girls giggled in the backseat, deciding who would marry Orlando Bloom and who would marry Josh Hartnett. I wasn't too thrilled with either candidate, since they were at least fifteen years older than my girls were. However, once Rachel declared that neither one could hold a candle to her Riley, I rallied behind Orlando Bloom. Even Mary told her she was insane. Matthew kept making explosion noises. Lots of spit required for those. Mary kept complaining about getting showered every time he blew something up. Why do little boys like to blow things up? Is there a blow-up gene? A blow-up chromosome? Maybe there's a blow-up property in testosterone. Rudy hummed some song, and I stewed in silence.

"What did you think of Lou Counts?" I asked finally.

"That lady was weird," Mary said.

"I'm not asking you, Mary," I said. "This is a big-people conversation. Okay?"

Which meant, of course, that the entire backseat suddenly grew very quiet.

"That was smooth," Rudy said.

"What did you think of her?" I asked.

"I'd say if Rambo ever wanted to get married, we've got the perfect bride for him."

"My sentiments exactly," I said.

"I'm not sure what Colin is thinking," he said. "Maybe she really is the best candidate."

"If the pickings are that slim, then he shouldn't be mayor. He should remain sheriff."

"Torie, you can't make the guy be sheriff if he really wants to be mayor," he said.

"I know. What are the requirements for being sheriff, anyway?"

"Why?"

"Because maybe I can think of someone else," I said.

"Well, she's not sheriff yet. Colin hasn't even won the mayor's race yet. So don't worry about it until it happens."

That is such a guy way of thinking.

We pulled into our driveway and got out of the car. I walked down to the mailbox and checked the mail, since I hadn't had time to pick it up earlier. I glanced out at the river. The moon reflected off the water, dusting everything with a pearly cast. Friday night would be a full moon. Perfect for a hayride. Then I glanced over at the mayor's house. Bill and his wife were home. The living room light was on. I was about to walk up my sidewalk to my house when I saw something glinting in the woods behind the mayor's house.

"Hey, Rudy," I said.

"What?" he said from the steps.

"Come here," I said.

"Just tell me what it is from there."

"Come here," I repeated.

He sighed heavily and walked with a frustrated swagger down the sidewalk to where I was standing. "What?" he said.

"Look," I said, and pointed to the light in the woods. It flickered every now and then, then disappeared for a few seconds. "What is that?"

"Reflection off of a deer's eye?"

"Awfully high off the ground to be a deer. Unless the deer have learned how to climb trees."

"Then an owl's eye," he said. "What does it matter?"

"I don't hear it hooting," I said.

"Torie. You're driving me crazy. You are driving me up the wall with your paranoia," he said.

"Hey," I said, "I have reasons to be paranoid. It's not like one day I just woke up and decided, 'Oh, hey, I think I'll be paranoid and make Rudy crazy.' It doesn't work that way. You work up to being paranoid because things happen, and you learn your lesson so that next time you'll be prepared. Paranoid. Besides, if I stop being paranoid, that's exactly when somebody will get me."

"Torie," he said, grabbing my hand, "I love you, but every time you see or hear something strange in the woods, it doesn't mean there's a bad guy waiting to fall out of a tree."

Just then I heard a loud snap, a rustle of leaves, and then a thud, followed by the muffled sound of somebody cussing a blue streak.

"Except this time," Rudy said.

By the time we got over to the tree, the man was gone.

Five

It was Sunday morning. The day of the parade. Stephanie, Helen Wickland, and I were all dressed in the antique reproduction dresses that we give the tours in, waiting for the parade to start. Sylvia had had dresses made for her and me years ago, so those were nearly antiques for real. I had a few new ones commissioned after Sylvia died, because Helen, Stephanie, and I were not all the same size, and since we were the three female officers of the historical society, we were the ones who would be using them.

"I can't breathe in this dress," Stephanie said.

"Imagine if you had to stay in it all day," Helen said.

"What do I do if I have to pee?" Stephanie asked.

"Hold it," Helen answered.

Stephanie gave Helen a horrified look. She

gave me an even more horrified one when I backed Helen up with a nod. Then she moved on to the next question. "So, did they ever catch the guy that was in the mayor's tree?" Stephanie asked.

"No," I said. "They found the broken limb and the binoculars that he dropped. Colin's hoping to get prints off of them."

Our float was behind the high school marching band. Riley and Rachel stood at attention, in full regalia, including plumes. I loved their uniforms. They were purple, black, and gold, with Sergeant Pepper's–style jackets. I was pretty proud of Rachel, because I don't think I could have stood at attention for a full five minutes. At least the weather was nice. It was a cool fifty degrees with blue skies dotted by big fluffy white clouds. The clouds were so white they nearly hurt your eyes to look at them. The air was crisp, and with every deep breath I took, I could feel it cleanse my lungs and mix with the thousands of roses on my float.

In front of the marching band was the big riverboat with the paddle wheel that I'd seen in the warehouse. It represented the maritime history of New Kassel and Granite County. Behind us were the Jaycees, and behind the Jaycees was the fire department. They'd hauled out one of the antique engines and put the dalmatian on it. Elmer had been torn between riding with the fire department and riding with us. I told him to ride with the fire department. Decisions have never been difficult for me.

So there we stood, waiting for Deputy Newsome to start off the parade by wailing the siren twice and then driving his squad car through town. I heard Mr. Gianino, the band director, call out, "Don't lock your knees!" to the marching band.

"So, what do you think the guy was doing in the tree in the first place?" Helen asked.

"I have no idea," I said.

"And you said that you saw a guy in their backyard the other day, too?"

"Yes," I said. "It's really weird. Colin swears it's not someone that he's hired."

"Why would he hire somebody to spy on the mayor?" Stephanie asked. She wore one of the new reproduction dresses. Hers was based on a pattern from 1756 with a supertight waist and tight sleeves, in a small flower print. We had to let the waist out, considering she'd just had a baby. We topped it off with a white bonnet. Steph is a bit taller than me, five years younger, and for my money a whole lot prettier. Our hazel eyes are the one feature we share. Our personalities, however, are more alike than either one of our husbands cares to admit.

"I don't know," I said. "To see what his next move is? It's silly, I know. I just can't think of any other reason there'd be somebody snooping in the mayor's backyard."

The siren started to wail, and you could see a lot of the band members let out a big breath. The crowd was huge, as crowds usually are for our events. Not only do a lot of the people in the county come for the celebrations, but we usually get a fair number of people from St. Louis — especially if there's food involved. If it's during tourist season, we get people from all over the country.

Helen went back to her spinning wheel and sat down. Stephanie and I braced ourselves for the float to start moving.

"I heard the sheriff brought somebody with him last night," Stephanie said. "To help on the investigation."

"Yes, GI Jane," I said.

"Torie," she said. "You know I have a cousin, a girl, who's in the marines, and she doesn't fit that stereotype."

"Oh, I totally agree, Steph," I said. "There are plenty of female military that don't fit this stereotype. But how shall I say this? Lou Counts is the prototype for the stereotype. I bet she eats her peas with a knife."

"Is she that bad?" Steph asked.

"Yes," I said.

The float gave a jerk and we were off. I started waving to all the tourists. People were taking pictures and waving back at us. "Safe to say she's never been to a Tupperware party," I added.

"Well, did you expect Martha Stewart as the next sheriff?" Stephanie asked.

"That would have been nice," I said. Stephanie looked incredulous. "I'm joking. No, I didn't expect Martha Stewart. I just didn't expect somebody completely devoid of personality and manners. You know, I wouldn't have cared if she'd had three guns strapped to her legs and a scorpion tattoo on her forehead if she had at least been nice when I was being nice! I don't care what people look like or what religion they are, and I don't care if they want to skin rattlesnakes every night for a hobby. But by golly, when somebody is trying to be nice and make small talk with them, they should at least be polite in return."

Stephanie smiled, and that was the end of our conversation, because the marching band started playing "Play That Funky Music." I'm not sure what that had to do with New Kassel or maritime adventures or anything historical, but the audience loved it, so who cares?

The riverboat in front of the band was having technical difficulties. They couldn't get the paddle wheel to turn. At least two people were climbing over the top of the boat to get to the wheel to try to check it out. I thought they probably shouldn't even bother. I mean, yes, it would be cool to see it spin, but if they weren't up there working on it, nobody in the audience would know the difference.

I spotted Sam Hill in the throng of people, taking notes and talking to the photographer next to him. I was sure he was here to cover the parade, but I had a sneaking suspicion that the main reason he was here was to see the floats for Colin and Bill. He stepped up to the rose-trimmed edge of my float, which I found strange, and then motioned me to bend down to him. There was no way I could bend down in this dress and on a moving float, so I got down on my knees. He grabbed my hand and pulled me close. "I need to talk with you as soon as the parade is over," he said.

I gave him a questioning look.

"Find me after the parade!" he shouted.

I nodded that I would and then stood back up, with Stephanie's help. I have the utmost respect for the women in any century prior to the twentieth. I have no idea how they could plow fields, wash clothes, bake bread, and scrub floors in these damn dresses and corsets when I couldn't even get up off of my knees without help.

The parade went on. The band was now playing "Funky Town." I guess the band teacher was going for a theme. Steph and I started dancing to the music. The people in the crowd were all clapping in time and egging us on. We linked arms and pretended to do a hoedown to the funk music. Cameras were snapping, people were laughing.

Suddenly there was a scream.

A blood-curdling, high-pitched, honest-to-goodness scared-to-death scream.

Stephanie and I came to a halt, tried to get our bearings, and looked around. There was a body lying on top of the paddle wheel on the riverboat float. It took me a minute to register what I was seeing. At first I thought one of the guys who had been working on the float had tripped and fallen onto the wheel, but then I saw both those guys standing on top of the boat, looking down at the body and the paddle wheel. The band had stopped playing, and the kids were all confused and looking around for instructions. A grinding-metal sound spurted from the boat, the wheel gave a jerk, and it spun and deposited the body right at the feet of my little girl.

Rachel screamed. Riley ran through the ranks of drummers, knocked over a sousaphone player, who lay on his back like a cockroach unable to get up, and made it to Rachel in seconds. He buried her face in his chest to shield her from the horror at her feet and called out for somebody to get the sheriff.

Once all the floats stopped, I managed to get off of mine, with the help of a few tourists, and I ran to where Rachel stood in the arms of her beloved. I glanced down at the body. A white male. Nice black suit. Shiny shoes. Head bashed in. Dead as a doornail.

"Rachel — oh, my God," I said.

She turned and found me. "Mom?" she said, and started to cry.

I gave her a hug, but before I could say anything soothing and maternal, Riley collected her again and headed off with her through the crowd. If I'd had a battering ram handy, or a strong young trumpet player of my own, I might have been able to follow them, but as it was, I didn't get far. When the body first appeared, the audience had given one big collective gasp and pulled back. Once they realized it wasn't going to jump up and dance, they had all inched forward. Nothing more interesting than a dead body that's not in a casket.

Just then Elmer appeared out of nowhere. He might be older than dirt, but he must have bionic wiring somewhere in that body. "Everybody stand back!" Elmer called out.

I looked up at the guys on the riverboat. "Get down from there. And don't touch anything!"

I heard Colin coming before I could see him. What I could see was people flying out of the way, as if he were literally picking them up and throwing them aside. He took one look at the body and then at me. Grabbing his walkie-talkie, he said, "Get me Newsome. And a CSU."

Then he looked back at me, with a look I'd really rather not see again. It was part fear, part irritation, part anger, and part I'm-gonna-rip-your-limbs-off.

"Hey, I didn't kill the guy," I said with my hands up.

"What happened?" he said.

"Evidently the body was stuck in the paddle wheel, and the float crew couldn't get the wheel to move, so they were messing with it. I guess they dislodged the body, and when the engine came on it dropped him here on the ground. In front of Rachel."

His gaze flickered from the body to me. "Rachel?"

"Yes," I said. "Riley took her somewhere."

"Where?"

"I don't know. Away from here."

"Right," he said.

After a moment I said, "Colin."

"Don't start with me, Torie."

"Colin, I'm almost positive this is the guy I saw running out of the warehouse the other day."

"Is this the guy you saw in the mayor's backyard?"

"No," I said. "For some reason there are several expensive suits running around New Kassel in shiny shoes."

"So it would seem," he said.

"And they have something to do with the mayor."

He thought long and hard about that statement. "You think this guy was in the warehouse?"

"Yes."

"Why did he come back? I mean, obviously, when you saw him he was alive and leaving. If it is the same guy, he had to go back in the warehouse for something."

"I know. And the first time I saw him, he was by this same float."

"Coincidence?" Colin asked.

"Could be," I said. "I don't know."

"As soon as CSU gets here, I'm going to

89

interview those two guys on the float. See what their story is," he said. "Maybe they even know the guy."

"Good idea," I said.

"Why am I telling you what my next move is?" Colin asked.

"I . . . You always do."

"Gotta stop that," he said, rubbing his forehead.

After all the chaos was over and I had Rachel safe and sound at home in bed with all her stuffed teddy bears and *Buffy the Vampire Slayer* in the DVD player, I took a long hot shower. When I got out of the bathroom, Mary was seated on my bed, looking quite pensive.

"Yes, dear?" I said. "You need something?"

"Was that really a dead body?"

"Yes."

"Why was it dead?" she asked.

"Because somebody killed it. Him. Somebody killed him."

"On purpose?"

"I'm not sure, Mary. In fact, it could have been a complete accident. We won't know until the autopsy."

"What's a hogsopy?"

"Autopsy?"

"Whatever," she said, rolling her eyes. "Is that where they cut your whole body open and look at your insides to see why you died?"

"Yes," I said. She knew how they did it, even if she couldn't pronounce it correctly. That was disturbing.

"People die because their hearts stop. Why do doctors have to cut them open to find that out?" she asked, and picked at her fingernail.

"Because they have to know what made the heart stop," I said. I ruffled her hair and went to my dresser to get some clothes. I was in my yellow terrycloth robe with my hair up in a towel.

"Did the body bounce when it fell? Rachel said the body bounced," Mary said.

"I don't think so," I said. In truth, I didn't want to know if it bounced.

"Did it feel anything?" she asked, her hazel eyes wide and horrified.

"No, honey. He didn't feel anything."

"That would be weird not feeling anything," she said.

"Yes," I said. "It would." I gave her a big hug and swiped the hair out of her eyes.

"Well, I'm gonna go call Cassidy. Tell her about the body."

"Mary," I said, "why don't you stop worrying about that body, okay? Think about happy things."

"Like kittens?" she asked.

"Yeah, kittens."

"All right," she said. "I'm still gonna go call Cassidy." Off she went.

There are some subjects that are too difficult to discuss with kids. I'd rather talk sex any day than dead bodies that bounce on the concrete.

I put on a pair of jeans and a sweatshirt that said WELCOME TO NEW KASSEL, MISSOURI. POPULATION 895. It showed River Pointe Road with the storefronts and the Gaheimer House. I had commissioned an artist to do the graphics last summer. The sweatshirts were a best seller in the gift shops. I tugged on my Skechers and then headed out to go see Sam Hill. It was nearly dinnertime, and I'd made plans with Rudy to meet at Chuck's for pizza with the kids. First, I wanted to see what Sam had thought was so important that he'd almost pulled me off a float to tell me.

As I walked down River Pointe Road, a car pulled up alongside me. It was the mayor's. "Torie," he said. "Nice parade. You won't get one next year."

I wasn't going to stop. In fact, I just kept on walking, eyes straight ahead, but then . . . I just couldn't let this egomaniac get the last word in. "We'll see about that, Bill. I'm sure Colin won't mind having a parade next year."

"Yes, but Colin won't be mayor."

"Awful cocksure, aren't you?"

"Yes," he said.

I stopped walking and placed my hands on the door of his car. If he decided to roll up his window, he'd cut off my fingers. "There's something fishy going on here, Bill. If I were you, I'd be watching my back."

He turned pale — at least, I thought he did. Maybe my empty threats weren't so empty. I mean, I said all sorts of things all the time, but usually I was bluffing. "And," I said, "we're having the parade next weekend. We're not going to disappoint all of those people who spent good money on their floats. Besides, think of the crowd we'll have. People will turn out by the thousands once they find out a body dropped out of the sky the last time we tried to have a parade. I can hear those cash registers ringing already. Can't you?"

"You can't just decide to have the parade next weekend without my permission."

"Sure I can," I said. "You wouldn't say no. Not when the mayor's office is on the line."

"It would be in bad taste to have the parade after what happened," he said.

Okay, he was probably right about that, but I wasn't about to let him win this argument. Besides, I'd never been accused of having good taste before. Why start now? "See you next weekend, Bill."

About ten minutes later I walked into Sam Hill's office at the *Gazette*.

"How's Rachel?" he asked.

"She's okay," I said. "I think she'll be fine."

"You know, my oldest was in the color guard," he said.

"Oh, that's right. Stacey. Wow, so she saw it firsthand, too."

"Yeah," he said. "Although the guy didn't land at her feet."

"I know. Rachel wouldn't even let me take her uniform home. She made me take it straight to the dry cleaner's. I don't think there was anything on it, but if it made her feel better, I'd have it dry cleaned twenty times," I said.

"It's just awful," he said and shook his head.

"So, Sam, what is it you wanted to see me about?"

"How long have you lived in this town?" he asked, making a steeple with his fingers.

"Forever. My parents were transplants, though."

"Do your parents remember Bill from their youth? Aren't they about the same age?"

"Actually, Bill's a little younger. Why do you ask?" I said.

"I've got a problem with this family tree, Torie." He motioned to the genealogical chart that I had brought over.

"What do you mean?" I asked.

"According to this family tree, Bill was born in New Kassel, and so were his parents," he said.

"Right. So?"

"My grandfather was born in this town. He says he can remember when Bill moved here, and he doesn't remember Bill's father at all. Now, Torie, you know as well as I do, in a town with a population as small as ours . . ."

"Right," I said. "It's virtually impossible for your grandfather not to have known Bill's father if he'd been born here."

"Can you check this out for me? I mean, I don't know the first thing about genealogy," Sam said. "I don't want to print something that is absolutely not true. Plus, it's only one source. I'll get reamed if I print something wrong and only had one source to go by."

There was something screaming inside of me not to do this. The part of me that my mother raised. The part that said, *Hey, it's none of your business.* At the same time, though, the other part of me, the part that told Mom and her common sense to jump off a bridge, was rubbing my hands and laughing *Tee-hee-hee, I get to climb up the mayor's family tree!* I guess I hesitated too long, because Sam jumped in.

"I suppose I could always do it myself," he said, "but I don't know where to start, and you do. I'll pay you for your time."

"Please, Sam. You know I don't need the money. That's not necessary," I said. "All right, I'll check into it."

"I don't mean to be pushy, but I kinda need this yesterday."

"All right," I said. "I'll go to my office right after dinner."

Six

I met Rudy and the kids at Velasco's Pizza. It's the best pizzeria in the county, and it just happens to be owned by my husband's best friend, Chuck Velasco. Chuck is a good ol' boy, never without his flannel shirt and work boots. He's one of my favorite people in the world, and for good reason. He's on Rudy's bowling team, along with Colin. They're great for comic relief.

We ordered a veggie deluxe pizza and a mushroom, green olive, and pepperoni pizza and ate happily in the 1950s décor to the sound of Elvis singing "Jailhouse Rock." The one food that Matthew eats more than he throws is pizza.

About halfway through dinner, Eleanore Murdoch came waltzing into the restaurant. She headed straight for our table, and I braced myself for whatever it was she was about to lay on me. She always seems red in the face, as though she were about to have a stroke, and she's unrealistically top-heavy. I really do worry about her health, even though at some point this evening I would probably wish she would drop off the face of the planet. I've come to the conclusion that she is oblivious to the fact that she is uncouth and really means no harm.

"What's the story on the body?" she asked as she reached us. The people behind us turned and glanced our way, and Rachel blanched.

"Nice to see you, Eleanore," I said. Eleanore is either color-blind or was born without taste. I'm thinking the latter, since in her own way she does coordinate things. Today she had on a pair of bright yellow and white checked stretchy pants, dark green shoes, and a big yellow shirt with a giant sunflower in the middle of it. The petals on the sunflower were 3-D. She wore big plastic green leaf earrings and bracelets. So, in her own way, she was perfectly coordinated.

"Hi," she said. "I've got a deadline. Going to press in the morning. I need an inside scoop."

Eleanore writes a little gossip column for the *Gazette*. I am convinced that the only reason the owner of the paper allows her to print her ridiculous . . . *news* is that he's her brother-in-law.

"Eleanore," I said, "why don't you leave this one to the professionals?"

"I am a professional," she said and turned her nose up. Then, quick as a flash, she leaned in to our table and whispered, "Did the body really bounce?"

"Mom," Rachel pleaded.

"Hey, Eleanore," Rudy said. "This is upsetting Rachel. Could you please not ask questions about what happened today?"

"Not ask questions?" she said, astonished. "What else do you want me to write about?"

"Well, maybe you could still write about it, but write from a philosophical angle, rather than a graphic one. Why don't you write about the effect this might have on the marching band, or the young people who were watching?" I said. "Or better yet, who was this poor man?"

"Yes," she said. "Who was this man? Is it true he fell out of a tree in the mayor's backyard?"

"I don't know," I said. "It depends on how long this guy was dead. If he was dead more than twenty-four hours, it couldn't have been the same guy. We just have to wait and find out. Really, Eleanore. We'd like to finish our dinner."

"Well, don't mind me," she said. She squeezed into the booth next to Rudy and took out her notepad. "You go right on ahead and eat."

By the time she was finished, she had interrogated each of us on exactly what we'd witnessed — except Rachel, who told her she could read her statement from the sheriff. Yes, there were days that Rachel reminded me of myself, no matter how much she looked like her father. Eleanore ordered some chicken wings while she "worked" and ate two pieces of our pizza. She informed us that she'd been too busy working on her column to bother with dinner. When we left, she was still sitting at our table.

I said good-bye to Rudy and the kids, who were headed to the video store and then for home, and went straight to my office. I unlocked the door to the Gaheimer House, reset the alarm behind me, and walked through the large glistening foyer and sitting room to the hallway and my office. Since Sylvia died, I'd had the soda machine taken out of the hallway and started stocking the refrigerator with Dr Pepper on a regular basis. Sylvia would never let me keep soda in the Gaheimer House fridge, but for some reason would allow a soda machine. I think it's because she made money off it. Sylvia had been incredibly generous, but if there was a way for a penny to be made, she made it.

I booted up my computer and ran to the kitchen to get a Dr Pepper. I checked my e-mail when I got back. A cousin had sent me one of those you-are-loved messages. I also got a note from a cousin in West Virginia saying he'd found yet another long-lost cousin on one of our branches. It was his mission in life to find every living descendant of our common ancestor. That's a pretty cool mission, if you ask me.

I logged off the Internet and then went to the family trees that I had on file and brought up Bill's. William Jarvis Castlereagh, born in July 1949 in New Kassel, Granite County, Missouri. There it was, plain as day. Could I have transcribed it wrong? His father was born in New Kassel and his mother was born in Kansas City, Missouri. He was the middle child of three.

I leaned back and tapped my pen on my lip. Well, all I could do was look at the original five-generation chart and see if I had typed it in wrong. Ugh. The originals were in the basement. I grabbed a flashlight and headed toward the kitchen. I opened the basement door and flipped on the light. I carried the flashlight as backup. The wiring

101

in the basement was so ancient I didn't trust it to hold for the ten minutes I'd be down in the dungeon. It wasn't one of those pleasantly finished basements, either. It was like a cellar. Concrete. Gray. Damp. Cold.

I made my way to the filing cabinets and opened up C. I found Bill's file and decided to carry the whole thing up the stairs with me rather than peek at it and run.

Years ago, Sylvia had asked every resident of New Kassel to fill out a five-generation chart to put on file with the historical society. Of course, not everybody did that, but plenty did. She also ran an ad in the paper asking people to donate their knowledge of their own personal history, and a lot of people responded. Some people even donated old family letters, books, and Bibles. When we modernized our records, it was my job to transcribe them all into the computer. I had help occasionally, but for the most part I did it alone. Now, if anybody contacts the historical society and wants to know if we have information on a John Smith, I can check and say yes or no. I've received letters from many people thanking the historical society for filling in gaps on their family trees.

I locked the basement door and made my way back to my office. I looked at Bill's handwritten charts. Bill had donated more than one five-generation chart. This was not unusual, especially for those who were serious about genealogy. I scanned all of his charts, just to see what I was dealing with. He definitely put his birthplace as New Kassel. He also put down New Kassel as his father's and grandfather's place of birth. He had a *Mayflower* ancestor. Alden. He also had a Civil War ancestor, a few Revolutionary War ancestors, a southern plantation owner ancestor, and two Native Americans. Both were from Algonquin tribes. Hmmm.

Well, this was actually pretty easy to solve. I went into the "library" room of the historical society. I call it a library, but we don't allow people to check anything out. Anybody can come in, however, and copy or look through whatever we have on file. I pulled out the telephone directory for 1949, looking for Jarvis Castlereagh, Bill's father. There was nobody with the last name Castlereagh living in New Kassel at all. I checked 1950, just to see if maybe they'd moved here right after Bill was born. Nope.

I took ten minutes and checked the telephone directories in order until I found a Castlereagh — 1969. Castlereagh, William J.

In 1969? Why would he claim that he was born somewhere he wasn't? And why would he put New Kassel down if he didn't even move here until he was twenty years old? I checked the marriage indexes for the county. He was married in 1970, so he was single when he moved here. I checked the marriage indexes all the way back as far as I had them, and there was not another Castlereagh married in Granite County. Bill's family never lived in Granite County.

It made no sense.

I picked up the phone and called Bill's house. "Mrs. Castlereagh?" I asked.

"Yes," she said.

"Hi," I said. "It's me, Torie."

"Yes, Torie, what can I do for you?" she said. "Before you say anything, though, you tell that daughter of yours how very sorry I am that she had to see such a horrible thing today."

"I will," I said. "Thank you."

"Poor thing. And she's such a sweet girl, too."

"Yes," I said. "But I was actually calling about something else. Um, I was wondering if I could ask you a question."

I knew better than to ask Bill anything, because, since I was doing the asking, I'd just get a stone wall. Bill wouldn't take the time to tell me the sky was falling. "Look, one of the reporters asked me to print out a five-generation chart on Bill. He wants to do some sort of profile on the two mayoral candidates. Anyway, um, he was looking at your husband's chart and noticed that Bill had put down that he was born here, along with his father and grandfather, and, well . . . there's no record of him living in this town before 1969."

There was dead silence on the other end of the line.

"I was wondering if he just got confused. I know those charts can be confusing as heck unless you're a bona fide genealogist," I said, trying to make it seem as though people did that sort of thing all of the time.

"Oh, uh . . ."

"Mrs. Castlereagh? Where was your husband born?"

"Really, Torie, I think this is highly unorthodox."

"I'm just doing this as a favor to Sam. Would you like for me to get this right, or would you rather Sam print something wrong?"

"I'd like to know why this is anybody's business?"

"Mrs. Castlereagh," I said, "when you run for a public office, or hold a public office, nothing is private anymore. Your whole history, including your family history, should be available to those you serve. Now, Bill knows this. I need to get this straightened out before Sam prints something that could come back and bite Bill in the butt later."

"I . . . I don't know what city Bill was born in," she said.

"What do you mean, you don't know? How can you not know where your husband was born?" I asked, incredulous. "What did he put down on your marriage license?"

"New Kassel."

"Didn't he have to have a birth certificate?"

"Yes," she said.

"What did it say?"

"I don't know," she said. "He just handed it over and that was that. I've never had to look at it for anything. In fact, I think it's in the safe deposit box at the bank, along with all of our other important papers."

"Look, I don't really want to talk to Bill about this, because you know he's just going to stonewall me. So why don't you hang up, tell him somebody from the paper was trying to verify this, and call me right back with his answer," I said.

Quiet again. "What do you want me to ask him?"

"Why he put New Kassel as his place of birth, and his father's and grandfather's place of birth, when there is no record of him or his ancestors ever living in this town prior to 1969. I'll check the tax records in the meantime," I said.

"You can do that?" she asked.

"This is America," I said and hung up.

I checked the tax records. Nobody by the name Castlereagh ever owned land in this county, until Bill.

I clicked my ballpoint pen nervously, tapping it every now and then for a change of pace. I all but pounced on the phone when it rang. "Hello?"

"Torie, it's me," Mrs. Castlereagh said.

"Yes?" I said. "What did he have to say?"

"He said he must have just made a mistake. So, see? It was nothing," she said. "I'll talk to you later."

With that she hung up. I called her right back. "Don't hang up," I said. "What do you mean, he made a mistake?"

"He said he thought his dad was born here, but evidently he wasn't."

"Okay, so I can buy that somebody could possibly not know where his parents were born," I said. "But he has to know where *he* was born."

I heard the phone rustle around, and then Bill was on the line. "Torie, it's nothing. When I filled out that damn stupid chart, I thought it would make me more appealing

107

to the voters if I was from their hometown. So I put down my family was from New Kassel."

"Bill, you had to know eventually somebody would go, 'Oh, hey, I don't remember Bill being in our senior class, do you?' I mean, come on. I'm not buying that for a minute."

"I honestly didn't think anybody was ever going to look, Torie. I just filled it out for the old bat because I was running for mayor, and how would that look if I didn't donate to you-all's little file?" he said.

"Bill, this makes no sense. Why didn't you just put down the truth?"

"Because I don't really know that much about my family. I wanted to appeal to the voters. Besides, we may not be from New Kassel, but we are from Granite County."

"Bill, I checked the tax records."

"So?"

"All right," I said. I didn't even have a chance to say good-bye. Bill hung up, and I was left staring at the phone. I went back to the library room and found the telephone directories for Wisteria. I went through them, year by year. No Castlereagh. Then I went through the ones I had for Meyersville. No Castlereagh. By the time I was finished it was nearly midnight. If Bill's family ever lived in this county, they didn't own land — which was possible. They also never had a phone — which, prior to 1949, would not have been that uncommon, but there were no Castlereaghs listed in any of those towns from 1949 to 1969, when they most likely would have had a phone. On the other hand, our esteemed mayor could have come from a family that was too poor to own a phone or land. There was only one way to find that out.

I'd have to check the index for the census records. If he thought I would just forget all about this, he didn't know me very well.

I grabbed the mayor's file from my desk, turned everything off, and went home. It occurred to me just as I stepped out onto the street that I hadn't driven. Walking is no big deal normally, even at midnight, but there'd been way too many strangers running around our town lately.

Rudy would kill me if I called him and asked him to come get me. I took out my cell phone and dialed the house. Rudy answered, groggy. I could hear the TV in the background, which meant he was sitting in his recliner, most likely snoring to *Everybody Loves Raymond.*

"Hey, it's me. I just want you to talk to me on the phone until I get to the house," I said.

"Huh?"

109

"I'm walking. It's midnight. Just stay on the line so I don't get kidnapped or anything," I said.

"How is that supposed to deter kidnappers?" he asked.

"Okay, fine. You win, come and get me," I said.

There's just a certain way you have to do things in a marriage. Rudy wouldn't be angry with me if it was his idea.

Seven

I slept very little last night. In fact, I stared at the ceiling so long I thought my eyes were going to run out of fluid and stick to my eyelids. I had to be really careful with this thing with the mayor. I might be reading something where there wasn't anything just because I dislike Bill Castlereagh, or there might really be something fishy going on.

The alarm went off at six, and I swear I hadn't moved all night. I think I had lain on my back, arms crossed at my stomach, for the five short hours I'd been in bed. Rudy rolled over and wrapped a hairy arm around me and put his right leg over both of mine. He knew I couldn't stand that. I'd wait twenty seconds and then put my legs on top of his. Hey, his legs weigh a great deal more than mine do.

Within a minute or two, he buried his nose

in my neck and kissed me. "Good morning," he said.

I reached over and twisted his hair around my fingers. "Good morning," I said.

"Is it really Monday?" he asked.

"Afraid so," I said.

He groaned, some pitiful sounding thing, and then squeezed me. "So that means I have to get up, right?"

"Right," I said.

"Ugh."

Actually, that was the most I'd heard Rudy say prior to a pound of caffeine in a long time. He dragged himself from the bed, and I watched as he disappeared into the bathroom, taking his pineapple-covered boxers with him. I managed to peel myself out of bed and go down and make everybody's breakfast. I usually wait until the last minute to wake Matthew up. The morning just goes smoother that way.

Mary ate her Frosted Flakes with her hair in her eyes. She might look more like me, but when it comes to morning she is definitely more like her father. She isn't even semi-human until she steps out of the car and onto school property, and I think that's more from fear than anything else. Mary doesn't like school all that much — unlike Rachel, who thrives on school. If she missed a day, the world would probably come to an end.

This morning, though, Rachel seemed quiet and reserved. She made her lunch without saying a word. In fact, she and Mary managed to get ready without saying anything to each other. This had never happened before in the history of . . . well, in the history of siblings. Period. Mary was supposed to yawn with her mouth full of cereal, and Rachel was supposed to call her a disgusting pig, at which point Mary was supposed to kick her under the table or pull her hair or spit the cereal out into the bowl. None of that happened. Mary didn't call Rachel a priss butt for staring in the mirror or fixing her hair. Rachel never told Mary that she had breath worse than a corpse.

What was going on here?

Was I actually complaining?

I filed it for future use. If this carried on for more than a day or two, I'd take them both in for a brain scan to see if aliens had invaded their bodies.

I managed to get the girls to school and dropped Matthew off at my mother's. Then, instead of going to the Gaheimer House, I went to the library. I dialed Steph's number from my cell phone. "Hey, Steph, it's Torie."

"Hey," she said.

"Just wanted to let you know you'll need

your key to get in the Gaheimer House. I probably won't be there until about noon. Listen, the alarm code is the Battle of Hastings."

"Okay," she said, "1066. Not a problem." We hung up.

That was the great thing about having a history teacher for a sister. She knew all the same major battle dates I did. That really is a cool thing, regardless of what you're thinking.

I got on the highway going north, then merged onto Highway 270. When I arrived at the main branch of the St. Louis County Library — and yes, St. Louis City and St. Louis County are separate in almost all things except the words "St. Louis" — I parked my car and went in. All of the genealogical records were kept upstairs. I loaded the machine with the Soundex for the name Castlereagh for the year 1920. The Soundex is a coded index for last names, which is a good thing because after 1880 you no longer have to know what county your ancestors lived in, just the state and their last name.

I had brought the mayor's charts with me, and I looked up the birth year of Jarvis Castlereagh: 1924. So he wouldn't be in the 1920 Soundex, but his father, Chester Jarvis

Castlereagh, would be. Since I already had the 1920 film in the machine, I went ahead and checked it. In fact, according to what Bill had claimed, Chester and his wife were married in 1918, so they should be listed in the 1920 Soundex as a family.

Sure enough, I found a Chester J. Castlereagh and wife, Isabel, listed in the 1920 Soundex for . . . St. Louis City. Not Granite County. Not even Jefferson County. He was living two or three counties away from where he should have been, according to Bill.

I checked the 1930 census, which is only available on the computer at the library, unless I wanted to pay a huge fee to access it from home. I found Chester and Isabel listed with four children, Jarvis being one of them, age six. Next I checked the index of marriages. Jarvis married a Lucy Stockwell in 1945 in the city of St. Louis. All of this matched what Bill had put on his five-generation chart except for the place. Why would he lie about where they were all born? Was it really just to appeal to voters?

That didn't even make sense. He must have known people would look at his family tree, and he should have realized that someone would figure out that the information was false. New Kassel was full of old people

115

who made elephants look forgetful. Could he really have known all of this information about his family but not have known where they were from?

I really don't know that much about my family. That's what he'd said. Then how could he have known he had a *Mayflower* ancestor and a Civil War ancestor? None of it made any sense.

I looked at Bill's chart. He had written that his father died in 1953 and his mother in 1968. I'd check the Social Security death index online when I got home. How many Jarvis Castlereaghs could there be in the state of Missouri who died in 1953? The index would tell me what county he died in. It would at least give me a little more leverage when I confronted the mayor with this again. I noticed that Bill hadn't put down what cemetery his parents were buried in. He didn't know that, either? Or was it just an oversight?

I glanced at the clock. Two hours had gone by already. I made copies of everything I found and then went out to my car and headed home. I stopped in South St. Louis County on Lindbergh Boulevard. I pulled off, made a right, and went down a ways until I came to a little place called P'sghetti's. The place has the best bread in

116

the world. I ordered a turkey and Swiss with some chips and a water, and an order of cheese garlic bread on the side. Way too much food for me to eat. In fact, I'd end up taking home half of the sandwich, and Rudy would take it to work the next day. I ate in silence, mulling everything over in my head. When I was finished eating I wrapped up my leftovers and drove the rest of the way to New Kassel.

I arrived a little after twelve, stopped at home to put my sandwich in the refrigerator and call Stephanie to tell her I was going to be even later. Then I drove out to Wisteria to the sheriff's office.

My stepfather's office is sort of bland, a lot of indoor-outdoor carpeting and a giant poster of all the NFL helmets. I knocked on his door, and he said to enter. When I went in I came to an abrupt stop because Lou Counts was standing in his office. She looked pretty much like she had the night she'd been at his house. She seemed to stiffen as I walked in.

"Hi," I said to her, and smiled. She just nodded. "Colin, um, I need to speak with you."

An odd expression crossed his face. I wasn't sure, but I got the feeling I was interrupting something or that he was embarrassed by my intrusion. For crying out loud, I'd knocked, which is more than I usually do.

"Sure," he said. "What is it?"

My gaze flicked to Lou, who had her thumbs shoved down in her belt loops. "It's . . . private," I said.

"Would you excuse us, Lou?" he said.

"Certainly," she said. "I'll be right outside your door, if you should need me."

What, like I could inflict harm on Colin? Jeez, if I could do that, I would have done it a long time ago.

Colin looked a bit peeved as Lou went out the door. He tossed a pen onto his desk. "What is it?" he asked again.

"Gosh," I said. "No need to be friendly."

"I'm working. Lou and I were going over her strategy for the polls."

"Oh," I said. "Well, I just wanted to run this by you. It's probably nothing, but Sam Hill had me bring in Bill's family tree. Actually, he asked for yours, too, but I only have half of it. I need to get what I can from you on the other half."

"Oh, I'll get right on that, Torie. Like there's nothing else on my plate other than my dead ancestors."

I flinched at his words. It wasn't so much what he said as how he said it. "Well, it's not for me. It's for Sam. He wants to do an

118

article. Anyway, Bill's family tree doesn't add up."

"What do you mean?" he asked.

"I mean, he's got the birthplaces of himself, his father, and his grandfather down as New Kassel, but none of them was actually born here," I said. "He says he filled out his chart to appeal to voters, but that doesn't make sense because too many people are alive to remember that his father never lived in New Kassel. So I don't know what's going on, but . . ."

"But what?" he asked. He looked a bit more interested now, since it pertained directly to his opponent.

"It could be completely unrelated, but first we find two guys snooping around Bill's house, and now I find these . . . lies on his family tree. It's just weird."

He considered what I said for a moment. "We have no reason to think the two are related in any way."

"I know," I said. "It just feels weird, and really, I'm wondering if Bill isn't hiding something. I found his ancestors in St. Louis. Same names, same dates, same people. Just living in different places."

"So what do you think he's hiding? Something that could damage his career?" Colin asked, a little too gleefully.

"Well, yeah. I mean, what if his grandfather did something bad, and Bill just thought that if he changed the places his family members were born on his family tree, nobody would ever connect his grandfather to the rest of them," I said.

"Something bad. As in how bad?"

"Colin!" I said. "I'm being serious."

"So am I. Do you know what this could mean for me? You have to find out what it is."

"So, since my ridiculous little hobby has turned up something you can use, suddenly you're all for my snooping. Is that it?" I asked.

"Torie, it's not like that."

"Forget it," I said. "Sorry I bothered you." I turned to leave and saw Lou Counts standing outside the door like some sort of presidential bodyguard. I took a deep breath and opened the door. My intention was to keep right on walking by her. I had no idea what this woman's problem was, but I wasn't going to disturb the hornet's nest, so to speak. She stopped me, though.

"Mrs. O'Shea," she said, "you really shouldn't bother the sheriff when he's working. You do your job and let him do his."

"You should really keep your nose where it belongs," I said to her. Okay, talk about the pot calling the kettle black, but, boy, did she tick me off. "What is your problem with me?"

"Everybody in three counties knows how you interfere with Colin's job. In fact, if he loses this election it will be because of his connection with you. He's weak. You've made him weak. And people see it."

"I'll have you know that more than a few of Colin's arrests and convictions were because of things I helped him find."

She tsked at me. She actually tsked. "I've met plenty of your kind, Mrs. O'Shea. The law enforcement wannabes."

"The *what?*" I screeched.

"When I'm sheriff —"

"You'll what?" I asked.

She stepped up close to me and shoved her shoulders back, trying to appear as intimidating as she could. I had news for her. She didn't need to shove her shoulders back to look intimidating. This woman was probably menacing in her sleep. "I'll fix it so that you can't even set foot in this building," she said.

"Really?" I said. "Well, you just push me, Ms. Counts. Go right on ahead. I'll make your life so miserable in this town, you'll wish you'd never heard of New Kassel."

"This happens to be Wisteria. And New

Kassel is just a little town in a little county, and how much attention I give it will be my prerogative."

"I think your underwear is too tight, *Ms. Counts.*"

"I oughta have you arrested," she said and moved a hand to her cuffs.

"Go ahead, it's not like I've never been arrested before." I held my hands out.

About that time, Deputy Miller came trotting down the hall. "Hey, hey, hey, ladies," he said, placing one hand on my shoulder and the other on Lou's. "Let's not do this."

"See ya," I said to Lou. I waved at her, a full five-fingered thank-you-very-much, and walked away. I don't know what came over me, but when I got to my car I just sat there and cried for several minutes. Colin was acting like . . . well, like the jerk I always thought he was. Guess that's what I got for starting to think he wasn't completely slug material. Now I had to go and pick up my son at my mother's and pretend her husband hadn't just hurt my feelings beyond belief.

And I needed serious help where Lou Counts was concerned.

Eight

"I'm going to hell," I said.

Father Bingham smiled and motioned for me to take a seat. Matthew ran and sat on his lap, and I cringed at just how stranger-phobic my son wasn't. Not that Father Bingham was a stranger, but still, it wasn't like Matthew had seen him every day of his life, either. The priest gave him a hug and then set him on the floor, pulling a piece of Juicy Fruit from his pocket and handing it to him. Matthew said thank you and immediately shoved the gum into his mouth. I knew he would swallow it within five minutes. He hadn't grasped the concept yet of something you chew without ingesting. He probably didn't see the point, actually.

"Now what's this all about?" Father Bingham asked. He had incredibly kind eyes behind his glasses. His office almost always smelled like pipe smoke.

For the record, I am not a Catholic. Rudy is a cradle Catholic, and we were married in the church, but I can't even remember the last time I actually went to a service, if you don't count funerals. Lately, though, I have found great solace in seeking out Father Bingham's advice. Gone are the days when you'd go into a confessional and get out your list of sins, check them off, say your Hail Marys, and leave. The priests actually give advice and offer help on issues that people are struggling with. And let me tell you, I've been doing a lot of struggling lately.

"I hate Lou Counts," I blurted. I explained to him who she was and what was going on. "I've tried to be nice to her. Twice. And she is so rude to me."

"Chances are she feels threatened by you," he said.

Matthew began running across the room as fast as he could, pretending he was blasting something, so spit was flying every which way. I took my cell phone out and set it on the game mode, and as he came by I grabbed his shirt collar and stopped him in midstride. "Here, play the game," I said.

"Oh," he said. He sat down on the floor, his eyes glazing over, and was happily lost in electronic land. Then I heard him gulp. There went the gum.

"Why should she feel threatened by me?" I asked. "The woman is *armed!* Do I look like I'm carrying an Uzi?"

"Because of your relationship with the townspeople and with the sheriff. You're his stepdaughter. You've known him a long time, and regardless of what you think, you do have an influence over him. So does your mother. He wouldn't be human if his family didn't have some influence."

"So? Why does that threaten her?"

"Maybe she thinks you're going to try to control her once she's in office."

Those words made me cringe. "Why would I do that? I don't control Colin, for crying out loud, or we wouldn't have half of the arguments that we have," I said.

"I'm not saying it's logical. I'm telling you the emotion that she is most likely feeling. She also sounds like a career woman. She probably wants to eliminate anything that might stand in the way of her success. That would be you," he said.

"Why me?"

"Torie," he said, "we all know your penchant for snooping."

"Oh," I said.

"Most people, when they are rude to you, or behave in an unfriendly or unkind manner, or even talk about you in a mean way to others, usually do so because they feel threatened or they're jealous. Simple as that."

"So what am I supposed to do about it? And why do I have to pay the price because she's too much of a baby to quit being jealous?" I said.

"We've had this discussion before," he said. "When your mother-in-law was in town, remember? I don't know what it will take to make Ms. Counts secure enough that she won't feel threatened. I'd like to think God could help her, or God's love, but I honestly don't know."

I was quiet a moment. "Do you think I've made Colin . . . weak?"

"Is that what she said to you?" he said. His face turned a shade darker.

"Yes," I said, fighting back tears. "Father, I never meant to —"

"Nonsense. What's the matter with that woman? You've not made Colin weak, Torie. No, you keep him honest."

"What do you mean?" I asked, feeling more confused by the minute.

"You've made him better at his job. You've made him look for things in places he never used to look," he said.

"Really?" I asked.

"That's not to say that you're not a busybody, because you are, but definitely you make him double-check his facts, and that's a good thing in law enforcement. That's a good thing in politics, too."

"So am I or am I not going to hell for hating this woman?" I asked.

"As always, Torie, you can't control how you feel about her, but you can control how you react to her," he said.

"You're so smart," I said.

"What? You think they hand these collars out in a Cracker Jack box?"

I thanked him for his help and left. I thought about what he'd said as I drove. I couldn't control how I felt about her, but I could control how I reacted to her.

I finally made it to the Gaheimer House long after dinner. I got online and looked up the Social Security death indexes. I did not find one for Chester Castlereagh, which is not unusual, because people born back when he was born did not always have a Social Security number. However, I did not find one for Jarvis, either, and he had been born in 1924. It could be that he died in a different state, or later than Bill had reported. I kept checking, and I finally found a listing for Jarvis Castlereagh in 1988 in St. Louis County. He was the only Jarvis Castlereagh that I found, so I knew it had to be him.

I've never been one for math, but it didn't

take a mathematician to figure out that 1953 and 1988 have a lot of years in between them. How on earth could Bill possibly have gotten the two years mixed up?

I checked the index for his mother, Lucy. Supposedly she had died in 1968. No listing. None whatsoever.

I got up and went to get a Dr Pepper. I came back to my desk and pondered everything I'd found. I realized that I was spending a lot of time on this and that I wasn't transcribing the church records like I should have been doing. Of course, the world wouldn't end if I didn't get the church records done, but I'd set a self-imposed deadline, and I hate missing a self-imposed anything. That's why I get things done. Of course, that's probably why I eat Mylanta tablets like candy, too.

I sighed heavily and heard a knock at the door. I ran through the sitting room and foyer to answer it. "Hi," Sam Hill said. "I saw your light was on. Can I come in?"

"Sure," I said. "Come on back to my office."

He followed me to the hallway, where I stopped. "Can I get you something to drink?" I asked.

"No, thanks," he said.

"Well, come on in, then," I said. "What can I do for you?"

"Well, I was sort of wondering where you

were at on that project I asked you to do," he said, scratching his head nonchalantly.

"Sam, I'm telling you, something's weird."

"I knew it," he said. "What did you find?"

"Well, nothing, really. That's the problem. I mean, these people on his family tree are real. Jarvis Castlereagh is his father, but he wasn't born in Granite County, he was born in St. Louis City, and now I've gone and found that he didn't die in the year Bill said he died."

"Why would he lie about when his father died?" Sam asked.

"Maybe he didn't want any of us to know his father was still alive."

"Why?" Sam asked, sitting in the chair opposite my desk. His eyes glistened with anticipation.

"I'm thinking his father wasn't all that respectable."

Sam smiled.

"Now, Sam," I said. "That's not nice. And I can't stand the guy."

"You don't understand," he said. "Bill has been an arrogant jerk since he took office in 1988. I've waited and waited for something to cook his goose with. Now I might actually have something. So, what do you think the nature of this is?"

I shrugged. "I think he didn't want anybody in this town to know who his parents were. I couldn't tell you the reason. In order to do that, I'd have pore through the St. Louis newspapers until I found something. And that," I said, "you can do yourself."

"What do you mean?" he asked.

"Hey, genealogy is my specialty. I'll continue with anything pertaining to genealogy and ancestors and cemeteries. The newspaper is your specialty. You go look up the names and see what you can find," I said.

"All right," he said. "That's fair. Give me the new dates."

I wrote down what I supposed was the correct date of death for Bill's father, as well as the addresses where his father and grandfather lived during the census years. I handed him the piece of paper and smiled. "How's Stacey?" I asked.

"I think she'll be okay," he said. "Any news on who the dead guy is?"

"No," I said. "At least if there is, Colin isn't sharing."

Sam raised his eyebrows and his forehead wrinkled. "Hmmm. Well, will you get back to me as soon as you find anything else?" he asked.

"Yes," I said. There was an awkward pause. "Sam, what's this really all about?"

Sam smiled at me and leaned forward and rested his elbows on his knees. "Intuition is

130

the greatest asset to a reporter. Actually, it's a pretty good asset to have if you're a politician or a doctor or a cop. I think it's served you pretty well, too. You ever get ahold of an ancestor on your tree or even somebody else's tree and you just think to yourself, *Something doesn't feel right?*"

"Yes. All the time," I said.

"I've been telling myself that something didn't feel right with Bill for about five years now. I'm not sure what it was. Maybe it's the fact that he conveniently has no family. Have you ever noticed that? He has two brothers. One lives in Alaska and the other one lives in Florida? Come on, what are the chances of that? Those are the farthest two points from St. Louis that you can get, except Hawaii. Both of his parents are dead. All of his grandparents are dead, and he doesn't seem to have one cousin or aunt or uncle, either. It just doesn't feel right," he said.

"That's why you asked for the family tree info, isn't it? Not because you wanted to write a piece but because you suspected something wasn't right with his family."

"I do want to write a piece, Torie. Don't get me wrong. I love this town. I love my job. But if I could actually write a story about something other than whose hog got first place at the county fair or how many cans of apple butter we sold at the last Octoberfest, I would die a happy man," he said.

"And the fact that you dislike the mayor — a lot — has nothing to do with it?"

"That doesn't hurt," he said.

"Well, I'll let you know the second I find out anything. You let me know what you uncover, too. Because you never know. It might lead me in the right direction to figure out what's going on."

"I will," he said. He stood then and headed for the door. "Hey, is your mother entering the recipe contest for best apple and pumpkin butter this year?"

"I'm fairly certain," I said.

"Man, that woman can cook," he said with a dreamy look.

"I know."

"Tell Rudy hello," he said.

"I will," I said.

He left, and I was back to staring at the computer screen wondering what I was missing. Sam Hill hadn't a clue how right he was. *Something just didn't feel right.*

The New Kassel Gazette
The News You Might Miss
By Eleanore Murdoch

I certainly hope that future parades do not end as abruptly or as violently as the one we had this year! I've decided to take a philosophical angle rather than a graphic one on this subject. What effect will this dead man have on our marching band? Who was the dead man who bounced on the concrete, after all? We must think long and hard on these engrossing questions. Since the judging for best float was done before the parade started, the Girl Scout troop won first place for the best float and second place was none other than our future mayor's, Colin Brooke!

Matilda Nichols is making her one-of-a-kind handmade Halloween costumes again this year. Make sure you get in line to get one. I went as a sunflower last year!

Everybody go on by and give a big New Kassel welcome to Tiny Tim Julep, the owner of the new shop, Tiny Tim's Tobacco.

And I hear from the grapevine that we are getting a new bead shop next month. Just in time to make gifts for Christmas!

Don't forget to vote!

Until next time,

Eleanore

Nine

The next few days went by without much incident. Rachel was a bit more withdrawn than usual but seemed to perk up when Riley was around. So, believe it or not, I actually invited Riley over for dinner one night. Of my own accord. It seemed to make things . . . *lighter.*

I drove out one morning to check on the builders and what would be our new house someday soon. The frame was up, the subfloor was finished, and it looked as though they were working on the roof. It was hard to believe it would actually look like a house and have drywall and carpeting in just a few short months. I pulled my car into the gravel and mud driveway. As soon as the guys saw me, they all stopped and waved.

The frame sat on fifteen acres of land. Of course, ten of that was woods, so Rudy would only have five acres to mow. I'd already picked out a spot for the chickens, and Rachel had more than once hinted at a great place for stables. She'd never actually asked to have a horse put in the stables, but I could only imagine that that would be the next request.

The house itself was nothing overly elaborate. I couldn't see the point in building a huge house with six bedrooms when Rachel would leave for college in four years. So we went with a three-bedroom, two-bath model, but with a finished basement where Rachel could have her room until she went off to college. I took the attic for my office because I liked to be up high, to be able to look out. I'd requested more closets and more storage, and it would be great not to have my desk in our bedroom anymore, but otherwise the main difference between the new house and the one we lived in now was that each room was a few feet bigger all around. That and the fact that I'd had a small mother-in-law's quarters built onto the back, and no, they aren't for my mother-in-law. They aren't even for my own mother. They're for my grandmother Gert. She's getting on, and I thought she'd like to live out in the country with family but still have privacy for the last years of her life.

It seems kind of silly to acquire so many

objects in life when in the end you downsize to "quarters" off somebody else's house or even just a room in one of your children's homes. I guess that's why I didn't really go all extravagant on this house, the way I could have. Sylvia's money — my inheritance — allowed me to have a huge house, even the big old Gothic thing that I dreamed about as a girl, but I no longer saw the point.

"How's it going, Eg?" I asked.

Egbert Hanshaw is a native of New Kassel and about six years older than I am. His little brother had been in my class. Eg owns Hanshaw Construction with his uncle Manley. He wears a shark tooth around his neck, wrapped with a piece of wire and hanging from a chain. Legend has it that it's the very tooth that he pulled out of his arm after being attacked by a shark in Hawaii. He really had been attacked. I've seen the scars.

"It's going great, Torie," he said. "Weather has been working with us. I think you'll be moving in shortly after the first of the year." He shoved his tan work boot into a clump of dried dirt.

"Wonderful," I said, and hugged myself. It was a bit chilly today, one of those silver-gray overcast days that remind me of death.

"We did have some theft, though," he said.

136

"I was going to call Rudy tonight and let him know about it."

"What was stolen? Did you call Colin?"

"Yeah, I called him. He said he'd send somebody out to check on it."

"Well, what did they take?" I asked, a little concerned.

"Five bags of concrete mix, some two-by-fours, coupla tools."

"Don't you lock everything up or take it with you?" I asked.

"Whoever did this did it at lunchtime. Yesterday, most of us went to Wisteria for a burger, left two guys here. Evidently the two guys decided to take a walk up the creek. You know, to stretch their legs and whatnot. When I got back, they were sitting out here on the backs of the trucks, so I didn't even know they'd left. Nobody realized anything was missing until it was time to go home. Then they fessed up that they hadn't been on-site the whole time," he said.

"Could they have been the ones who stole the stuff in the first place?" I asked, blowing warm breath into my fingers.

"I thought that, too. I checked their trucks. If they stole it, they had somebody come and get the stuff, or they drove it off the property before we all got back from lunch. I really don't think they did it, but I guess you never know," he said.

"Huh," I said and looked around.

"Really, the stuff probably didn't come to two hundred bucks. Not sure you wanna press charges and all that even if they catch whoever it was," he said.

"Well, the tools aren't mine," I said. "They're yours. The concrete and wood are the only things I paid for."

"That's true," he said. He looked eager to get back to the job. Even though he had on one of those thick, heavy flannel shirts and a hooded sweatshirt under it, he seemed to be a bit chilled. Moving around would warm him up, so I let him get back to work.

"I just want to look around a second, okay? Then I'll be out of your hair."

"Not a problem," he said. He handed me a hard hat.

I plopped it on my head and walked around where the back of the house would be. The clear water in the creek meandered about an acre away from what would be the back patio. The front of the house had a big white porch. I walked around the side of the house and through an opening in the frame. I waved at one of the workers and went into the house and up two flights of stairs. Guys kept telling me to watch my step as I went, because the stairs weren't enclosed yet.

When I reached the "attic," I looked out across the land and was happy. A peaceful feeling settled in my chest despite the fact that since there were no walls, all I had to do was step through the two-by-fours and I would free-fall three stories to the ground. I realized that I was going to get to see this gorgeous sight every time I looked out my office window.

The orange and red leaves of autumn splotched across the woods, almost like flowers in bloom. An opening in the trees, right behind the creek, became a pasture. That was ours, too. I looked to the right and saw the road run in front of what would be the yard. A large, cleared pasture was across the county road from our property. Ironically, it was part of Eg Hanshaw's land. He owns about thirty acres. If you drove half a mile down the road by his mailbox, you'd find his unique, self-built mansion sitting among several large oak trees and about four outbuildings. I couldn't see his house from ours because of the swell of a few hills. I guessed Eg would make sure my house looked good, though, since he'd have to look at it every day when he came and went from his property.

I sighed, content. Then I went down the stairs, gave back the hard hat, and went to work. Friday night we were having the hayrides to kick off the second weekend of the Octoberfest. I needed to make sure everything was in order and that we had plenty of volunteers to drive the tractors and ride the horses and keep the bonfire burning.

I arrived at the Gaheimer House just after ten, and Stephanie greeted me at the door with Jimmy wrapped in a sling. "Hi, sweetie," I said to the baby. He smiled and, of course, I smiled. I find it impossible not to smile at a baby who's smiling at me. For one thing, it's one of the purest moments in a person's life. When else can you take a person's emotion at face value? Only with a baby. Babies have no hidden agendas. None whatsoever.

"You got a package from your aunt up in Minnesota," Stephanie said.

"Wonder why she sent it here instead of the house?" I asked.

"Maybe she thought you might have moved already, and she just wanted to make sure you got it," she said.

We made our way back to the office, where I found a very large box sitting on my desk. "You're probably right," I said. I opened the box. Inside were six bottles of wine from Northern Vineyards. "Oh, how sweet."

I pulled out a bottle and read the label.

"When Rudy and I were up there last time, she served some of this at dinner. We loved it, and you can only get it from the winery. None of the stores down here carry it," I said. "Or can order it, for that matter."

I read the note.

Was at the winery the other day and thought of you.

Hope things are good with you and Rudy. Please visit again soon.

Love, Aunt Sissy.

"Wow," I said. "I miss her."

"I haven't gotten to meet her yet," Steph said.

I suddenly felt horrible. I sometimes forgot that my dad's family was her family, too. I reached in and took one of the bottles of wine out of the case and handed it to her. "Here," I said. "It's from Aunt Sissy."

"That's okay," she said. "I got my own box."

"What?" I said.

"She sent me a sampler box and told me to come up and visit her some time," she said. She bit her lip as if the thought made her both nervous and giddy.

"Oh, that was really sweet. See why she's my favorite aunt?" I said. "Well, we'll just all have to go up together and see her."

"Really? You mean it? You'll go up with me? Because I would feel really weird going up to visit her without having met her first, but if you and Rudy are along, it won't seem so weird," she said.

"Yes, um, do you want to go in the winter and see snow?" I asked.

She laughed. "You'll do anything to see snow, won't you?"

"Well, I wouldn't commit murder," I said.

"Speaking of which," Colin said from the doorway.

I jumped, Stephanie squealed, and Jimmy started crying.

"Jesus, Colin. Look, you made the baby cry. What do you want?" I asked.

"Just wanted to let you know that an ID came back on the body that fell from the float. He had a record a mile long," he said, leaning up against the doorframe. "I mean, we're talking extortion, three counts of assault and battery, two counts of manslaughter that conveniently got thrown out on a technicality. All sorts of stuff."

My mouth was open. I glanced at Stephanie, and so was hers. Jimmy's was open, too, but that was because he was wailing. "What was he doing in New Kassel? What was he doing in the parade?" I asked.

"I don't know," Colin said. "I'm working on that."

"What about the prints on the binoculars you found in the mayor's backyard?" I asked.

"They don't match the dead guy's," he said. "So far, I haven't found a match for them in the system."

"Huh," I said.

"Weird part," he said. "The dead guy was from Chicago. I mean, his current driver's license was from Illinois. Chicago! He wasn't even from Missouri. Why would a guy from Chicago, Illinois, be snooping around in our warehouse with floats for a parade, and why would he end up dead?"

"Tourist?" Stephanie asked.

"Well, if he was a tourist, he was completely alone, dressed in an expensive suit — damned Armani suit, to boot — and, as far as I can tell, didn't even have a hotel room. There was a call that came in about an abandoned rental car," Colin said.

"Where?" I asked.

"Up in Arnold. At Richardson Road and Highway 55. You know that commuter parking lot right there?" he said.

"Yeah," I said.

"That's where they found it. It was his."

"So, does this dead guy have a name?" I asked.

"Vincent Ricardo Baietto. Better known as Vinnie 'the Gun' Baietto."

"Huh?" Stephanie asked.

"What?" I sat down.

"A hit man. From Chicago. In New Kassel," Colin said.

"Oh, I really hope he was just in town for the fudge and the hayrides," I said, and gulped.

"I suppose stranger things have happened," Colin said, "but something tells me he wasn't here for the fudge."

"Why?" Stephanie asked.

"Well, because he's dead, for one thing," Colin stated with such matter-of-factness that I almost laughed.

"This is surreal," I said, rubbing my forehead.

"Tell me about it," he said. "Look, Torie, have you seen anything strange going on in town, other than the guys you've seen spying on Bill?"

"Isn't that enough?" I asked.

Just then my phone rang. I answered it, and Stephanie excused herself to try to get Jimmy to stop crying. Colin sat down in the chair opposite my desk and played with the fraying edges of the upholstery. He was in full uniform today. I wondered how many more times I'd get to see that before he became mayor — because as much as I wanted him to stay sheriff, I was voting for him for mayor, and so was everybody else I knew.

"It's Eleanore," a voice said. I was so lost in my thoughts, I'd forgotten I'd actually picked up and answered the phone.

"Yeah?" I said. "What can I do for you?"

"A hit man just checked into my bed-and-breakfast," she said in a panic. "Torie? Do hit men stay in bed-and-breakfasts? I mean, I thought they stayed in sleazy highway motels with cockroaches and stained toilets."

"Wait, wait, slow down. What makes you think this guy is a hit man?" I asked. Colin almost jumped out of the chair.

"His name is Tito de Rosa, he paid in cash, and he's wearing expensive cologne and shiny shoes."

"Eleanore, he could be a salesman, for crying out loud."

"How many salesmen pack a Gluck? Huh? Tell me that one, Miss Know-It-All."

"You mean a Glock?"

"Yes, a Glock."

"I'll be right over."

Colin looked at me as if I'd just announced the Virgin Mary was going to be on Letterman.

"Eleanore has a hit man staying in her bed-and-breakfast." I couldn't believe I kept a straight face.

Eleanore met us at the front door of the Murdoch Inn. I love the Murdoch Inn. It's one of those buildings that, as a child, you think is magical and full of princesses. It has turrets and latticework and climbing roses. Then you grow up and realize that crazy women who wear clothes that look like plants actually live in them.

"Act casual," Eleanore said as we approached.

"Eleanore," Colin said, "Torie mentioned he had a weapon?"

She nodded her head, and her pumpkin earrings bounced. "Yes. A Gluck."

"How do you know what kind of weapon it is?" I asked.

"Really, Torie. I have a satellite dish. Don't you?"

Actually, no. I have cable, and that just came about in the last year or two.

Colin sighed heavily and placed his thumb on his gun holster. He always does that when he's concerned. It's like a mental check that yes, his weapon is still there. "All right, you stay here, Torie. I'm going to go up and have a talk with him."

"I'm not staying here," I said. "Colin, this is my chance to see a real live hit man! When will that ever happen again?"

"You don't know that he's a hit man," Colin said. "You're not going."

"Why not?" I asked, and stomped my foot.

"You are not a deputy," he said. "At all."

"You could deputize me right now," I said.

He laughed. "Not on your life!"

I crossed my arms, completely unhappy with his decision.

He disappeared into the Murdoch Inn, and Eleanore and I exchanged worried glances. "I'm afraid," she said. "What if the guy kills me in my sleep?"

"Well, look at it this way, Eleanore. At least we'll know who did it."

"That's true," she said. "And oddly comforting."

A few minutes later, Colin emerged from the Murdoch Inn, looking really ticked off. I've seen that look before, sort of a mixture of anger and determination — a serious combination in a man of his size. "The gun is registered." He held it out in a hand towel.

"Hey, that's one of the towels from the inn!" Eleanore said.

"I'll return it," Colin said. "I promise. I told him I wanted to keep the gun until he left town. He didn't argue with me. Claims he's an insurance salesman and carries the gun for protection."

"Jeez, the guy never heard of pepper spray?" I asked.

"He also happens to be a gun collector," Colin said.

"You buy that?" I asked.

"Not one bit," he said. "But, he's surrendered his weapon. All I can do is sit and wait to see what he does. I'll put Deputy Counts on him."

My heart stopped in my throat. "D-did you say Deputy Counts?"

"Yeah," he said. "She decided to jump ship now. Said even if I lost the mayor's race and she didn't get to become sheriff, she wanted to work for me. She's now a bona fide deputy of Granite County."

Colin walked off down the steps, and I just sat down on the porch, right where I was. Eleanore patted me on the head. "You want some Scotch?" she asked.

Ten

I was sitting at the kitchen table reading a book on the history of gypsies in medieval Europe when Rachel came in and sat down across from me. She didn't say a word, she only sighed. My mom-sense went into overdrive almost immediately. For one thing, a sigh is a big deal in teenage land, and for another, Rachel usually sits down and starts rattling on about people at school, favorite movies or actors, or what horrible atrocity her siblings have subjected her to recently. Whether I want to hear these things or not. No matter if I'm reading, on the phone, or hanging upside down and gagged. Rachel talks. Period. Something was definitely up. I placed my gas receipt in the book as a bookmark and looked up at her. "What's up?" I asked.

"Nothing."

"You've been my kid for how long?" I asked.

"Ever since I was born," she said, giggling.

"You really think that big dramatic sigh and then a 'nothing' is going to fly with me? Huh?" I asked.

"No," she said. Her face turned red. My first instinct was to think of Riley. Of course. Had he been squeezing something other than her hands? I'd kill him. Okay, I wouldn't really, but this is a very small town, and I can inflict damage.

"I've been thinking about that dead guy," she said.

"I thought you might," I said, relieved that Riley had not acted improperly. At least, if he had, that wasn't what she wanted to talk about. Now that I thought about it, I wasn't so sure being relieved was appropriate.

"I just can't seem to get him out of my mind. I mean, Mary took twelve pairs of my earrings the other day, and I didn't even yell at her. I feel like I don't have the energy to yell at my own sister," she said.

"What did you do about it?"

"I just went over and dumped out her book bag and took them back."

"And this is bad?" I asked, thinking that, finally, I would get some peace in the house.

Rachel rolled her eyes. "When I don't even feel like yelling at my brat sister for taking something that was clearly mine, there is something wrong," she said.

I chose my words carefully. I didn't want to scare her off. "Well, what is it that you think is wrong?" I asked.

She burst into tears. Big fat tears rolled down her face, and that damn chin trembled — which usually does me in — and then she swiped at the streaks on her face and took a deep breath. "Do you think he was somebody's dad?" she asked.

I couldn't help it. The tears welled in my eyes. I had to fight to keep them in check. She was so sincere, and even if the guy was a hit man from Chicago, Rachel clearly saw him as a person. I reached over and squeezed her hand. "Oh, baby, I don't know if he had kids or not," I said.

"But he was somebody's son. Everybody comes from someone," she said.

"Yes, that's true," I said.

"It's just creeping me out that somebody's son or dad or brother bounced on the concrete in front of me. *Dead*. But it's not only that, Mom. I'm sad that somebody's son bounced at all. It makes me so sad, I just don't know what to do about it," she said, and sobbed.

I got up and hugged her then. "It's okay," I said.

"All the kids are making fun of me," she

said through snot. It was like her face had suddenly turned into a lawn sprinkler. There was wet stuff coming from everywhere. I jumped up to get her a paper towel. It was the only thing handy.

"Why? You can't help it if Mr. Gianino put you in the front line."

"No, because I'm sad over it. Every time I start crying over this whole thing, they all make fun of me."

"Well, honey, they're just callous," I said.

"Riley doesn't make fun of me, though. He told me that he'd like to kill the guy for being dead and scaring me," she said, and laughed through the tears. "I told him that was hardly possible and would only add to the problem."

"Well, I'm glad Riley is standing behind you," I said. I really was happy about that. He'd proven to me that he really cared about Rachel, and that was all I could ever ask of anybody involved with my children.

"I just can't get it out of my mind. I've tried reading or playing board games or video games. None of it helps. About the only time I don't think of it is when I'm watching a really good movie or something," she said.

"It'll get better. I swear," I said.

"You promise?" she asked.

"I promise," I said.

With that, she got up and took the entire container of cookie-dough ice cream out of the freezer, got a spoon, and headed off to the living room. I had to do something or her mind would turn to mush and she'd gain twenty pounds. I'd bought ice cream five times since Saturday, and she'd eaten all of it.

I picked up the phone and dialed Eg Hanshaw. "Eg," I said, "I need to talk to you about building a stable."

Later, after eating dinner and helping the girls with their homework, I was upstairs seated at my desk. I booted up the computer and then went to Google and typed in some of the names on Bill's family tree. I discovered that one of his ancestors connected him back to Charlemagne. I checked a few of my books on royal genealogy, just to make sure whoever posted the family on the Net had the lineage correct. Bill did not have this info down on his charts. It was possible that he didn't have a clue about it. Well, if he didn't know he was descended from kings, I sure as hell wasn't going to tell him. All I needed was Bill feeling justified in his Henry VIII behavior.

I surfed the Net for a while, looking for quarter horse breeders in Missouri. Then I checked out some breeders of draft horses. We wouldn't really have any need for a draft horse, of course, but they're so sweet-natured, at least in my experience. I found a few breeders and saved their Web sites to my favorite places. Rudy would probably have a fit when I told him I was thinking of buying the kids a horse, but I thought it would be good for them. Rachel certainly needed something right now to throw herself into, other than television and mountains of ice cream.

I checked my e-mail. Colin had sent me a link to his brand new Web site. I clicked on it and up came a picture of Colin in his uniform. There was a photograph of all of us at his wedding. Interesting to see me listed on his Web site under "family." There was also a great picture of him and my mother on the cruise they took last year. Colin had wanted to go to the Bahamas, but my mother had wanted to go to Greece. My mother won.

It was bizarre to see my mother in the context of somebody's wife. She'd been my mother for so many years that it was almost startling to think of her any other way. She was my mom, she was a grandma, and she was an artist, but she hadn't been some-body's wife in so long, I'd forgotten that was an option. I studied the photograph of them on the boat. Her gray hair had multiplied tenfold in the past few years, and she had crow's-feet, but her skin was gorgeous, and her oval face and brown eyes were just as beautiful as ever. Hardly up to Hollywood standards of beauty, yet there she was, smiling out at the camera. Beautiful. Proof that true beauty doesn't come in a bottle or at the end of a knife.

Colin's Web site happened to make me think of Bill's. I typed in Bill's name, and his site unfolded. He'd gotten his oldest daughter, Karri, to write the introduction. "Hi, all! This is my father, the mayor of New Kassel." Karri has such finely tempered features that her face is calming to look at. She got her looks from her mother, for certain, because Mrs. Castlereagh has that same calming nature about her. I maneuvered around the Web page and finally clicked on the bio section.

I come from a tiny town down in Granite County, Missouri, called New Kassel. I graduated from St. Louis University in 1970 with a major in political science and a minor in business.

I didn't really want to hear about his accomplishments. I was afraid there'd be a saving-a-baby-from-a-burning-building story, and then I'd throw up all over my desk. I skipped on down.

As a child, I can remember looking out on the Mississippi River, thinking it was the most beautiful thing I'd ever seen. It was the giver and taker of life. I remember long lazy summer days, drinking lemonade and running through fields of cornflowers and daisies, thinking that the world was indeed a charmed place. As mayor, that's what I think of every day when I go to work. I want to preserve that way of life for all of those children growing up in the generations after me.

Oh, brother, I was going to throw up anyway.

I was about ready to log off when I saw a column about things of interest in New Kassel. I clicked on it. He had several shops listed, along with places to stay. Several icons were devoted to our festivals and events. There were even photographs posted of our last Strawberry Festival. He had a link to the hunting and fishing Web site of Granite County. Last but not least was the historical society. He mentioned Sylvia and Wilma Pershing, the founders of the historical society and for decades the president and vice president. He did not mention me or any of the other current officers. Not that I expected him to. No, this was exactly what I expected from him.

The mayor hides in his office on most days and does nothing. He reaps the benefits of the very hardworking staffs of the historical society and the events coordinator board. Yes, I happen to be on both staffs, but they are made up of more than just me. I can think of twenty people right now who are responsible for all the tourist events that make our town money.

You'd never know it from the mayor's Web site.

Now I was angry *and* nauseated.

I clicked on his photo icon. I know, I should have stopped, because all that I was achieving by any of this was getting myself angrier by the minute, but it was like a train wreck unfolding before my eyes — I had to keep looking. The photo icon brought up his high school picture. His wedding picture. A picture of him standing in a boat holding up a fifteen-pound catfish with a link to the wildlife and game commission. A photograph of him signing some piece of paper in his office — like he ever really did anything but sign his own checks.

There was a picture of him as a little boy. The caption read, "Me, one summer evening in my front yard, in front of Old Man River." He was about four years old in the photograph, wearing a pair of bib overalls and a hat, barefoot and shirtless. He had been cuter than cute, I had to admit.

Well, I was disgusted enough for one night. I clicked off the computer, made some phone calls to make sure we had enough tractors and horses for the hayrides tomorrow night, and then went to bed. Rudy came up some time later, because I heard him stub his toe and cuss a blue streak.

At about three in the morning, I was awakened by a noise. I got up and looked out the window that faced the mayor's house. I didn't see anything unusual. The trees swayed in the breeze and made dark, spidery shadows against the mayor's house. I walked over and looked out the window that showed me the river. That was habit. If ever I woke up in the middle of the night, I would go and watch the boats and barges going up and down the river. This would be the thing I missed the most when we moved into the new house. When I looked out that window, though, I sucked in a breath and jumped behind my curtain.

Down below I could see two figures standing in front of the railroad tracks with the river flowing behind them. I couldn't tell who they were from this distance. It was far too dark. I opened my window just a crack, kneeled down, and placed my ear next to the sill, trying to hear what was being said — as if their words would be carried across the road and my yard and float up to my window. Nosy people know no bounds.

Then the strangest thing happened. They started shouting, and suddenly I could hear their words. Well, at least some of them. The two people looked angry. Arms started flailing about. One shoved the other and then pointed a finger at him. The one being threatened backed up, but then he lunged, leaning into the other guy's face. Who was doing the threatening? I couldn't tell.

"What in the hell are you doing?" Rudy said.

I shrieked, started, and knocked into a bookcase, dislodging one of the shelves. About fifteen books came crashing to the ground. Several of them landed on the backs of my legs.

"Shhh!" I said, and glanced back out the window. About that time, the two men separated. One walked down River Pointe Road toward the center of town, and the other walked . . . into the mayor's yard, opened the mayor's front door, and stepped inside!

One of the men had been the mayor.

"Torie, what are you doing?" Rudy said again.

"Looking for my contact."

"In the middle of the night?"

"Yes."

"Why don't you just admit that you're spying on the neighbors?" he asked, and went back to bed.

"Oh, my God, Rudy," I said, shutting the window and then running for the bed. "I just saw Bill outside arguing with somebody."

"Hurrah. The man has enemies."

"At three in the morning?" I asked, rubbing the backs of my legs.

"Is it three in the morning?" he snapped, sitting straight up.

"It . . . could be," I said.

He flopped back down on the bed and groaned. Then he covered his face with his pillow and motioned for me to go away.

"Who argues outside at three in the morning?" I asked.

"Somebody whose enemy is pissed off at three in the morning. Speaking of which . . ."

"All right," I said. "I get the picture."

I lay back down and nestled under the covers, but I did not go back to sleep.

Eleven

The next morning, before I even took the kids to school, I went over and knocked on the mayor's front door. Nobody answered. I tiptoed through the dew-wet grass to the garage and peeked inside. Bill's car was gone, but Mrs. Castlereagh should have been at home.

"Maybe she's sleeping," Rudy said from behind me.

I jumped. "Oh, jeez. Will you *please* stop doing that!"

"Sure," he said. "When you stop snooping on everybody. Torie, what is the matter with you?"

"What do you mean? I've snooped on our neighbors for years, and suddenly it bothers you?" I asked.

He motioned for me to come out of the mayor's yard. "Come here," he said. He looked like somebody who was trying to get a stray dog into the Humane Society truck. I glanced back at the mayor's house and then went to stand by my husband.

"What?" I asked.

"Look, I know you go a little wacky where the mayor is concerned," he said, making a circle by his ear with his finger. "It's difficult when you live right next door to the very person who can destroy you. Not in a literal sense, of course. But you have to stop this. He's going to press charges one of these days. We only have a few months to go before we'll be far away from him, and our chickens will no longer be threatened by the big bad man. Okay?"

I blinked at him. "No," I said. "What is the matter with *you?*" I asked. "You've been so condescending to me . . . well, ever since I fell through the chicken house."

"And what were you doing at the time you fell through the chicken house?" he asked.

"That's beside the point," I said.

"No, that *is* the point."

I gestured at the mayor's house. "Look, something is going on in there. We've got two different people snooping around his house —"

"And you would make number three —"

"And now he was fighting with somebody last night at three in the morning," I said.

162

"I've got a feeling about this, Rudy."

He rubbed his forehead.

"You know what your problem is?" I asked. "Your problem is that you know that when I get these feelings, I'm usually right. You can't stand it."

"I just want to be normal," he said.

"Well, snap out of it, because we're not." End of conversation. I went and got the kids ready for school, dropped them off, and then headed over to the fire station to check on the stuff for the hayrides.

Elmer met me on the front lawn of the firehouse with a big smile and a slight lilt in his gait. "Hey, Torie," he said. "We had a couple more tractor donations for the weekend. We should be able to run eight different hayrides an hour. Last year we could only run five."

"Well, that's wonderful," I said. "What about horses?"

"We've got four wagons to be hitched up to the horses, so that makes a total of twelve. And I spoke to Ron Burgermeister, and he said he's got reservations already for the horses all night long. The tractor-pulled hayrides are first come, first serve."

"Well, that's great," I said.

"Should be a success."

"What about the bonfire? You've got one

163

of your engines on standby, right?" I asked.

"We're going to take the old one out to the field. Let the kids climb on it and what not. Then, if the bonfire gets away from Chuck, we'll be there to step in. I think we've dotted all of our i's and crossed all of our t's," Elmer said.

"Well, good," I said.

"Are we doing the parade again tomorrow?"

"No," I said. "My mother informed me that it would be in bad taste, and once Jalena Brooke has spoken, you kinda have to go with it. At least on matters of good taste."

"Isn't that what mothers are for?" he asked.

I agreed and then sighed. "Well, then. I'll see you tonight."

"Oh, and that new guy . . . Tiny Tim something-or-other," he said.

It took me a minute to remember who he was talking about. The new shop owner in town. "What about him?"

"He's having his grand opening this coming week and wanted to know if he could hand out fliers at the hayrides."

"Tell him, only when the tourists are coming back from the rides. Not on the way out to the bonfire, or I'll be picking up fliers for a week. If he gives them the fliers on the way out of town, then they leave them in their car for a month, and that means no trouble for me."

"I'll tell him," Elmer said. "See you tonight."

I ran a few more errands and then stopped at Fraulein Krista's Speishaus for lunch. I love the food there, but there's also just something incredibly appealing about grown men and women running around in Hansel and Gretel outfits. Or maybe it's just me. Whenever I step into the restaurant, it's like stepping into a restaurant deep in the Black Forest. Bavarian music poured out of the overhead speakers, and Sylvia, the great stuffed bear, sat at the end of the bar with an emerald green scarf tied around her neck. Sylvia had become the town's mascot.

I sat in my usual booth and ordered my lunch. I was busy not being a busybody for once. Sam Hill walked in and headed straight for my booth. The whole town knows I'm here on most weekdays between twelve and one. If I'm not here, they start speculating about where I am.

"Hi, Sam," I said, and wiped my mouth. "Have a seat."

Most of the time, I get my privacy here. I usually bring a book or some work from the historical society with me, but quite often I will be graced with a visitor at lunch. I like that, actually. Well, I complain about it a lot if I'm trying to work or trying to disappear, but in reality it's quite a compliment, and I feel like I stay connected with my fellow townspeople this way.

"Hey, Torie."

Sam sat down, and I noticed slight purple smudges beneath his wide brown eyes. Something told me he'd been up all night. "What's going on?" I asked.

He ran his fingers through his hair and gave a disgusted sigh. It was one of those I-give-up sighs. "I can't find anything incriminating on the Castlereagh family."

"You say that like it's a bad thing," I said with a smile.

The waiter came over to ask if Sam would be eating. Sam ordered an iced tea and a piece of lemon meringue pie.

"Well, I thought I would find something that would tell us why Bill would lie about his father and grandfather," he said. Then he glanced around and lowered his voice considerably. "There has to be a reason."

"It may be nothing more than arrogance," I said, although I felt deep down inside that wasn't the truth. The argument Bill had had last night was very real. I had thought about it during the remaining hours of the night, and the only realistic scenario I could come up with was that somebody was trying to blackmail the mayor. But what information was the mayor trying to protect?

"How so?" he asked.

"I was all over his Web site last night," I said. "He's got the lie up there for everybody to read. Talking about how he came from New Kassel and how he tiptoed through fields of cornflowers during the long summer days of his childhood and all that crap. I mean, he's put the lie out there for everybody to see. Now he has to make sure he keeps the truth hidden or he's going to look like a fool."

"So you're saying you think he just made up the lie so that he seemed to be a hometown boy?"

"It may be nothing more than that," I said.

"Then how do we explain the two men snooping around his house?"

"I'm not sure," I said, and took a bite of my sliced turkey. "You've come up empty, right?"

"I can't find anything in the papers that alludes to his parents having been mass murderers or anything," he said.

"Maybe they were just losers and he was ashamed of them," I said. "I'd like to get his wife to talk about her in-laws, but she's very

167

careful about what she says. I think she would flat-out deny me answers if I asked questions, anyway."

He slumped back just as the waiter brought his iced tea and lemon pie. "So my story is gone."

"Not necessarily," I said. "The mayor still lied about where he was from, and it's on the Web, so it's not like he can deny it."

He rubbed his eyes and then took a bite of pie. "Maybe this is why I work for a small-town paper. I don't have what it takes to find the answers."

"Have you checked the court records?"

"For what?"

"I don't know," I said, "but the civil court records are available to anyone. The Castlereaghs might have been sued by some-body or brought up on charges for some-thing. At this point, you need to check every-thing."

He smiled at me and took another bite of pie.

"Of course, you'll have to go to downtown St. Louis, because the records you'll need are there," I said.

"I knew that," he said.

"Did you find an obituary for Jarvis?"

"Yes," he said. "I did, but there was noth-ing in it that would give me a reason to think he was a terrorist or anything."

We ate in silence for a while. I waved to Krista, the owner, as she went behind the bar to make the drinks for another table. Sam finished his pie and then drank his iced tea. "What have you discovered?" he said.

"That the mayor is a jerk," I said. He laughed and gave me a look as if to say, *What else is new?*

"Hey, I've been meaning to ask you," he said.

"What?"

"I've been thinking about opening a microbrewery," he said. There was already a wine shop in town, the Grapes of Kath, owned by Kathy Schlemper.

"Do you plan on serving food, too?"

"Just like pub food. You know, burgers, fries, chicken wings, nachos, onion rings. I mean, nothing gourmet," he said.

"I think that would be great," I said. "You might want to talk to Elmer about space, though. You'd need a pretty good-sized building."

"All right, I will," he said. "After I get rid of our mayor."

We both laughed, and then he left with the promise of getting back to me as soon as he'd checked the courthouse records — which of course would have to wait until

Monday. I finished my lunch, talked to Krista for a while, and then went to the Gaheimer House to do some transcribing until the festivities started this evening.

At six o'clock, my best friend since childhood walked into my office. "Collette!" I said, surprised to see her. I jumped up and gave her a hug and was immediately engulfed in her sea of perfume. It was some expensive stuff from Nordstrom, but it made me sneeze the same as Avon. I guess allergies don't differentiate.

Collette is a reporter for the *St. Louis Post-Dispatch*. She was born and raised in New Kassel. Unlike me, she couldn't wait to get out of the small and claustrophobic confines of a small town where everybody knows everybody else's business. That's her description of New Kassel, not mine. The only reason she ever comes back to visit is me and my family.

Today she was dressed in a red wool suit that had huge gold buttons down the jacket, with black pumps and black hose. Her big blondish hair spilled all around her shoulders. "What brings you here?" I asked.

"Oh, I've been suspended from the paper," she said.

She dropped that piece of news as if she were telling me the temperature outside.

"Collette," I said. "I'm sorry. What happened?"

"I deserved it," she said. "I came by because I might be moving to Arizona. There are a few papers there that are interested in my work."

"Arizona?" I said, shocked. "When?"

"It might be as early as three weeks," she said. "So I wanted to come down and spend a weekend in my old hometown."

"That is the biggest line of crap I've ever heard. You are not the least bit sentimental," I said. On the other hand, I'm overly sentimental. We seemed to balance each other fairly well. I kept her out of trouble — a lot — and she got me into trouble. Okay, well, I get myself into trouble plenty, but Collette got me into a different kind of trouble.

"I got a room at the Murdoch," she said. "I really just wanted to come down and see you."

"You can stay at the house," I said.

"No," she said. She moved a stray hair from her face with one perfectly manicured brilliant red nail. "It's not like I called or anything."

"That's okay," I said. "So, Arizona?"

Collette had lived in Seattle for a few years after we graduated, and she'd gone to college in Chicago, so it's not like she hadn't lived away before. She'd moved back to Missouri to be with her father when he was dying. She ended up staying ten years after that.

"I'm due for a change," she said.

"Well, I'll miss you."

"I'm not sure yet," she said. "There's also a paper in Durham, North Carolina, that's interested. One in Miami, too. But I think if I move to Miami I'll get into too much trouble."

All right, there was more to this story than she was telling me, but I wasn't going to push. She'd tell me eventually, because she'd burst if she didn't. I could tell the difference between something she didn't want to talk about at all, something she wasn't ready to talk about, and something she wanted me to ask about. This was something she'd get around to telling me about on her own.

"Well, I'm glad you're here. Tonight we're having hayrides and a bonfire," I said, smiling from ear to ear.

She rolled her eyes. "God, don't you people know how to have fun in this town?" she asked.

"Yes," I answered. "Why do you think we're having a bonfire and hayrides? You'll need jeans and sneakers. Preferably boots, but I bet you don't have any."

"I brought sneakers," she said. "I know how this town is."

"Good," I said. "I need to go home and feed the kids and be back at the firehouse by seven. You're welcome to join us for dinner, but I'll warn you, it's probably going to be some palatal insult like weenies and beans."

"I'll meet you at the firehouse," she said. "Is Krista's still good?"

"Yeah, and Ye Olde Train Depot still has the best lasagna in town."

"I'm in the mood for steak," she said.

"Then the Train Depot or the Old Mill Stream is the place for steak."

"All right, I'll meet you at the firehouse. In my sneakers."

"Okay, see you then," I said, and gave her a quick hug.

At precisely seven the bonfire was lit out of town on the Maeder farm. In town, Elmer, Stephanie, Helen, Colin, Tobias Thorley, Oscar Murdoch, and Charity Burgermeister were all loading up passengers to take them on their hayrides. There was just one problem. We were a few people short to drive the horses and tractors. Riley stepped up and volunteered to drive a tractor, and Rachel sat herself permanently in the back of his wagon. Colin took Matthew and Mary with him while my mother took people's tickets and money.

Collette showed up a few minutes past seven, and the line for the hayrides was so long it meandered all the way down to the Smells Good Café. We were still short four drivers. Rudy put his baseball cap on backward, rubbed his hands together, and climbed up on a tractor.

About that time Father Bingham and Eleanore Murdoch showed up to help my mother sell tickets and to try to keep the people in line happy. Other people were working the refreshment stand and the kettle for the popcorn. Kettle corn just makes the whole event.

My mother's sister Emily had come in for the event, too. She owns a farm with her husband, Ben, out on Highway P. Aunt Em could, of course, drive a tractor, so I put her right to work. That left one horse-drawn wagon and one tractor. I looked at Collette.

"What?" she said.

"I need you to drive the tractor."

"What? Not on your life!" she said. "I'd rather eat your cooking for a week."

"Fine, you want to take the horse?"

"Oh, God, no! I'll take the tractor," she said. She cussed me the whole way to the tractor, and even after she got up in the seat she was still calling me names under her breath. I was laughing the whole time as I got up on the wagon and picked up the reins of the horses.

"Just follow me," I said. "We go out to the bonfire. Drop off passengers and then come back and get the next group. If there's anybody at the bonfire who wants to come back to town, then we bring them back. The ride is about fifteen minutes one way."

"I don't believe this," she said. "If I break a nail —"

"You'll break a nail," I said. "You can fix it on Monday."

I slapped the reins, and the horses began to pull the wagon slowly. Collette really would get over it. She'd been mad at me a dozen times in her life, and I mean seriously mad at me, and she always got over it. She says it's because nobody loves her as unconditionally as I do. Pretty sad considering she has a mother.

In the wagon were bales of hay and lots of passengers. Some were locals, some were tourists. Teenagers from the surrounding towns always came out in droves for this event, and tonight was no different, but it always amazed me how the teenagers were from all walks of life — in my wagon alone for instance. I had the captain of the football team. I knew he was captain because his mother was on the events committee with me, not to mention Rachel had had the biggest crush on him a long time ago — like in August. Seated next to him was the requisite cheerleader, who was also his girlfriend. Next to them was a kid who had long black hair, a John Deere hat, tattoos on his left hand, and safety pins in his lip. His girlfriend basically looked like he did but with breasts. So it didn't matter who you were. Hayrides were just good old-fashioned fun.

I looked over my shoulder. Collette was behind me, not smiling in the least. She really needs to learn to appreciate the little things in life — because sometimes the little things are all you're going to get.

I took a left and made it to the New Kassel Outer Road. I passed Stephanie's tractor coming the other way. I waved. As she came by me, she called out, "This is so much fun!"

I'd brought a camera along, so I picked it up off of the seat next to me and snapped her picture as she went by. It was starting to get dark. The sun had just disappeared behind the line of trees. I figured we had probably twenty minutes before it was too dark to see.

We made it to the Maeder farm. The Maeders had decorated the field with witches and ghosts, lots of pumpkins, and stalks of hay. After we dropped off our passengers, I snapped some pictures of the kids and Colin, a couple of Rachel and Riley, a few of various people from town, and one of Collette driving the tractor. I mean, I had to have a picture of Collette driving a tractor. Then the drivers went back to New Kassel to get the next load.

By the time we headed back out to the bonfire with our next group of people, it was dark and getting cooler. I was glad I'd worn another layer under my flannel shirt. My cheeks and hands were chilled, but not uncomfortably. Just the way I liked it, actually. The moon was full tonight. A big, glowing white orb hovering out there in space. When I was a kid I couldn't understand why it didn't just fall and crash to the earth.

The tractors had headlights, but the horses didn't — that's one of the drawbacks of real live creatures — so Elmer had lined the road with Tiki Torches. He said he'd gone to fifteen different stores to find enough. The moon was bright enough that I probably could have seen the road without the Tiki Torches, but I was happy they were there, all the same.

Riley passed me, with Rachel still in the back. She waved at me as she went by.

When Riley realized who I was, he tipped his baseball cap at me. I wasn't sure if he really was that grown up or if he just pretended for my sake. Either way, the kid was slowly winning me over. As long as he kept his hands to himself, there would be peace in New Kassel. Colin's wagon came next. I saw Mary, but Matthew was no longer in the back. I slowed the horses. "Hey, where's Matthew?"

Colin turned around quickly. "He's not back there?"

My heart jumped to my throat.

Then Colin started laughing. "Your grandma is at the bonfire," he said. "I left him with her."

I suppose the look on my face was one of pure fear, because he quickly added, "He wanted to stay with her. He said, 'I want to stay with the grandma with the cracks in her face.'" I stared at him, not believing that he'd leave my son with a woman who took fifteen minutes to get up out of a chair. "Mary said it was okay."

"Oh, Mary said it was okay. Well, then that makes it all right," I said, wondering if my son was roaming around the wilderness by himself by now and curious as to when Mary had suddenly become an authority in Colin's eyes. I love my grandma, but she's old and can't exactly run after a toddler if he decides to take off.

When we dropped off our passengers, I spotted Matthew and Grandma. He seemed to be enthralled with the fire and was sitting quietly on the hay next to her. It was the first time I'd seen him not in perpetual motion in a week at least. She caught my eye and gestured to Matthew, and she gave me a thumbs-up to say she was fine with him. All right, I felt adventurous tonight.

We made the trip back to New Kassel, and Collette seemed to be getting more comfortable behind the wheel of the tractor. I noticed a group of guys on motorcycles and pushed it to the back of my mind. We often get motorcycle groups through New Kassel, because of the scenic two-lane roads along the river. Especially in autumn. We picked up another group of people and headed back out to the Outer Road. I had a particularly rowdy bunch this time. They were singing songs and laughing. The horses didn't seem to mind. They just plodded along. I was loving my job and my town at the moment. In fact, I was so pleased with my life that I'd totally forgotten that in a few short months, Lou Counts could be the new sheriff.

That's why when the shots rang out I was completely dumbfounded.

Twelve

People started screaming, and I heard Collette cussing a blue streak at the top of her lungs. My horses twitched, shook their heads, and whinnied. I knew any second they were going to take off. "What the hell is going on?" a passenger from behind asked me.

I spun around in my seat, trying to see something. Behind Collette's tractor were two motorcyclists gaining speed — and leveling guns. "Collette!" I shrieked. "Speed up!"

"I can't!" she screamed. "This damn thing will only go slow and slower!"

My horses kicked it into gear as the motorcycles got closer, and the last thing I remember before complete chaos took over was watching Collette's tractor get smaller and smaller as I left her in the dust. I didn't know what to do. Should I just let the horses run, or should I stop them? If I stopped them, were the gunmen going to pull over and kill us all?

These thoughts were shooting through my mind at record speed. I was amazed I could actually separate one thought from the other. It turned out that I didn't have any choice in the matter, because the horses took out a Tiki Torch and ran off the road into the field. All I needed was for one of the horses to break a leg and go down. The whole wagonload of people would go flying and the horse would be hurt. As it was, people were jumping off the wagon behind me, and I was pulling on the reins, yelling for the horses to stop. I must have said "whoa" a hundred times at least, and no matter how many times I whoaed, they just kept on going. I couldn't see where we were headed. Only the occasional hay bale or fence post was illuminated enough by the moon that I could make out what it was as I flew by it. I suppose the horses could see in the dark, because they'd swerve at the last minute and miss whatever it was.

My heart hammered in my chest, and sweat broke out along my back and on my hands. I could barely grab the reins. The horses turned and jerked so fast that I was almost thrown from my seat. I would have just let them run it out, but a field in the dark is a very dangerous place for a horse. I glanced back over my shoulder. There were a few people left in my wagon, hanging on for dear life, praying and squealing. Except one guy who was laughing his butt off. I was sincerely happy that there was some insane human being who could find the lighter side to this situation.

Suddenly the horses made a sharp left and we were headed back to the Tiki Torches and the road. Collette's wagon was stopped, and another wagon that had been coming from the opposite direction had pulled over.

The horses picked the worst place to come back on the road, because at that point the road swelled on a rise, and the horses and my wagon were going to have to go up a steep incline of about ten feet. Visions of me toppling through the air crowded my mind, and I pulled on the reins and shouted, "Stop, you stupid animals!"

They didn't stop. They took that incline like there was no tomorrow. As I glanced behind me at the wagon, I saw the last three or four remaining passengers tumble out of the back, the hay bales falling after them. The laughing idiot was among those who bit the dust on that last hill. I squeezed my eyes shut and grabbed onto those reins so tight I could feel the leather cutting into my hands.

Then the horses just stopped. They couldn't make it the rest of the way up onto the road with the wagon attached. They stumbled backward and whinnied furiously, and when they did, I saw a few people scuttle down off the road and come after the horses. Several people grabbed hold of the horses' bridles or bits or manes, wherever they could get some leverage, and stopped them. I jumped down off of that seat so quickly you would have thought I was an Olympic athlete.

Then I just stood and shook for several minutes.

When the sirens began to wail in the distance, I remembered the gunshots. People who had been in my wagon were strewn all over the field. Some were bleeding, some hobbling. When I crested the swell of the road, I ran for Collette's wagon. "Collette!" I called out.

I found her sitting in the road at the base of the tractor wheel, tears streaming down her face. "Are you all right?" I asked.

She said nothing. I glanced around at the other passengers. The ambulances pulled up one, two, three. Somebody from Collette's wagon had been shot in the calf. There was a bullet hole on the side of the wagon, and one of the tractor tires had gone flat. I assumed a bullet had hit it. "Collette," I said.

She still said nothing. Finally she grabbed my hand and stood up. "I have always hated this town!" she cried. Then she collapsed into sobs in my arms.

Colin stepped up to me then. He'd been driving the other tractor that had stopped to help them. He looked as though he'd just received the worst news of his life, and instantly my whole body went weak. Mary! She'd been in his wagon. "Mare?" I said and swallowed.

"She's fine," he said. He pointed down the road, where one of the motorcycles was lying as if some child had just casually discarded one of his toys. The driver lay on the concrete with a pool of blood slowly trailing from his body. My eyes searched Colin's for an explanation.

"I shot him," he said and hung his head. Colin never had gotten used to this part of his job.

"But you weren't even on duty," I said.

"Ever since the stuff with the mayor . . . I've been carrying my weapon even off duty," he said. "It's a good thing. Well, in a way."

Mary came running up to me. She slammed into me so hard she almost knocked me over. "Mommy!" she squealed.

"Mary," I said. "It's all right." I picked her up and hugged her close.

"Oh, my God," she said. "You should have seen it. Grandpa was, like, brilliant. He just stood up like this and then he did this and then *kapow, kapow.* The guy did a somersault off of his bike and landed in the road! And he bounced! Dead people really do bounce!"

She was breathless, her eyes wide. "Are you all right?" I asked.

"I'm fine. It was the coolest thing I have ever seen," she said.

Clearly she had no clue that her life had been in danger, or even that the guy on the motorcycle would not be getting back up. I mean, she knew he was dead, she'd said he was dead, but I don't think she completely understood that he was dead — and that her grandpa had taken his life.

"Mary, honey," Collette said. "You come with me." They went off to sit in the back of somebody's pickup truck.

"Are you all right?" I asked Colin.

"No, I'm not all right. Dammit, Torie, what the hell is going on here? We've had the occasional poisoning and breaking and entering in our town, but we've never had somebody shooting at our people or our tourists. This has gone too far!" he said.

185

"This is my family, my friends, my home. No, I am not all right. And if Mary . . . When she realizes I killed that man . . ."

"All right," I said. By this time there were three ambulances, three squad cars, and a boatload of people who had been passing by and stopped to see what was going on or to ask if they could help. "What do we know?"

"I'll tell you what I know. The damn mayor was in Collette's wagon, that's what I know!" he screamed.

I glanced around, and sure enough, I saw Bill and his wife sitting on the side of the road, unscathed but shaken. "You think this was an attempt . . . You think this was a hit?" I asked.

"That's exactly what I think," he said. "Completely unsubstantiated guess, but that's exactly what I think."

"Wow," I said. "Why didn't they just use a car bomb?"

"In case you haven't noticed, Bill's cars — yes, both of them — have been in the shop recently. He and his wife have walked everywhere. I haven't seen him in a car in over a week," he said.

"Are you suggesting . . . ?"

"I am suggesting that he knows his life is in danger," he said. "And I intend to find out right now."

"Wait," I said. I filled Colin in on the argument I'd witnessed the night before between Bill and the stranger. He squeezed the bridge of his nose and shook his head. "Brilliant, that's just brilliant."

"Why doesn't Bill just run? Go into hiding? I mean, wouldn't you, if you knew somebody was trying to kill you?" I asked.

"I don't know, but I'm going to find out." Colin headed over toward Bill, and I followed on his heels. I did it quietly, hoping he wouldn't even notice that I was there.

When we reached the spot where Bill and his wife were sitting, the mayor looked up from his shaking hands and said, "What do you want?"

"I want to know what's going on here, Bill," Colin said.

"What makes you think I know anything about this?" he snapped back. Mrs. Castlereagh's eyes suggested he did, though.

"I hear there was a domestic disturbance at your home last night," Colin said.

Oops. Bill, of course, looked over Colin's shoulder to me. I was right, Colin hadn't realized that I was standing there. He glanced over his shoulder, sighed heavily and motioned with his head for me to leave. I did as he instructed, trying to walk as slowly and listen as intently as I could. It turned out that I didn't really need to, because the mayor started yelling at Colin, which I was not prepared for. I don't think Colin was much prepared for it, either.

"Just stay out of this!" Bill yelled.

Colin said something that I couldn't hear.

"I don't know what you're talking about." Bill again.

Colin kept his cool, and as a result, I couldn't hear a word he said.

"Tell her," Bill said, pointing at me, "that what happens in front of my house is my business. Who the hell is up at that time looking out the window, anyway?"

At that, I tucked tail and headed back to the truck where Mary and Collette were. Before I could get there, Bill and his wife walked briskly over to one of the townsfolk, asked for a ride, and left.

Colin came back over to me, with his swagger exaggerated just a little. "You really know how to piss people off," he said.

"It's an art," I said. "So what do you think he did to warrant this?"

"Gambling debt, maybe? I mean, it's the simplest, most common thing I can think of. I think he borrowed money from someone for something and then stiffed them," he said.

"Have you checked his banking records?"

"Not yet. His whole financial history is at the top of my list now," he said.

"You know he's not going to talk," I said.

"No, probably not," Colin said. "And really, I have no evidence that they were after Bill. Guess I'll have more leverage once I know who these clowns on the bikes actually were."

"Where's the other one?"

"Got away."

"Are Tito de Rosa's whereabouts accounted for?"

"We'll find out," he said. He stormed off and went to the closest squad car.

I walked over and hugged Mary, who was still babbling on about the guy doing the flip over his motorcycle. Her eyes were glassy and I realized that she was in a mild state of shock. Collette lay on her back, staring up at the stars, still cussing. Most of those cuss words had either my name or New Kassel attached to them.

"Hey, Colin!" I called.

He turned around. "What?"

"Can you get somebody to drive Mary and me to the hospital? I think she's going to need a sedative or something."

Colin came running over to the truck. "Why? What's the matter with her?"

"Nothing, physically. I mean, she's not

hurt. I think she's going into shock."

She was shaking all over, her mouth still spewing words at a thousand miles an hour. He glanced around and saw Chuck standing by his truck. "Chuck! Take Torie and Mary to the hospital, now!"

"Colin," I said, "don't push Bill. Not tonight. Put him under surveillance. I might be wrong, but I don't think this has anything to do with his finances. He hasn't been acting like somebody in debt for gambling."

"What do you know?" Colin asked.

It's difficult when you live right next door to the very person who can destroy you. Rudy's words came back to me, only in reverse. What if I could destroy the mayor?

"Whatever it is I know, I don't know I know it yet. But there's something else going on here," I said.

Rudy almost took the hospital doors off the hinges as he came bursting through them. He ran up to me and hugged me close. "How's Mary?"

"She's fine, now," I said. "They gave her a sedative, and they want to watch her overnight."

"I don't believe this," he said. Then he glanced around the room and saw Chuck sitting in a chair.

"Chuck drove Mary and me over here," I said.

Chuck got up and grabbed Rudy by the shoulder and gave him one of those man-to-man hugs. "Thanks, Chuck," Rudy said.

"My pleasure," he said. "I didn't want to leave until you got here, but I'm going to go ahead and go now."

We both watched Chuck walk out of the hospital doors, and then Rudy turned to me, taking a deep breath. "What is going on?"

"Well, Colin seems to think it was an attempted hit on the mayor," I said.

The color drained from his face. "I just saw Bill at his house. He had a taxi meet him."

"We don't have taxis in New Kassel," I said.

"I know. He called a St. Louis cab to come all the way down here and get him."

"The jerk is afraid to even use his own car to run," I said. "Rudy, this is serious."

"Well, if he's gone now, I'm not going to worry about it. As long as he's out of my town and away from my family, I don't care," he said.

But I did care. There was no love lost between the mayor and me. In fact, I despised him most of the time. For some reason, though, I knew I could figure this out and

191

felt bound to do so. I don't know, maybe it was because I knew his daughter Karri fairly well, and even though I didn't like him, he was still her father. I was reminded of Rachel having been worried about Vinnie Baietto being somebody's dad. Or son. Well, I knew for a fact that Bill had children.

And I felt sorry for them.

I glanced around the hospital emergency room. Wisteria was the closest emergency room, so all of the victims from tonight's fiasco had been brought here. The room was in utter chaos. The waiting room was in just as much disarray. Other than the person who'd been shot in the calf, most of the injuries were not serious. Bumps on the heads, cuts, scrapes, and a few broken bones. A few hours after the incident and I was noticing that my butt cheeks were incredibly sore and it felt like one of my shoulders sat higher than the other.

Out of nowhere Rudy grabbed me and hugged me even closer. "You were right," he said.

"About what?"

"That there was something going on with the mayor," he said. "I'm sorry I didn't believe you."

"That's all right," I said.

He said nothing, but I felt as though he

wanted to say more. Something in his body language. I'd let it go for now. Rudy was like anybody else. If you pushed him too much he'd clam up and be stubborn. He was stubborn enough anyway that I didn't want to give him any extra reasons to be.

So I did something I rarely did. I shut up and hugged him back, pretending that everything was okay. But everything wasn't okay. Something was very, very wrong in my town.

Thirteen

The next day came whether I was ready for it or not. I would have loved nothing better than for the sun to have taken the day off for a change, but it rose. I can't sleep once it's daylight, and since we didn't get home until eight in the morning, there would be no sleep for me. Rachel had gone to Riley's for a few hours, but was home by noon. Mary had curled up in bed with her daddy, both of them drooling onto my snowmen flannel sheets quite nicely. About ten that morning, Helen Wickland called and said that she would give my tours for the day. So I lay around and watched the Lord of the Rings trilogy on DVD with Rachel until my eyes were red and glassy and I was seeing pointy ears and hairy feet everywhere I looked. We ordered pizza in.

By the time the end credits rolled on the third movie, the living room looked like a movie theater, with soda cans strewn about, empty microwave popcorn bags on the end tables, and something sticky on the coffee table. I glanced around at the room and sighed. I'd have to clean it. Tomorrow. For now it was dark, and maybe I could finally sleep. So I toddled off to bed, but I jumped at every sound. It was the most fitful night of sleep I think I've ever had.

That damn sun rose the next morning, too. On a Monday! Rudy and Mary had literally slept all Saturday and Sunday and all night last night, although Mary had gotten up about five this morning for good. The morning had gone by in a fairly normal fashion. Rudy went to work. Rachel and Mary went to school. I was so sleepy I was stupid.

I had two choices. I could either stay at home and stare at four walls or I could go to work and stare at four walls and at least have the opportunity of an interruption to break my stupor. So I grabbed Matthew and took him to work with me rather than taking him to my mother's. There I sat, trying desperately to work, but my mind kept wandering. I'd had to comfort two different children in the past week because of violence that they had witnessed. There were no two ways about it. I was pissed off.

The Catholic church records would have

to wait. I snatched my purse, threw Matthew on my hip, turned off my computer, and went into the kitchen at the Gaheimer House to get a bottle of water. Stephanie was standing at the sink trying to get a stain out of a doily that normally graced one of the upstairs chests. Somehow Elmer had managed to knock over a cup of coffee when he was giving a tour last week — although he still swears that the coffee wasn't his. Stephanie had left Jimmy at her mother's today. I think she was afraid to bring him into town.

"Hey, you want to run down to the library with me? I'm just going to one of the branches in South County. They have a book there with St. Louis wills from 1920 to 1960. I need to look for one."

"Sure," she said.

"Oh, good. Because I'm honestly in no shape to drive."

We locked up and then headed to South St. Louis County in Stephanie's car. We pulled off in Arnold and got sandwiches and fries from the drive-through at Lion's Choice and were back on the highway in a flash. Matthew was in heaven, shoving fries into his mouth faster than I could stop him, since I couldn't reach him in the backseat. For once, he could eat as piggishly as he wanted. When we reached the Tesson Ferry branch of the library, we still weren't finished eating, so we sat outside with the windows rolled down and finished our food. The air was so cool and clean, it was almost as if it separated all of my nose hairs as I breathed it in.

"So, what's up with your friend Collette?" she asked. "She's moving?"

"She says she might be," I said. "With Collette, you never honestly know until it happens. That's why I try not to get too worked up over things until I know for sure. But she's right. She is due for a change. Long overdue, so I expect her to move somewhere. Even if it's not Arizona."

"I have a cousin like that. She moves all over the country. Every three to four years she moves, just because she needs a change," she said. "Me? It takes me three or four years just to get to know my neighbors."

"Well, maybe that's why your cousin moves," I said. "She finally gets to know the neighbors."

She smiled and agreed that was a possibility.

"So, are you freaked by what happened?" I asked.

"A little," she said. "You know, I've been thinking."

"You want to quit?"

She laughed and swallowed a fry. "No," she said. "What's changed recently? I mean, Bill has been the mayor for all of these years. Why would somebody be after him now? What has the mayor got to hide that's just become apparent recently?"

"I dunno," I said. "I don't live in his house."

"No, I mean in town. What's changed?"

I thought about it a moment. "For one thing, he's about ready to lose his job, and I think he knows it," I said.

I thought some more and finished off my sandwich. "Sam Hill suddenly got really interested in the mayor's family history. I wonder if he knows something that I don't and he's not sharing?"

"Could be," Steph said.

"Uh . . . Lou Counts is deputy and might be sheriff. Maybe she and the mayor have some bad blood. Or maybe she knows something and is blackmailing him. Gosh, it could be anything. We've got a new shop opening up. A tobacco shop. The only other thing I can think of that I know has to do with the mayor is that he put up a Web site. I can't think of anything else," I said.

Stephanie thought it over while she finished her fries. "Maybe I was wrong, then. It just seems weird that everything has been fine all of these years and now suddenly it's not."

"Yeah," I said. I like my sister. Our minds work in a similar way. I wonder how much damage we would have done to New Kassel if we had been raised together. I'm not sure New Kassel could have handled two of me as a teenager. Of course, she's five years younger, so we probably wouldn't have been at the truly crazy stage at the same time.

"Well, let's go in and look for this will," I said. "I hope it's here. But first, I have to clean up the monster back there." I jumped into the backseat, armed with wet wipes, and got Matthew cleaned up. There was a piece of a fry left in the bag, and he had a fit when he thought I might actually throw it away. The kid loves food.

"Has Sam not come up with anything new in his search?" Stephanie asked me.

"I think it's really hard when you're not sure what you're looking for. I mean, if he knew for a fact that Bill's mother had done something . . . oh, I don't know, something specific, then he'd sort of know where to look and what to look for. But we have no idea what it is the mayor is trying to hide. All we know is that it has something to do with his family."

In the library, I went to the reference

room, scanning the shelf with my index finger until I found what I was after. I pulled the book out, went through the index, and found Castlereagh, Jarvis. 1953.

"Here we go," I said. I skimmed the will, reading out loud but not every word. I'm sure that was fairly annoying to Stephanie. I didn't find what I was looking for, so I read it again, this time reading every word.

"Well?" she asked. "Does it tell you anything?"

"It tells me that Jarvis Castlereagh didn't leave Bill anything in his will. I mean, not one dollar. He doesn't mention him at all," I said.

"Why do you think that is?" she asked.

I didn't have a clue and I said so. Bill was born in 1949, so he was only four years old when his father died. I wouldn't ordinarily expect anything to be left to an offspring at that age. Most of the time people leave everything to their spouse, unless it's a second spouse and they want to make sure a specific amount or a specific item goes to their children. That wasn't the case with this family. So it wasn't the fact that Bill didn't receive anything from his father that bothered me. What bothered me was that both of his brothers did inherit part of the estate. That meant that Bill had been singled out for a reason. Bill's older brother was left money for a college fund, a comic book collection, and a chair that had belonged to Jarvis's grandfather. The youngest son was left money for college, a baseball card collection, and a set of china that had been Jarvis's mother's. The rest went to his wife, who was to split it among their children when she died.

"This makes no sense," I said.

"Well, maybe Bill and his father had a falling-out and his father left him out of the will. That's a pretty common thing, actually," she said.

"How could he have had a falling-out with a four-year-old?" I asked.

"Oh," she said. Obviously she hadn't realized that Bill had only been four when his father died. "That is odd."

I made a copy of the will on the copier and then returned the book to the shelf. My brow was furrowed, my mind racing at just what this could mean. Why would Jarvis Castlereagh disinherit one of his own children?

"I don't understand," she said.

"I just . . . I can't think."

Dinner was bizarre. Rachel was quiet. She was setting a world's record for quietness in a solid week. Yes, believe it or not, I was actually wishing she'd talk incessantly like she usually does. Mary was off-the-wall hyper and downright evil. She'd stuck her tongue out at Matthew at least three times, flipped mashed potatoes at Rachel, and called her father a wanker. Of course, she had no clue what that word meant; she just thought it sounded appropriate. I had to stifle a laugh and pat Rudy on the back so that he wouldn't choke on his peas. Rachel calmly wiped the mashed potatoes from the front of her shirt and went on eating. Rudy was still fuming over what had happened on the hayride. A faraway look entered his eyes if he wasn't in the middle of a conversation, and even then I'd lose him halfway through a sentence half of the time. The only person acting perfectly normal was Matthew. He had free rein to be completely himself, because the other two kids were barely aware that he was there.

Give him three more days and he'd notice he was being ignored by his sisters, and then he would start acting up.

"Rachel, you wash the dishes. Mary, you dry," Rudy said.

Neither one fought him over it. Rachel just got up and did it, and Mary jumped up on her chair and did the football-wide-receiver-dance and yelled, "Oh, yeah. Oh, yeah."

I wanted my children back.

A knock at the door was the only thing that kept me from going over the edge with worry. I answered it and found Colin standing on my front porch with *her*. The über-deputy, Lou Counts.

"Hi," I said to both of them, making sure I had a nice smile on my face — but not overdoing it, or Lou would think I was trying to butter her up. We sure as heck didn't want that. "Come on in."

"I just wanted to let you know that the mayor is gone," Colin said from the porch. They made no move to actually set foot in my house, so I went out to them and instantly wished I had shoes on. The floor of the front porch was cold, and the shock of it shot all the way up to my knees.

"Yes, he took a cab out of town," I said.

"We contacted Karri. She says nobody's heard from her parents," Colin said.

"So what are you thinking?" I asked. "Are you going to search his house?"

"Well, he hasn't been missing a full twenty-four hours, and I have no proof of any foul play."

"Colin!"

"Let him do his job, Mrs. O'Shea. He's doing this one by the book," Lou interrupted.

"Oh, as opposed to all the jobs he's done against the book?" I asked. "You know, Colin might be unorthodox in his approach to his job, but he's never just out and out broken the law or gone against the book, as you put it."

"Torie," he said, "Karri said that her parents have done this before."

"Done what?"

"They've taken off for a little three-day holiday without telling anybody they were going," he said. "Until Karri gets worried or until I can connect the trouble on the hayride to him, I'm gonna leave it be."

"Colin," I said.

"If he hasn't shown up at the end of three days, I'll check into it. I just wanted to let you know that he is definitely gone."

"Did he close out his checking account? What about credit card use? That'll tell you where he is," I said. Lou rolled her eyes at me and shifted her weight to one hip.

"I'll check tomorrow," he said. "Don't worry, I'm on it."

"Colin, you know as well as I do that Bill would not leave in the middle of a political race," I said, hugging myself close to ward off the chill. "You know something is up. Election day is a week from Tuesday! He would not just leave, and you know it."

"I've made up my mind," he said, stern-faced. "Don't push me on it."

"Fine," I said, and held my hands up. He tipped his hat and turned to leave, and Lou Counts gave me the snootiest look I've ever seen. I swear it was the adult equivalent of sticking her tongue out at me. I just glared at her, wishing I had Superman's powers for half a minute.

I went to bed at eight thirty, exhausted. I only slept a few hours before my dreams woke me.

Fourteen

It's funny, the things that you become accustomed to without even realizing it. I've become incredibly conditioned to the noises in and around my house. If I hear them at a certain time of day, it's normal and I don't react. If those same benign noises are heard at midnight, an alarm deep in my consciousness goes off. Like tonight. I woke up out of a dream-ridden sleep with a start, panting and sweaty. I had been dreaming that I was tied to a paddle wheel and every time it went around I was dunked into the murky, muddy river. I think I'd been holding my breath in my sleep, for whatever reason, and that was the real reason I woke up. As soon as I did, I heard my chickens cluck and Fritz give a little bark. Chickens clucking at midnight could mean a stray dog or a coyote. Or maybe it meant somebody was next door at the mayor's house.

I stood and stretched, amazingly alert for only having had four hours of sleep. I went to the window that showed the view of my backyard and the mayor's house. I could see part of his house over my fence, because my bedroom was on the top floor. There were no lights on at the mayor's residence. Nothing that would tell me he was hiding inside or that he'd fled the country. I glanced out the other window. The one that the moonlight shone through and showed that black-silver highway of water. The Mississippi. Old Man River. God, I was going to miss this view when we moved. A sense of calm lay across everything. Whatever had been bothering my chickens had now passed. Most likely it had been a stray dog or cat.

I went back to bed and tucked my feet under Rudy's legs to get warm. He jerked at first but then got over it. Fritz, being a wiener dog, can't jump up on the bed without help. His little legs are too short. My arm lay over the edge of the bed, and I felt his wet nose on my fingers. I opened one eye, which he saw, so he immediately wagged his tail and gave me what I call a doggy smile. I leaned over, scooped him up, and kissed the top of his head. Then I laid him down next to Rudy's warm back, pulled the covers off, and went over to my computer. There was no way I was going to go back to sleep.

I waited patiently, staring out the window, as my computer booted up. The computer decided to run some stupid analysis, so I went downstairs, grabbed the near-empty carton of ice cream and a spoon, and ran back up the steps in time to see the computer screen ready for me. I logged on to the Internet, waited for it to make those annoying noises, and then heard, "You've got mail."

My cousin in West Virginia had sent me a typed-up version of a will he'd found for one of our ancestors. I printed it out to read later. I waded through the junk mail and sighed. I just want to say for the record that I hate spam, and I think all those who send it should have to endure some torturous event, like having their eyelashes plucked. I delete everything that has an address I don't recognize. It was hard to type and shovel ice cream at the same time, but I managed. I went to Bill's Web site and waited for everything to load.

I went to the section that had the photographs from when he was younger. I read the blurb about running through fields of flowers again. For some reason, it bothered me this time. Well, it had bothered me the first time I read it because I thought it was horse manure, but this time it bugged me for a different reason. At first I'd just thought that he'd made it up, that he'd lied, but now . . . My brain let go of something it had been holding on to, and I was almost certain that I'd read those words somewhere before.

The picture of him sitting in his front yard, with the Mississippi behind him, kept drawing my attention. There was something wrong with it. Actually, there were a few things wrong with it. If this was his front yard, then the sun was setting on the wrong side of the river. If this was taken in New Kassel, as he claimed, then New Kassel was on the east side of the river, and we all know that New Kassel and all of Missouri is on the west side of the Mississippi. This photograph had been taken in Illinois or Mississippi or somewhere on the east side of the river.

There was something else. I looked at the bottom of the shoes of the little boy in the picture. They were hard to see because the picture was so small, but there were initials there. In big families, sometimes people would write the name or initials on the bottoms of the little kids' shoes, especially if the children were close in age. I couldn't make out what it said, but I was almost certain that the first initial was not a *W.* I saved the page to my favorites and then sent it to Colin in an e-mail, telling him to call me as soon as he got it.

Then I went to my bookshelves and started combing through books on New Kassel and Granite County. Two hours later I found what I had been looking for. In *A Biographical Sketch of Noted Personalities of Granite County, Missouri*, published in 1911, I found what had been plaguing me. The foreword was an autobiographical piece written by the editor of the book.

As a child, I can remember looking out on the Mississippi River thinking it was the most beautiful thing I'd ever seen. It was the giver and taker of life. I remember long lazy summer days, drinking lemonade and running through fields of cornflowers and daisies, thinking that the world was indeed a charmed place.

I slammed the book shut and stomped my foot. That son-of-a-bitch had plagiarized a hundred-year-old book for his stupid Web site! That was my first reaction. My second reaction was to wonder how he ever got the smarts to do it in the first place. I mean, this would have actually required some research on his part. I was impressed — but I was ticked at the same time. Rudy, who had heard me slamming and stomping, rolled over and buried his head under his pillow.

Then the phone rang. I glanced at the clock on my desk. 2:40 a.m. I grabbed it before it could ring a third time. "Yeah?"

"It's Colin. You said to call as soon as I got the e-mail."

"Colin, it's nearly three in the morning," I said, incredulous. I shook my head at his audacity.

"You sent it at almost one in the morning. I figured you'd still be up," he said. "I've seen Bill's Web site. Remember? I'm the one who told you about it."

"Okay, something is seriously wrong with this situation," I said in a whisper.

"Shut up!" Rudy roared from the bed.

"What did you find out?" Colin asked.

"Well, first of all, that whole bit he's got on his Web site about running through cornflowers, et cetera, was written in 1911 by a man who edited a collection of biographical sketches of Granite County residents. I mean, word for word. So he stole that. That's not really one of his childhood memories."

Rudy tossed a pillow at me. It hit the floor.

"So he plagiarizes. We know the guy's a jerk," Colin said. "We know he'll stop at nothing to get votes."

"Yes, but —"

Another pillow went whizzing by my head and nearly knocked over my sand-castle sculpture. "All right, I'm going!" I said to Rudy. I went down to the kitchen, with the cordless phone still in my hand. I was afraid I would wake up the kids if I stood in the kitchen and talked, so I went out on the back porch. I kept the door cracked, and Fritz came slithering through to join me. Immediately the chickens started to stir. "The picture of Bill as a baby. It was taken on the east side of the Mississippi," I said into the phone.

"So? Maybe he was at his grandmother's house when he took it. Or maybe he just forgot what time of day it was when he posted it on the Internet."

"Colin!"

"Look, I'm on your side, Torie. I don't believe Bill was born and raised anywhere near here any more than you do, but that hardly proves anything. I'm playing devil's advocate. This is what he'll tell you. He'll say, 'Oh, I was at my great-aunt's house' or whatever. This doesn't prove anything," Colin said. His voice sounded strained.

"No, but it does prove that he's lying. We know he's lying, regardless of what stupid excuse he comes up with. Also, on the bottom of his right shoe, in the picture, if you look close enough . . ."

"What?" he said. I heard him click some buttons. Evidently he had the computer on in front of him. He had two phone lines in his house.

"I think it's initials written on the bottom of his shoes," I said. I explained my theory to him. "I think if you had somebody in the lab enhance it, we might be able to figure out what the initials are."

"So?" he asked.

"So, if the initials aren't *WJC,* we'll know —"

"Know what? They could be hand-me-down shoes," he said. "His cousin's shoes."

"Well, you could still check," I said. Of course, I knew he was right. In fact, I'd just given Stephanie a whole bag of clothes for my new nephew, and some of them had Matthew's initials on the tags. One jacket had his whole name in it. Sometimes things get mixed up on the playground at the park or what have you, so it was best to mark your stuff. I knew Colin was right, but I didn't want to believe him.

"I will," he said. "I'll have somebody try to enhance it. I'm just telling you that none of this proves anything. It only makes our suspicions stronger. But we don't know anything else, not even what to be suspicious of."

"Well," I said, taking a deep breath and smelling woodsmoke on the air, "that's something."

"I suppose."

"All right, Colin, I'm freezing, so, I'm going inside now, which means I have to hang up."

"All right," he said.

"Let me know what you find out."

He didn't acknowledge what I said in any way. He just said good-bye and hung up. I pushed the button on the phone and then called Fritz back onto the porch, making that smoochy sound that dogs love. As I looked up to see him coming, I saw a person standing at the end of my yard. Now, our backyard has the privacy fence so that the mayor doesn't have to see our chickens, but we don't have a fence that goes all the way around the house. I jumped, startled, when I saw the person. Fritz growled at the stranger with all his might. Who said a dog that's only four inches off the ground couldn't be a good watchdog?

Then the person just walked around the back of my porch, as if he owned the place. I turned to go into the house and run like lightning when I heard a voice. It was Lou Counts.

"What in the hell are you doing in my

backyard?" I asked, furious with her but relieved at the same time. My thumb was on the nine button on the phone; if she came two steps closer I was calling 911.

"Just making sure you stay on your own property," she said.

I was so confused I didn't know what to think. "I am on my property. Speaking of which, you're on it, too. You'd better get off."

"Go ahead, call 911," she said. "I am the responding officer."

"No," I said. "Miller is on duty. I know the sheriff's department schedule."

"Then I was never here. Like to see you prove that I was," she said.

It was going to be like that, huh? "Fine," I said. "It rained last night. It's muddy. I'm sure your footprints will be easy enough to cast."

She laughed a little, but it was more to try to make her look smart than anything else. She knew I was right. "Stay away from the mayor's house," she said. "Colin doesn't want you over there. I'm just doing some moonlighting, to make sure his wishes are met."

"Oh, did he put you up to this?"

She shuffled her feet. I couldn't see her expression in the dark, just the glint of the moon off her cropped hair. "There are so

215

many things going on right under your nose and you're too self-absorbed to see any of them," she said.

"Like what?"

"Like the fact that the sheriff really doesn't want you snooping where you don't belong. He told me, in no uncertain terms, that if it weren't for his wife, he'd have as little to do with you as possible. He puts up with you only because his wife would be heartbroken if he didn't. He also told me he felt sorry for your husband."

"Everybody feels sorry for Rudy. That's no big secret."

"They bowl together," she declared.

"Yes, I'm aware. Boy, you're a regular detective."

"It's the only thing you're aware of. At the bowling alley last week, Rudy told his friend and fellow bowler Chuck that he wished you guys would move to California."

"What?" I said.

"That was right after the guys in the bowling alley were calling him some not too complimentary names and making fun of him."

"About what?" I asked. A lump rose in my throat, but I swallowed it down. I couldn't trust anything this woman said. Not one word. Somehow, though, she'd managed to touch on my one area of insecurity. Now the seed was planted.

"About his marriage," she scoffed. "Must you have everything spelled out for you?"

"You know what?" I said. "It's three in the morning. You're in my backyard uninvited, I'm barefoot, my teeth are chattering, and I have to pee. I don't believe a word you're saying. I believe you'd say whatever you could to distract me. So just go on home."

"Distract you from what? Investigating a nonexistent crime that is none of your business?" she said.

"There'd have to be a crime in order for it to be none of my business." Was I really having this conversation at three in the morning? On my back porch? "Besides, two guys on motorcycles were shooting guns in my town. That's hardly a nonexistent crime."

"I was referring to your mayor."

Something wasn't right. I could not for the life of me see what was going on here, but something wasn't right. Everybody from Sam Hill to the mayor to this . . . this woman. There was something I was missing.

"Good night, Lou."

"That's Deputy Counts to you," she said.

"Good night, Lou. I catch you in my yard again and you'll be sorry," I said.

She turned, hands clasped behind her

back, and walked out of the yard. I was so furious with her I could have spit, but I was probably more furious with her for keeping me away from the mayor's house. Until I saw her round the corner of my house, I had been entertaining the idea of snooping around over there.

I really, really hated that woman.

The New Kassel Gazette
The News You Might Miss
By Eleanore Murdoch

The hayrides and bonfire were a huge success! Well, other than the fact that people got shot at and such. We made a lot of money off of that event, and one man wrote us a letter saying it was the most fun he'd ever had in his life. Two weekends in a row we've had rip-roaring events! Has anybody else noticed the television crew trucks parked around town?

Oh, Tobias Thorley wants me to publish a thank-you for whoever it was who sewed up his knickers.

Father Bingham wants to encourage all of us to pray for the safe and speedy return of our mayor and his beloved wife.

Leftover apple cider from the weekend's event can be bought at the general store for half price. My husband says it's a great laxative.

One last thing. Elmer wants to have an audition for new members of the New Kassel adult marching band. Seems some of the members have had too many hip replacements to be able to march in time anymore. So see Elmer at the firehouse.

Can't wait to see what happens on Halloween.

Until next time,
Eleanore

Fifteen

The next morning brought a head full of doubt and a gut full of conflict. There was a part of me that didn't believe a single thing Lou Counts had said to me, but there was also a part of me that knew I was head-strong, belligerent at times, nosy, and a real pain in the butt to live with. Rudy had his hands full. Of that, there was no doubt. That's why I loved him — because he knew my light side and he knew my dark side and still loved me. At least that's what I'd thought. Or could this be what I sensed from him the other night? The sense that some-thing wasn't right between us and I was just too blind to see it? But wouldn't he tell me if something was wrong? In my mind, I kept going back and forth with this argument. Then I'd think that Lou really was all those names that I'd spent the night calling her in my head. In fact, I'd fallen back asleep last night thinking up ingenious new names for the woman.

Then I'd think, why would Lou Counts lie? What would she have to gain from it? She wanted me out of the way, but out of the way of what? Unless she was seriously worried about my influence over the voters. Well, if she wanted to find out just who had the power in this town, I'd show her.

It was Eleanore Murdoch. Hands down. A few strategically dropped sentences and Eleanore would destroy Lou all on her own, or at least make things difficult for her. All I'd have to do was take the wrapping off the present. Gosh, all this time I thought I'd missed my calling and should have been a detective. I really should have been a politician. Somewhere in the back of my mind, I knew Father Bingham would have some rather discouraging words to say about what I planned to do, but darn it, this called for the big guns — and nothing was bigger than Eleanore's mouth.

Rudy had gotten up and gone to work, just like every other day, and hadn't acted as though he had some deeply hidden marriage-breaking secret in his heart. So after I dropped the girls off at school and Matthew off at my mother's, I drove back to New Kassel, convinced more than ever that

Lou Counts was just playing me — or trying to. A Sheryl Crow song was playing on the radio, and I sang along. For a moment I forgot all about what had happened over the weekend. It was just me and Sheryl and the gently rolling hills and meadows in their full autumnal blaze.

I arrived at the Gaheimer House and made some phone calls. One was to Eleanore. Did she know that I'd found that peculiar Lou Counts stalking around my backyard last night? Yes, it made me feel very creepy. Yes, Lou certainly had a lot of sway where the sheriff was concerned. That was all there was to it. Eleanore would take care of the rest. Surprisingly, I didn't feel as guilty as I thought I would.

Then I started calling every high school in Granite County. I didn't speak to people in administration because they would have told me that the information was confidential. I called up the librarians and asked them to check the yearbooks. "Yes, I'm planning a surprise birthday party for my father-in-law, Bill Castlereagh, and I wanted to come in and check your yearbooks for pictures of him that I could blow up and use at the party. I can't ask him for his yearbooks or he'll get suspicious. I think he graduated in 1967. Could you check and make sure before I drive down there? What? No Bill Castlereagh? What about 1966 and 1968? No? Well, I'm certainly glad I called first. Thank you." Again, simple as that. Surely there was a place reserved in Hades for somebody who could lie that easily. It had my name on it. A throne, carved out in brimstone. I shook my head and rid myself of that vision.

By the time I was finished I had found out nothing, which was exactly what I was after. I had found out that nobody by the name of Bill Castlereagh had graduated from any high school in Granite County. Now he couldn't even use the old I-came-from-the-area line.

The phone rang, and I answered it. It was my sister. Today was her day off. "Hey," she said. "Look, Jimmy's got a fever. If he's not better by tomorrow, I may not be able to come in. I'll ask my mother to watch him, but I'm not sure she can."

"Okay," I said. "Not a big deal."

We talked a few more minutes, and then Collette sauntered into my office and plopped down in the chair across from me, one leg thrown over the arm of the chair as if she owned the whole damn place. That's the thing with Collette. She can make any place feel like hers in nothing flat. There's an art to that. Of course, she looked completely out of place in a room where the walls are decorated with my Rose of Sharon quilt and framed historical maps of the town and the county that have yellowed with age. She wore unbelievably spiked black heels, a black miniskirt with black hose, and a royal blue silk blouse. Still, she'd claimed the place as hers from the moment she swung that leg over the arm of the chair.

"Collette, I can see your underwear," I said with my hand over the phone.

"Oh, like you've never seen it before," she said and moved her leg around.

I said good-bye to Steph, hung up the phone, and stared at my best friend, who looked as though she'd had the worst night of her life. Her clothes might have been spiffy, but her hair looked sort of dirty, like from too much hair spray, and her makeup was smudged beneath her eyes. My assumption must have registered on my face.

"Don't blame me. I'm traumatized. I had to drown my sorrows in something."

"What are you talking about?" I asked.

"Well, I was so distraught after what happened to me Friday night that I've been on a shopping spree ever since," she said. "I'm officially out of money."

"Credit?"

"Maxed," she said.

I had been so wrapped up in myself and my kids that it hadn't even occurred to me that Collette might have been having some difficulty with what happened, too. Of course, Collette lived for excuses to go on shopping sprees, so I wasn't going to feel too guilty over it.

"Hope you have enough money left to pay Eleanore," I said.

"She made me pay for my room up front," she said, and rolled her eyes. "She doesn't trust anybody."

"Nope. Not a soul."

"I've got another check coming from the paper, and my severance pay. Otherwise, I'll be dipping into my savings."

"Have you decided where you're going?"

"I heard back from Tucson. They want to do a face-to-face interview. So that's good," she said. Then horror crossed her face. "God, I'll need a new suit and a manicure."

"You'll live."

"Only if I get the new suit and manicure," she said.

We were laughing when I heard the front door to the Gaheimer House open. Now, there's a sign posted outside that gives the days and times we give tours, but tourists see a big old red brick building in this town and automatically assume we're open. I've had people come in thinking we were an antique store. I had one woman who had an offer all ready for the sideboard and dining room furniture. She was quite upset when she found out none of the contents of the Gaheimer House were for sale. So I didn't think much of it when I heard the door open, but then I realized that Stephanie wasn't here, so I got up to go and see who it was. Before I could make it out of my office, a man appeared at the door. He wore a charcoal gray pinstripe suit, a silk shirt, and shiny shoes. His dark black hair was slicked back, and he had a nervous twitch in one shoulder.

"Tito de Rosa," he said, and extended a hand.

I almost said, *Oh, the hit man,* but caught myself just in time. "Hello," I said.

"I'm looking for Victory O'Shea," he said.

"That would be me."

"You're Torie O'Shea?" he asked, looking me up and down.

"Yes," I said. I'm not sure what he expected, but I suppose a short woman with sneakers, Levi's, and a T-shirt that read NOBODY CAN EAT PIES LIKE I CAN EAT PIES wasn't exactly his idea of the person who would run the historical society. The T-shirt was from a pie-eating contest that my husband had won a few years back. It had fake pie stains splattered all over it. I often wear my husband's things. That's one thing husbands are for. Opening jars, killing bugs — although Rudy is as scared of spiders as I am — warming your feet on in the middle of the night, and lending you their extra-big clothes.

"And I would be her best friend and trusty sidekick." Collette stood and held her hand out. *Right,* I thought. *Just as long as there aren't any tractors involved.* "You can call me Collette."

He smiled and kissed her hand. Then he looked back to me.

"What can I do for you?" I asked, and then wondered if that was a good thing to say to a hit man or not. Probably not. I wondered if I should add "within reason." Mr. de Rosa sat in the chair that Collette had just vacated. He adjusted the button on his jacket and then checked for dirt under his nails.

I wasn't about to offer my assistance again. I'd wait him out. Finally he smiled, and I swear a spark of light glinted off one of his front teeth. "Rumor has it that you're the woman to see around here, Torie. Do you mind if I call you Torie?"

"Uh . . ."

"I want you to keep an eye on Tiny Tim for me."

"The tobacco shop owner?" I asked.

"Yes," he said. "I can make it very much worth your while."

"I don't need any money, Tito. Can I call you Tito?" There was no doubt that the way to stay one step ahead of crooks was to make sure that you didn't owe them anything or need what they were offering. This man thought I could be bought, because most people can be, but he had nothing on me.

"All right, then, if you watch Tiny Tim for me, I'll make sure nothing bad befalls your family," he said.

Okay, there was that.

Collette just stood there with her mouth open, gaping at this man.

"What exactly do you mean by 'watch him'?" I asked.

"I have reason to believe that Tiny Tim is conducting business in this town," he said.

I played stupid. I played like I did not suspect him of being a mafioso. I played like I had no idea Colin had confiscated his Glock. I did not for one second think that this man didn't have another weapon with him. "Yes, he's opened a tobacco shop," I said, and smiled at him sweetly.

He smiled back at me, but it never reached his eyes. In fact, I saw genuine malice behind those dark lashes of his. "Let me rephrase that. I believe he's conducting illegal business in this town."

Collette laughed with her mouth open, slapped her hand on her knee, and then struggled to regain control when she realized she was the only one laughing. "In New Kassel?" she asked. "Nothing illegal ever happens here."

I glared at her.

"Okay, well the occasional murder," she said, "but nothing else. In fact, I happen to know that everybody in this town actually pays their taxes on time."

Mental note to self: Inquire about Collette's sources.

"At any rate, Torie," he said, "Tiny Tim's business is my business. Well, let me just say that I believe something he's involved in is directly related to something that I'm involved in. His actions could alter my actions. I need you to let me know if he begins to behave unusually."

"First of all, I don't know any two-bit crooks, so I won't know if his behavior is weird. I have nothing to compare it to," I said. Tito de Rosa began stroking his chin. It looked like it might be a nervous habit, something he would do just before he whacked somebody. "Second of all . . . well,

I had something else to say, but now I seem to have forgotten it."

He smiled, and then I remembered. "Oh, and the sheriff has sicced his new deputy on Tiny Tim. So if I'm caught snooping on Tim, she'll know and go tell the sheriff."

He seemed to think about that for a minute, as though it could be a serious kink in his plans, or maybe I read something there that wasn't there. "Just tell me what you see," he said.

"Like what?" I asked.

"A late-night rendezvous. If he fails to open his store on time. If he leaves town. If he begins to have some . . . unseemly company in his shop. Call me."

"Unseemly," I said.

"He means more of his type," Collette said. "Shiny shoes and suits."

Shiny shoes did seem to be a dead giveaway. I don't think any man I know in this town has shiny shoes — except maybe the pair that Tobias uses for church, but he only wears them on Sunday. Shiny shoes on Sunday seem to be acceptable. Of course, in other parts of the world, the corporate world, for example, men with shiny shoes are an everyday occurrence, but not here in New Kassel. Shiny shoes in New Kassel mean shifty.

"Oh," I said. "Let me ask you, then. There have been a couple of shiny-shoed individuals in town lately. One we found dead on a float. One fell out of a tree but managed to escape. Two more shot at my best friend here, and one of them was killed by the sheriff. Well, those two were wearing motorcycle boots at the time, but I'll bet their street shoes were shiny. Are these your people?"

"Just let me know about Tiny, Mrs. O'Shea," he said, and stood and stretched.

"Hey," I said. "I have a job. I can't just snoop on Tiny Tim all week. Besides, you're better at surveillance than I am, certainly. I mean, isn't that part of your job description?"

He just looked back over his shoulder and smiled as he walked out of my office. The nerve of him! Collette and I exchanged exasperated glances. I got up and followed him to the door. "Who do you think you are?"

He spun on me then, and I knew that he had been playing nice up to this point and that I didn't have a clue what I was up against. There was no mistaking the venom in his eyes. He all but pinned me to the wall, nearly knocking over a porcelain vase. A cold wind seemed to wrap him up. It would not surprise me to learn that the man actually had no heart. He moved so quickly and so precisely, and yet I couldn't even so much as see a pulse beneath his skin. He never blinked when he spoke. "I can make those that you love disappear. Hell, Torie, I can make this whole town disappear. So do as I say and quit being cute." His chin jutted out at the end of his speech.

I swallowed a sob, and tears stung the back of my eyes. I completely believed his threat.

"Don't go telling that stepfather of yours about our little collaboration, either. Okay? And I'll see to it his bowling league stays intact," he said. "Even though they need to be put out of their misery. Capiche?"

"Right," I said.

With that he left the Gaheimer House, and the tears flowed down my face.

So much for staying one step ahead of the crook.

Sixteen

It was not lost on me that Tito de Rosa had used the word "collaboration." In the movies, any time a person does a favor for the mob, they own you for life. Or you end up at the bottom of the river, wearing cement shoes. Collette came running out of my office to find me in a shaking heap on the foyer floor.

"Oh, my God," she said and ran to me. "Are you all right?"

"Yeah," I said. My chin trembled. "I'm just really scared."

"I can get some of my friends at the paper to see what they can find out on this guy, if you want me to," she said.

"I don't want you involved," I said.

"I'm already involved. I was there when the pact went down."

"His name is Tito de Rosa. We think he might be Chicago mob."

Her face blanched. She helped me up off the floor. "The de Rosa family. As in Victor 'Papa' de Rosa? He belongs to that family? Is he Victor de Rosa's son?"

"I don't know," I said, irritated. "I don't make it a habit to trace the family trees of the Mafia. I mean, I don't even know the names of any, except the obvious ones. Like Bugsy Malone and Al Capone."

"This century, sweetheart," she said.

My mind drew a blank.

"See, this is why you need to get out in the world. Get to the big city once in a while," she said.

"Why? So I can meet the thugs face-to-face? No, thank you. One of the reasons I live in New Kassel is so they remain just names on the television," I said.

"Yeah, but you have to turn the blasted thing on once in a while," she said.

I'd concede that point to her.

The phone rang in my office. I just stared down the hall at the doorway. Collette looked at me, and then she looked at my office, too.

"It's probably Rudy," I said.

"Right. Probably not the Godfather calling in a favor," she said.

"Collette!"

"Sorry," she said. "I'll get it."

She ran for my office to get the phone, and I trailed along behind her as if I'd just been caught in a tornado. I don't know what I had thought Tito was made of, but obviously I hadn't taken him seriously enough. I cringed when I thought of the way I'd made fun of him in the office. *Can I call you Tito?* My God, it was a miracle that he hadn't shot me right then and there.

A wave of anxiety washed over me as I realized he was probably not alone in town — unless he was cocky and thought that some little podunk town like New Kassel wouldn't require much manpower. He could handle us hicks. Nah, guys like that didn't live to be thirty by being stupid. He had backup in town. I'd bet on it.

"It's Colin," Collette called out.

I made it to the door just as Collette was about to tell him that Tito de Rosa had paid us a visit. I stifled a screech and grabbed the phone from her, shaking my head at her as I did. Tito had been specific. Colin was not to know about our meeting.

"Hey, Colin," I said.

"You okay?" he asked. "You sound . . . shook up."

"Fine," I said, and started fake-panting for breath. "I just ran all the way from the back-yard."

235

Man, those lies just kept tripping off my tongue. Collette looked at me and rolled her eyes. Somehow when Collette rolls her eyes, it's much more insulting than when anybody else does it.

"You need to get more exercise," he said. "I can put you on a regimen."

Coming from the man who could no longer see his toes . . . I wanted to punch him, but I let it go. "What's up?"

"I just wanted to make sure you were still at the office. I want to come by and talk to you," he said.

"Are you bringing your watchdog? The she-wolf?"

"No," he said. "It's her day off, anyway."

"You mean she takes a day off? I bet she's out target practicing. Or doing like five thousand sit-ups or something," I said.

"Just sit tight."

Colin was at the Gaheimer House in about fifteen minutes. In that time I had filled Collette in on what had gone on between Tito and me in the foyer. She promised not to tell anybody. Then she filled me in on the de Rosa family of Chicago. Papa de Rosa indeed sounded like a gem. Back in the seventies, his right-hand man had accidentally allowed one of his dogs to be poisoned. Papa de Rosa loved his dogs so much that he made the guy eat dog food for a week. On the last day he gave him a big steak dinner — and poisoned him. I shivered. She had just opened a can of Pepsi and I had just opened a Dr Pepper when Colin came in.

"It doesn't mean anything conclusive," he said. He held up a photograph of a fingerprint. "In fact, I'm not sure what the hell it means."

"What is it?"

"The fingerprints came back on those binoculars," he said.

"And?"

"They belong to Tiny Tim Julep," he said. "The guy who owns the new tobacco shop."

My heart sank, and Collette almost choked. She waved her hands in front of her face and then found her Pepsi can on my desk and took a drink. "Drainage," she said to Colin. "Been trying to get rid of it for a week."

Colin only gave her a peculiar look. "Why would the new tobacconist be hiding in a tree snooping on the mayor?" he asked. "It makes no sense."

"Well, it explains why the branch broke. Tiny Tim is huge," I said.

"I'm going over there to talk to him now. See what his explanation is for this," he said.

"Did he have a rap sheet?" Collette asked.

"Racketeering. Tax evasion. A few things. Assault and battery. Managed not to spend too much time in prison for any of it, though. Funny how those guys rack up a list of crimes a mile long but do under five years' time total. What I want to know is why a man like that would come to New Kassel to open up shop. There's a connection to the mayor. That's for sure. If only I knew what Bill was hiding," he said.

Collette and I exchanged worried glances. I was not about to offer my opinion on what, who, or why Tiny Tim Julep was in our town.

"Hang on a second," I said to Colin. I logged on to the Internet and brought up Bill's Web site. While I was at it, I explained quickly to Collette what was going on — or what we thought was going on — with Bill. "Nobody's seen him since the hayride," I finished up.

"Maybe he just needed a shopping binge, too," she said.

"Very possible," I said, "but I'm thinking not."

We all crowded around the computer screen and studied the Web page. "What do you think he's hiding?" Colin said.

"Maybe one of his kids is a homosexual.

You know, that could ruin his political career," Collette said.

Colin shot her a quizzical glance.

"This is the Midwest," she justified.

"Well, as far as I can tell," I said, "your children's sexual preferences don't seem to hurt your career. It does hurt your career if it's *your* sexual preference. Which is odd, since I'm sure there are plenty of heterosexual deviants in places of power and nobody's the wiser, but that's neither here nor there."

"I'm just trying to help," Collette said. "As I said before, this is the Midwest."

"I think there's more to it than that," I said.

"Wait," she said. "This bio says that he was born in 1949 and graduated from college in 1970. Unlikely, he would have graduated from college a year early. Not impossible, but not likely."

She was right. There on the computer screen, Bill had written that he had graduated in 1970. "Good job, Collette," I said.

"See? I'm good for something," she said.

"I'll bet he never even attended that college. Did I tell you that I checked every high school in the county? He did not graduate from any of them. So he either went to school in Granite County and dropped out without graduating, or he went to school somewhere else. I mean, the jig is definitely up."

"No kidding," Colin said.

"He's got a lot to answer for, and there's no way he's going to be reelected. He's finished. Washed up," I said.

Colin was unusually quiet, and I eyed him curiously. "What is it? I thought you'd be thrilled."

Colin shrugged. "Well, I just kinda wanted to beat him fair and square, you know? Because I was the better person."

"The guy has lied about everything. I think that makes you the better person, you dork," Collette said.

She was right. Regardless of what his reasons were, Bill was a liar and had misled our entire community. I checked my e-mail quickly. Force of habit. Another message blinked at me from my cousin in West Virginia. I'd read it when I got home.

"Well, I'm going," Colin said. "You want me to drive you home?"

"Sure," I said. "I'll be right with you. I just have to close up here." As soon as he was out the door, I turned off the computer and then raised a finger to my lips. "Collette," I whispered. "Find out what you can on the de Rosa family. Get back to me tonight or tomorrow. The mayor has lied about everything, and somebody from the de Rosa family is in our town. Too much of a coincidence, if you ask me."

"I will. I'll see what I can find on this Tiny Tim Julep fellow, too," she said. "Maybe Bill was part of the witness relocation program."

"Well, if he is, remind me never to turn state's evidence."

"Why?"

"Because our government didn't do a very good job of relocating him. Besides, he doesn't have a whole new identity. He just fudged the one he's got. No, there's more to this than that. Something is so not right here that it actually hurts my head to think about it," I said. I stuck my head out of my office and glanced through the ballroom. Colin had shut the front door behind him. "I've got to go. Call me tonight."

"I will," she said. She grabbed her purse, turned off my office light, and walked out through the ballroom and the foyer with me. Once outside, she went right, in the direction of the Murdoch. Colin and I went left, in the direction of my house. He dropped me off at my driveway and waited there until I had shut the door.

At dinner the kids acted a little more like themselves, but things still weren't the way they should be. Rudy was kind of quiet, but perturbed at the same time, like every little thing irritated him. Of course, maybe it was because he got very little sleep last night, what with me up at three in the morning. I chose not to push anybody about how he or she was feeling.

I decided to give Matthew a bath. He was safe territory. He wasn't old enough to be hiding things from me. Whatever Matthew was feeling was what I got. No guessing games. I washed his hair, which was a chore since he wiggled more than a baby pig. Then he began to play like he was a pirate. "Man overboard!" he called out, and fell face first in the water, narrowly missing the spout by an inch. The second time he did it, he drenched me, and I jerked his arm and told him to stop.

"It's fun," he said. I'm sure adults come across as the biggest party poopers in the universe to a three-year-old child.

"I gotta potty!" Mary called out, and came running into the bathroom.

"Use ours upstairs," I said. She reluctantly left the bathroom, running with her legs squeezed together. Matthew thought that was funny and chuckled. I turned around long enough to grab his towel from the cabinet, and he did the man-overboard thing again and this time smacked his head on the

242

spout. He landed in the water and sucked in a big gulp and came up coughing and spewing. A big knot formed on his head almost instantly.

"Aww," I said, and dragged him out of the water onto my lap, soaking wet. "This is why mommies tell you not to do stuff that's stupid." I raised his arms over his head to try to clear the water out of his lungs. I'm not sure if that really works, but my mother always did it to me, and anytime anybody is choking my grandmother always yells out, "Raise their arms over their head!" So I did it, regardless. For all I knew, I could actually be making it worse. He coughed and sputtered some more. It was kind of funny, because he desperately wanted to wail and cry, but he couldn't stop coughing long enough.

I dried him off, put his jammies on him, and led him by the hand out to the kitchen, where I put some ice cubes in a Ziploc bag and told him to hold it on his forehead.

Rudy came in and took one look at me and laughed. "You jump in with him?" Then he saw Matthew's head. "What happened?"

"He walked the plank and hit his head," I said.

"Here, you come watch Spider-Man with Daddy," he said. "All right?"

I let Rudy take Matthew to the sanctuary

of the living room recliner, and I went upstairs and changed my clothes, passing Mary on the way down. She took the stairs two at a time, and when she skipped one, she ran all the way back up and did it over.

After I'd changed into my own jammies I, of course, booted up the computer and began looking at the files on Bill's family tree. I glanced down at the handwritten ones and then looked at the ones on the computer. There were no transcription mistakes. Whoever had transcribed Bill's tree (most likely me) had done so exactly as it had originally been written. I knew that when all of this finally fell into place I was going to feel like an idiot.

The phone rang. I answered it. It was Elmer. "Torie," he said, "I just wanted to know about this weekend."

"As far as I know, everything is still set to go on the bonfire-cookout-bluegrass-Octoberfest," I said.

"I thought maybe because of what happened . . ."

"Well, we may not have anybody show up, but it's still a go," I said.

"How are your girls?" he asked.

"Better," I said. "Thanks for asking."

"That's good," he said. "I'll talk to you later, then."

I hung up the phone and rubbed my eyes. The last of the day's sunlight filtered through the window that faced Bill's house. In another three weeks it would be dark right after dinner. I couldn't help but wonder what Sylvia would think of all of this mess with the mayor, if she were alive. Of course, if Sylvia were alive, she might actually know something that would help me. I'd found out firsthand that her shoes were too big to fill. I might have the money and the property and the title, but I would never have the memories and the knowledge that she had held in her mind.

I glanced down at Bill's handwritten charts and realized something with startling clarity. The handwriting on Bill's charts . . . It was too old-fashioned looking to be his. I opened a drawer and pulled out some photographs that had been Sylvia's. She'd written on the back of them before she died. The handwriting matched that on Bill's charts. Sylvia had filled out the mayor's family group sheets and his five-generation charts.

Was that possible? Well, of course it was possible — but why would she?

I began cross-referencing Bill's charts on the computer. By the time I was finished, I'd figured out one very important detail. From four generations back, Bill's family tree was

. . . too perfect, for lack of a better term. It was as if somebody had added his great-grandparents' names to the lists of the most prestigious families in American history. I mean, there wasn't one single woman living in a poorhouse, no average ordinary coal miner or dirt-poor farmer.

I logged on to Google and typed in a few of the different families that he was descended from. A few Web sites came up, and I checked the group sheets for each of them.

A "group sheet" is a family data sheet of a particular ancestor and his family. For example, my group sheet would list Rudy, me, Rachel, Mary, and Matthew with our birth dates, places of birth, etc. It would also list Rudy's parents and mine, and has a place for death dates, cemetery record, and info like occupation.

People from all over the world have compiled family group sheets on specific families on the Internet.

So, basically, I was checking Bill's family tree to see how they matched up to the genealogies online.

Bill's great-grandmother on his mother's mother's side, for example, was supposedly one of the children of a Samuel Baldwin in Massachusetts. I found the right Samuel Baldwin — who, by the way, was descended from Charlemagne through the Bruen family — but Bill's great-grandmother was not one of his children. I typed in more names and found more of the same. Somebody had connected the names on Bill's charts to all of these families with illustrious pedigrees. His family tree, for certain, was a completely fraudulent piece of work from the fourth generation on back!

I didn't for one second believe that Bill was smart enough to do this on his own.

So who did that leave? It hurt my head to think about it any more, so I went downstairs and told Rudy and the kids good night. Matthew was asleep on Rudy's lap, drooling to his heart's content. I shuffled back up the stairs and fell asleep almost the second my head hit the pillow.

Seventeen

Something woke me up at ten past midnight. Maybe it was just my internal alarm clock suddenly warning that it was after midnight and Rudy was still not in bed. He should have thrown his big hairy leg over my hip by now and made grinding noises with his teeth. The simple fact was, if Rudy had come to bed, I would still have been asleep.

I pulled the covers back and spent five minutes trying to find my robe. I still couldn't find it, so I threw on one of Rudy's sweatshirts and padded down the stairs to go and rescue the recliner from Rudy's butt. I rounded the kitchen and saw the light from the television flickering on the walls. Sure enough, Rudy was still in the recliner, our son on his lap. Both snored with their mouths open, breathing deep and even.

I moved Rudy's hands, picked Matthew up, and carried him to bed. The knot on his head had turned purple in the few hours since his run-in with the bathtub faucet. I tucked him in, scavenged around on the floor around his bed until I found his favorite stuffed bear, and nestled it under his arm. Then I headed back out to the living room to turn off the television and try to get Rudy to come up to bed.

The television was showing wrestling. I shook my head. What in the world was he teaching my son? Wrestling, for God's sake? Well, maybe it had come on after he was asleep and he was none the wiser. Yeah, I'd give him the benefit of the doubt, because otherwise the implications were just far too disturbing.

As I reached for the remote, I heard a noise outside. Thinking maybe the mayor had returned home, I ran to the front door, opened it, and stepped out barefoot onto the porch. There was nothing. No taxicab or car. I thought about Mrs. Castlereagh and wondered just how much she knew about her husband. Had she been lying to me, or had she really not known the truth? If she was clueless about the mayor's secrets, I couldn't help but think that she was probably good and scared right now. Wherever she was.

My porch light was off, so it was pretty

dark outside. Then I heard another noise. It was definitely coming from the mayor's house. Maybe he had returned without a taxi. Maybe the taxi had dropped him off up the road and he and his wife had simply walked back to their house because he knew I'd hear him come home if he arrived in a car. Boy, I think you'd have to be slightly demented to think that way, which didn't bode well for me, since I'd thought of it, too.

I stepped to the end of the porch, hugged myself close, and peeked around the edge of my house. I saw a light flicker in the mayor's living room. That son-of-a-gun was back. He thought he could just slip in under our noses and . . . do what, exactly? What would he accomplish by that? Maybe he had come back for something.

I ran across the side yard and across the mayor's driveway and up onto his porch, wiping my damp feet on his rug. I peeked into the living room and saw him moving around. I rang the doorbell, and the figure stopped. Then I knocked. There was no way I was letting him get out of here without finding out the truth. I was going to make him answer for all of his lies. "Bill! Open up! The sheriff's looking for you!"

The figure left the living room. What kind of idiot did he think I was? I banged on the

250

door some more. No response. "Bill! Open. This. Door."

A crashing sound came from somewhere in the back of the house. Or was it the back door? Was he trying to run again? I ran around to the backyard in time to see a huge figure running across the yard, jumping over the fence and into the woods. The mayor's back door was standing wide open and one of those big terra-cotta planters had been turned over and broken. Obviously, I was a pretty big idiot. It hadn't been the mayor at all. There was only one person I knew who was that big, and that was Tiny Tim Julep.

I stepped inside Bill's house, ran to the phone on the kitchen wall, and called Colin at the office. This was his only night shift of the week. "Brooke," he said.

"It's me, Torie," I said.

Instantly his voice took on a note of concern. It was after midnight, after all, and I'm sure I sounded a bit rattled. "What is it?"

"I'm in Bill's house."

"You're *what?*" he exclaimed.

"Don't be mad," I said. "I heard somebody over here, and I thought Bill had come home. When I got here the back door was open, and I saw Tiny Tim jumping the fence."

"I'll be right there. Don't move. Don't touch anything," he said.

"Right."

"I mean it. Don't touch anything!"

"Sure thing," I said. As soon as I hung up the phone, I knew that I would never have this opportunity again. I was alone in the mayor's house. Can I just say that he had lousy taste? On the wall in his living room were two of those big golden plate-looking things from the seventies. His couch had big rust- and gold-colored flowers all over it. His curtains were green paisley, and an ottoman with no fewer than three pieces of duct tape slapped on it was shoved haphazardly against the recliner. It was like stepping into my aunt's California apartment in 1969. The dining room furniture was made of faux wood, Formica or something. The kitchen had dark brown cabinets, probably pressed board. The refrigerator was a dark pea-soup color. I suppose none of the things in his house would have looked that bad if they all hadn't been thrown in the same pot together.

I started rifling through kitchen cabinets and drawers. Nothing. I checked the freezer. Don't ask me why, but it seemed like a good place to hide something. Of course, then his wife would have had to know about it, because most women know what's in their freezer. No, if the mayor was going to hide something from his wife, where would he hide it? Not between the mattresses, because women are also the ones who usually change the sheets. I'm not saying there aren't men in the world who change sheets, because there are. It's a statistical anomaly.

So where?

The garage. I know I don't set foot in my garage if I don't have to. Immediately, I ran for the door that led to the garage from the living room, opened it, and stepped inside. It seemed really big, but I guess since both of the mayor's cars were gone, it would seem as though it had too much room. I checked under the workbench for anything that might have been taped underneath. Nothing. There was a supply cabinet, an old rusty metal one, standing in the corner. I opened it and was confronted with jumper cables and extension cords and . . . just boy stuff. It all smelled like motor oil and paint. I checked under each shelf. Nothing. Then I noticed, in the very bottom, a sliver of paper sticking up between the floor and the wall of the cabinet. I tugged on it, but it would not budge.

I got down on my knees on the cold concrete floor of the mayor's garage and tugged some more. I could hear a siren in the distance and knew my time was limited. I rummaged around on the workbench until I found a screwdriver and then went back to the cabinet. I wiggled the screwdriver into the seam of the floor of the cabinet and shoved, and the floor popped up. Just as I caught sight of the stash of papers in the secret compartment, I heard Colin's squad car. I saw his lights flashing on the walls of the garage through the little windows in the garage door.

Darn it! I shoved the fake bottom back on top of the papers, tossed the screwdriver onto the workbench, ran through the house, and flopped down on Bill's couch just as Colin came striding through the front door, Lou Counts right behind him.

"I can't believe you did this!" he said to me.

"Really? I figured this was exactly what you expected from me," I said. He gave me a dirty look and ran his hands through his hair. Lou Counts looked down at my knees. I glanced down to see what she was looking at. I had dirt stains on the knees of my p.j. bottoms. I said nothing, but her eyes locked with mine, and I knew there was no story I could give her that she would believe.

"What are you doing in here?" Colin

asked, pacing the living room floor.

"I thought I heard Bill come home. I came over and heard a crash in the back. Must have been the guy knocking over that big potted plant on the patio. Then I called you," I said, crossing my arms.

"What if the guy had come back?" Colin asked.

"As fast as he was running, that didn't seem likely," I said. Lou put her thumbs in her belt loops and looked around the room. The door to the garage was cracked. She glanced back at me.

"You go in the garage, Mrs. O'Shea?" she asked.

"Why would I?" I asked.

"Just answer the question," she said.

To lie or not to lie? Oh, boy. My soul was in deep trouble. "I don't remember," I said, wincing internally. I was going to hell. No two ways about it. "Maybe Tiny Tim was in there."

Colin's gaze traveled around the room, landing on the garage door and then on me. "You expect me to believe you've just been sitting here on the couch like an angel waiting for me?" he said. "You were alone in the mayor's house. Your dream come true."

"I'm going home. I held down the fort for you guys," I said. Then I locked eyes with

Lou Counts once again. "Now you guys can do your jobs."

"I want the place dusted for prints," Lou said to Colin. "Then we'll know exactly who was where."

I stormed out of the mayor's house, ticked off without really having any reason to be angry. I mean, no, I hadn't waited calmly on the couch. I had been alone in the mayor's house and taken advantage of it. I had been in the garage snooping. They were accurate in their assumptions, and my fingerprints were everywhere to prove it. I had no reason to be angry. So why was I angry?

I charged across the yard, across my driveway, onto the porch, into the house, and past Rudy. "Rudy, get up and come to bed!" I called out, and smacked him on the shoulder as I made my way to the stairs. I heard him say something to the television as he woke up. When I made it to the second floor, I threw myself into bed. Then I realized I had on disgusting p.j. bottoms, pulled them off, tried to find new ones and couldn't, and so decided just to go to bed in a T-shirt. Then I realized my feet were filthy, so I had to go in the bathroom and wash them in the tub.

Rudy came in then, scratching his head and yawning. He looked at me and at my feet and back at me. "Why are you washing only your feet?" he asked.

"They were dirty," I said.

"Oh," he said, and crawled into bed.

I looked at myself in the mirror and cringed at the gray hair. I still hadn't managed to color it yet. I really was getting old. Mother Nature was not going to endow me with some special gift as I subconsciously had assumed she would throughout my youth.

Why was I so angry?

I knew why I was angry.

I was angry because they had interrupted me before I could snatch whatever was in the bottom of that utility cabinet.

Eighteen

The next day as I left the house, I noticed the crime-scene tape wrapped crookedly around the mayor's house. There were still officers there. One of those officers had dusted for fingerprints and would find mine. I supposed I could lie some more and tell them that the fingerprints had been left at some other time, but other than to stand just inside the door, I'd never been in the mayor's house much. Maybe years ago, but prints from those visits would have been wiped away by now.

I drove through town and dropped the girls off at school. I cracked the driver's-side window, just because I love the smell of autumn, not because I was hot. In fact, I've been known to turn the heat up on the floorboard and roll the window down at the same time. I took Matthew to my mother's and promised her that we'd come for dinner this

Friday. Then I went out to the construction site to see how things were going with our house. They actually had the windows in now.

Egbert Hanshaw met me at the driveway with a smile on his face. "Hey," he said as I got out of the car. "Whatcha think?"

I glanced up at the house. It was a beautiful sight. To think Rudy and I had designed it ourselves was pretty satisfying. Every little detail that went into the house, Rudy and I had decided. And as much as I was going to miss our view of the Mississippi, I was looking forward to moving into the new house. "Wonderful," I said.

"Should get the walls up on the stables pretty soon," he said.

"Yeah, about that. I was wondering if you could put me in contact with anybody who sells quarter horses. I found a few Web sites, but I don't know. I think I'd kind of like to deal with somebody who's not a total stranger."

"Actually, I do know of somebody. Cousin of mine, named Hank Hanshaw. If you take Highway P down about ten miles, he owns that Mississippi Valley Ranch. I bought all four of my horses from him. Let me tell you, Lady is an unbelievable horse. Hank's the best in the area."

"Oh," I said. "Yes, I've passed that property a thousand times. I never knew that was your cousin's."

"He's only owned it for about a year. Bought it from old man Jenkins," he said. "Jenkins decided to move to Taos."

"Good," I said. "I'll go by there later."

"Is there anything you wanted, or are you just here to look around?"

"Just checking in," I said. "Ever find out about those tools and concrete mix?"

"We gave a statement," he said. He shrugged his shoulders as if that were all there was to it.

"Have you had any more problems or theft?" I asked.

"Not a bit," he said.

"All right," I said. "I'll let you get back to work." I went into the house, nodding at the construction crew as I went. Some of the guys on the crew I knew better than others, because some were from New Kassel. A few were from Wisteria, and a couple of guys were from up in Arnold.

I climbed the stairs to where my office was going to be. With the windows in, it gave the room a feeling of nearly being finished, even though there wasn't any drywall or finished flooring. I glanced out my window at what had already become my favorite view. A hawk swooped down and landed in the top of a tree. My window was about as high as that first line of trees in the backyard. The hawk moved his head from side to side and then spread his gorgeous wings and soared into the pasture to catch his prey. Wow. If I was going to get to witness hawk activity like that all the time, I would be a happy woman.

Down to the left was where the stable was going to be. The workers had already laid the subflooring for it. I had a good view of it from here.

I was probably crazy for buying a horse. Fritz was the only pet I'd ever managed to not kill. With that thought, I turned to go and caught a snippet of a conversation between the construction workers.

"Well, that poor bastard needs to have an upper hand somehow," said one of the workers with a deep voice. "She has the upper hand on everything."

"Yeah, moving out here was definitely his doing. Said it took him lots of smooth talking to get her to agree to it," the other one said.

"I'll bet. That woman probably argues over what toilet paper to buy," the deep voice said.

"He thinks moving her out here will get her away from all the goings on in the town.

You know, like she won't have her nose in everything."

"Well," said the deep voice, "I hope he gets some peace. Rudy's a nice guy."

The two men crossed in front of the stairway, carrying a sawhorse into the living room. They glanced up to see me staring, struck still at the sight of them. One looked away; the other one made a gesture that made me think he was going to apologize for what I'd overheard. I held a hand up at him. "Don't bother."

I rushed past him, tears streaming down my face. Eg saw me leaving and waved. Turning the knob on the stereo, I tried to use the radio to drown out their voices in my head, but I couldn't find anything harsh enough to do the job. I kept flipping channels and getting soft rock songs or, worse yet, elevator music. I can't believe they actually have a radio station that plays elevator music. Finally I landed on a station that was playing some Zeppelin, and I cranked it as loud as I could without completely distorting the sound.

Trees flew by the window. Spotted cows moved their mouths to moo at me, but I just cranked that music and sang along. I came to the ranch that Eg had told me about and pulled in. Off in the fenced field I saw no fewer than a dozen horses grazing. I didn't see anybody around outside, so I knocked on the door of the house.

Hank Hanshaw answered. "Ms. O'Shea," he said, "what can I do for you?"

"I'd like to buy a horse. Or two," I said.

"Well, sure," he said. "Let me get on my shoes." He disappeared for a second and then came back to the door and took me out into the field. I said a silent thank-you to the powers that be that I'd had the foresight to wear my Doc Martens and not my sneakers. There was horse manure everywhere.

Hank was a small, wiry guy. I would not have known he and Eg were related, except that Eg had told me so and they had a similar way of holding themselves. Shoulders thrown back and elbows far away from their sides. A couple of horses trotted by, and a few just stood where they were. Hank put a hand on the hip of a beautiful buttery-colored horse. "Hey, girl," he said. "I'm here."

I watched him as he slid his hand down her back and eventually up to her mane. He pulled her face around, showed me her teeth, and gave me what amounted to a twelve-point check of things to look for in a horse. I just saw that it wasn't swaybacked and went, "Oooh, pretty horse."

While we were standing there, a dark wine-colored horse with a black mane came up and nuzzled the back of my head with his nose. "That's Cutter," Hank said. "I think he likes you."

I reached around and petted the horse's face. The smell of cut hay was thick in the air, and the sun kept playing hide-and-seek with the clouds. A breeze picked up and blew across my face gently. I stroked Cutter's neck, and the horse blinked at me, sniffing my hair. Just standing that close to something that big was magical. He fluttered his nostrils and made a funny noise. I'm not sure how long I stood there, soothed by the presence of the animal, before Hank finally broke the spell with idle chatter about whether or not it would be a bad winter.

An hour later Hank had shown me all of the horses that were for sale and told me which ones he thought would be best for a family that had small children and had never taken care of anything larger than a wiener dog. He told me the prices and said he had a special going: Buy two, get the third one half price. I only wanted two, though.

Finally the meeting ended with me writing him a check to hold Cutter and Moonstone, the buttery-colored one. "I'll be back with

Rudy. See if he likes these two horses," I said.

"Well, all right, Ms. O'Shea. I'll be seein' ya, then." He glanced down at the check in his hand and smiled. "We have a summer camp for the kids. Teach them about grooming and proper care and all that."

"Reserve a spot for three," I said.

"That boy of yours is too young," he said.

"Then I'll be the third kid. I have no idea what I'm doing, either."

Just as I was about to get in the car and leave, a small, sporty-looking red car pulled into Hank's driveway and threw gravel all over my car, chipping the paint. Hank looked a bit confused for a second. "City slickers come down and buy horses they ain't got no place to keep. Don't ride 'em or nothing," he said. "Women love horses. Guys like this just like to say they got horses, so the women think they're sensitive."

I nearly choked as Tito de Rosa got out of the car and walked toward us. I glanced nervously at Hank. "Oh, Hank, I think he's looking for me," I said and put my hand out. "Thanks for all of your help."

"Well, all right," he said. "See you later."

Hank headed toward his house, glancing over his shoulder several times at Tito and me. I knew that once he was in the house, he would stand at the window and watch what happened. That's what I would have done. And really, curiosity is rampant in all of us. Some just have better self-control than others.

"What do you want?" I asked.

"You saw Tiny Tim last night and didn't tell me?" he said. "Can't tell you how angry that makes me."

I swallowed. "I was going to call you as soon as I got to work," I said. "There were cops all over when I left the house. Deputy Counts is suspicious as it is. I just wanted to make sure I wasn't being watched or followed."

Tito smiled at me.

"Obviously, I'm no good at telling whether or not I'm being followed," I said.

"What happened?"

"About midnight, I heard a noise over at the mayor's house. I went over because I thought it was Bill coming home. But it was Tiny Tim."

"What was he doing there?" he asked.

"I'm not sure. I interrupted him before he really got a chance to do much," I said.

Tito leaned into me, and I backed up until I found the edge of my car with my hands. "I swear," I said. "That's all I saw. He took off into the woods."

266

"Have you seen him since?"

"No," I said. "Look, if you already knew about Tiny Tim, why do you need me to watch him?"

"The only reason I found about it is because that loudmouthed idiot that I rent the room from told me all about it at breakfast," he said. "Imagine my surprise."

I swallowed again. My heart seemed to have relocated to my head. My palms began to sweat, and breathing became something that I had to concentrate on.

"Maybe I should make her keep tabs on Tiny Tim," he said.

As much as I would have loved to pass the torch, I couldn't let Eleanore get mixed up in this any more than she already was. "No," I said. "She's a complete innocent. I swear I was going to tell you this morning. Just as soon as I got back to the Gaheimer House."

His gaze flicked past me to the horses in the field beyond. "You just had to buy a horse first? What, you think a horse is more important than our agreement?"

"No," I said. "I came out here to buy the horse to try to . . . cool off. The guys at the construction site had made me angry. That's all."

A slanty, almost curious smile crossed his face. "Did it work?" he asked.

267

"Surprisingly well," I said.

"Play your cards right, and you'll get to be a happy horse owner. Got it?"

I nodded my head, because I couldn't seem to actually speak words. "Let me know if you see Tiny Tim again," he said. "Right away. No excuses this time."

"Of course," I said. "But I'm not sure he'll be coming back."

"Well," Tito said and lit up one of those dark, skinny cigarettes. "He never was very smart. Maybe he'll surprise us." He got back in his little red sports car and drove away, kicking up more gravel in the process. I wasn't sure if that was for effect or if it was because Tito had never driven on a gravel road before and didn't know how to handle the car.

I reached into my pocket, got out my keys, and tried to unlock the car door. My hands shook entirely too much, and I had to stop and take a deep breath and try again. On the third try, I got the key into the lock, and I all but fell into the front seat. I jumped and squealed as the radio blared when I turned over the engine. I'd forgotten I'd turned the car off when the radio had been on. Quickly, I turned it down. This time, I searched the stations for something soothing.

★ ★ ★

A few hours later, I was seated at the Gaheimer House, staring at the quilt on my wall, wondering just how many stitches were in it, when the phone rang. I'd been sitting there for a few hours, unable to do anything but trace the little curvy lines of stitches with my eyes. Stephanie had come into my office twice to see if there was anything she could do for me, but since she had no clue what was going on, she really couldn't help. She gave the afternoon tours, and still I sat there.

I picked up the phone, anticipation rising in my chest. There was a lot of noise on the line, and the sound of music in the background. "Torie, it's Sam Hill."

"Sam," I said, relieved that it wasn't Tito or anybody else in the Mafia. "What can I do for you?"

"Meet me at the Corner Bar," he said. "I've got news."

"All right," I said and hung up. I called out to Stephanie that I was heading over to the Corner Bar for a second. I walked out of the house and down the street and turned and walked some more. The Corner Bar is just that, a bar situated on the corner. Every town has one. Heck, up in St. Louis, there's one on every other corner in some neighborhoods. New Kassel just has the one, but we

269

really don't need any more than that.

A Pabst Blue Ribbon signed flickered on and off in the window, and the *p* was out on the OPEN sign. I stepped into the smoky bar and immediately had to adjust my eyes, since it was dark inside. I think it has to be dark inside a bar during the day because it must be really hard to get tanked on cheap beer in the daylight. At least it would be for me.

Just as I walked in the door, the first chords of Waylon Jennings singing "Are You Sure Hank Done It This Way?" came on the jukebox. The bartender nodded at me. His mother plays bridge with my mother. He knew I wouldn't be drinking, so he didn't bother to come over and ask. I found Sam Hill sitting in the corner booth, nursing a dark brew of some sort. On closer inspection I decided it was a Black and Tan. I was impressed that he could get that in this bar.

"Sam?" I said as I sat down. "I was unaware that this was a hangout of yours."

"It's not usually," he said, "but I just had to come and celebrate."

Little prickles danced down my neck and spine. "Celebrate what?" I asked.

"I hit the jackpot," he said, leaning forward. He slid a large manila envelope across the table to me. "I've found out what it is that Bill has been trying to hide all of this time. I know what it is that he is so ashamed of. And believe, me, Torie, it's a doozy."

"What?" I asked, opening the envelope. Inside were photocopies of newspaper articles. "Don't make me read them, Sam. Tell me."

"His mother was a murderer," he said, and smiled. He took a big drink of his beer and sighed heavily. "It doesn't get any better than that. Does it?"

I was a little disturbed at his glee over the fact that somebody, not to mention somebody's mother, was a murderer. I glanced around the smoky room. There were two men in flannel shirts sitting at the bar. A woman, Jessi Dunn to be exact, was sitting at a table in the middle of the place, flirting ostentatiously with some guy I didn't recognize. Jessi had graduated with me. Five kids and seven husbands later, this was her domain. She picked her next Mr. Dunns here. "Lower your voice, Sam. This is the mayor we're talking about."

He waved a hand at me. "Not for long, Torie. Not for long." He took another drink of his beer. This time he burped. "Oh, jeez. Sorry."

"Okay, all right, tell me already," I said.

"Lucy Castlereagh was arrested and brought up on charges for killing her infant

271

child," he said. "The baby was only a day or two old. It didn't even have a name."

"How?" I asked.

"Supposedly she suffocated it with a pillow. The article mentions all of the other children at home being scared out of their wits. Jesus, Torie. They even went to foster homes for six months. Bill was in a foster home because his mother was being held without bail for killing his brother!"

"What do you mean, supposedly?" I asked. This was incredible. Two people sat down in the booth behind us. I didn't get a good look at them, because I didn't want to turn around and stare. The less attention Sam and I got at this point, the better. Yes, I was paranoid, and it would probably get worse before it got better.

"I mean the charges were dropped because ultimately they couldn't prove it." He shrugged and seemed disappointed with that one little detail of his discovery.

"I don't know what to say," I said.

Sam rambled on. "They don't mention the children's names in the article, I guess to protect the innocent and all that, but it's the right family. It's Lucy Castlereagh and her husband Jarvis, and the address is the same address you gave me for where they lived in the census."

"Well, Sam. You did it. You found what you were looking for," I said.

"I found way more than I was looking for," he said. "I could have only dreamed of a jackpot this big. You don't seem too thrilled about it, though."

Something was niggling at me, and I had no idea what it was. "No," I said. "I am . . . thrilled for you, really. But I was wondering. Could you maybe not run this story for a few days?"

"What? Torie, you expect me to sit on this?" he exclaimed. "Not a chance. What's the matter with you?"

"I'm just saying that maybe you should get a little more proof. Get some more witnesses or something," I said.

"I doubt that any of Bill's brothers will speak to me, even if I could run them down in the next few days. Torie, I can't believe you," he said.

"Fine," I said, and held my hands up. "You're the reporter, not me. I don't know how these things are done, obviously. Congratulations."

Sam said something in response, but I didn't hear him. I was too busy trying to catch the conversation in the booth behind me. "It's quite a coup for Rudy," the voice said. It was a familiar voice, but I couldn't place it. I suppose I was in denial. I held my breath waiting to hear what came next. "I cannot believe he got her to move out of this town." I couldn't make out what the other person said to that. "Oh, no doubt. One small step for man."

"Excuse me, Sam," I said. I stood up and turned to see who was sitting in the booth behind me. It was Colin, having a beer with a man I recognized but couldn't place by name. Obviously, Colin wasn't on duty, and when he looked up and saw me standing at the end of his booth, he flinched.

"Oh, Jesus, Torie."

"No, I'm certain I've never been mistaken for Jesus," I said. I looked at the man sitting across from him and nodded. "Glad to see you've got this whole thing wrapped up with the mayor so you can spend valuable time sitting here having a beer and gossiping about your stepdaughter."

"Torie," he said.

"Shut up, Colin," I said. There were a bunch of things I wanted to say to him. In fact, my mind flooded with all of the things I needed to say. Somehow, though I couldn't form the words. What was this feeling in my chest? Was that . . . hurt? If it was hurt, then that must mean that at some point I'd learned to trust Colin. He'd become family.

Finally all I could think of was a ridiculous insult. "I've never understood what my mother sees in you," I said. And I took his mug of beer and dumped it right in his lap. I walked out of the bar and straight to the Gaheimer House to get my car, without even so much as glancing back.

Nineteen

"I want you guys to take a ride with me," I said.

Rudy and the kids stared at me over the dirty dishes. We'd just finished eating homemade enchiladas. Rudy rubbed his stomach and said, "I don't know, Torie. All those beans cooped up in the same car. Is it a long ride?"

Mary laughed, and Rachel gave her father the oh-puhleeze look. "You can wear a mask," I said to him.

"Where are we going?" Rudy asked.

"You'll see," I said. Half an hour later we turned into the driveway of Hank Hanshaw's ranch. Hank saw us pull up and came out onto the porch with his napkin still tucked in his shirt, his cowboy boots clanking on the front porch. I waved to him. "We're just here to see the horses."

"Sure," he said. "Let me get on my boots,

so as you got someone with you."

Mary and Rachel each gave me a quizzical look, obviously cautious because they didn't want to read something into this trip that wasn't there. Little did they know that what they were reading into it was exactly what they were getting.

The girls ran ahead into the field to the horses, with Hank leading the way, and Matthew dragging behind. His little legs couldn't quite keep up with them, but he was certainly determined to make it to the horses. "Don't sneak up behind the horses!" I called out. "They'll kick you!"

"What's this all about?" Rudy asked.

"If you wanted to move, why didn't you just say so?" I asked. "Why couldn't you just be honest and say, 'Torie, I want to build a house away from town'? Why did you have to make me think this was my idea?"

"I don't know what you're talking about," Rudy said as we walked out through the field. It was obvious from the expression on his face that this was the last thing he had expected from me.

"Okay, all right, I'll play that way, Rudy. Then let me ask you this. If you were going to complain to half of the town about your life and your wife, then why weren't you smart enough just now to answer the first question honestly, so that I wouldn't have to tell you that I know you're lying?"

He looked down at his feet but kept walking. "Torie, I —"

"I'm hurt, Rudy. Look, I know I'm a pain in the ass," I said.

"You don't know the half of it," he said.

I stopped in my tracks then. "Why, you —" I would not call him names, even though I wanted to. "We're married. We're a team. No matter how much I would have fought you and no matter how many sleepless nights it would have taken, why didn't you just come to me and say, 'I want to move out of town, because I think it would be best for our marriage'? Because now it's going to take me months, Rudy, months to get over this. If ever."

"You're overreacting," he said.

"Rudy!" I snapped. His head shot up, and he looked at me with guilt in his eyes. "This is a small town. Lou Counts knew. I overheard the guys working on our house talking about me like . . . well, like I'm your mother! You've made me out to be some horrible . . . thing! You're the saint. Nobody hears about how many times I tuck a blanket under you because you fell asleep in the recliner in front of the television, yet again. Come on, every marriage has its compromises. Ours is no different. Just next time, tell me before you complain and then brag to half of the damn town."

I started to walk toward the girls, but Rudy shot a hand out and grabbed my arm. "We're a team?" he asked.

"Yes."

"Then what is this? You've already got the horses picked out. You just bring me in on the tail end of it to make it seem as though I had some say-so in it. You know for a fact that if I stood here and said, 'No. We're not getting a horse,' you'd still get the horse. You are always off doing things that I don't have any clue about."

"Well, first of all," I said raising my voice, "I came out here and picked out the horses without you because you'd made me so angry! But secondly, you're not interested in what I do. None of it. You've got your world of bowling and fishing and that WWF stuff, and I've got mine."

"Yes, and yours is dangerous. God help me," he said and looked to the heavens. "If I had known that being a genealogist would put you in harm's way, I would have married somebody else!"

We were quiet a moment, the wind whipping our hair around. In the distance I could hear the children's laughter and the horses' hooves and whinnies. The whole time, Rudy and I just stared at each other. "I didn't mean that," he said.

"Yes, you did," I spat.

"I didn't marry a cop, Torie. I wouldn't have married a cop."

"But, Rudy, I help people. I don't see how you think I can just sit back and not help Colin, when sometimes I'm the only one who sees the things I see."

"Like right now with the mayor," he said. "You just had to get your nose in there."

"Rudy, I can solve this. I can do it. I mean, I don't know if I can find out where Bill is, but I can sure as hell find out what this is all about, and then that could help Colin," I said.

"You don't do this for other people. You do this because you can't stand not to be in the middle of things," he said.

"That was uncalled for," I said, holding back tears. "Right now I've got some stupid Mafia guy breathing down my neck. I haven't had a decent night's sleep in weeks. I'm trying to keep my stepfather from making a terrible mistake by endorsing Lou Counts, and I'm trying to keep Sam Hill from committing career suicide. On top of that I'm trying to figure out where the mayor's gone, what he's hiding, and why dead bodies keep turning up in our town. You think that's all for me? You think I do all of that for me, Rudy? I don't even like the mayor!"

Rudy hung his head then.

"Dammit, Rudy. At least I do something." Tears were rolling down my face now. I swiped at them angrily and hoped that the kids were far enough away not to notice.

Rudy sighed and looked around the field, then kicked the pile of horse manure in front of him. "Which horses did you pick out?" he asked.

I pointed to Cutter. "That one," I said. "And that yellow one over there."

"Pretty," he said.

"Sweet-natured, too," I said.

We walked over to the kids. Rachel had found a brush on the fence and had taken it down and was brushing one of the horses. She glanced up at us, a twinkle in her eye that I hadn't seen since the parade. She was vibrant and glowing, her cheeks flushed with exactly what should be on the face of a youth. Life and happiness. Matthew was squatted beneath one of the horses, stepping whenever the horse did. He'd get a real rude awakening if the horse decided to take a whiz. Mary held her hand out and she had three horses following her all the way through the field. Wherever she went they followed.

I hadn't seen either one of the girls so calm and . . . normal in weeks. The horses were a good idea.

"So, we're horse owners," Rudy said.

"Looks like it," I said. "Unless, of course, you really don't want to do this."

He glanced at the kids. "Are you kidding? Look at them."

"I know," I said.

"But I want three. That way one of the adults can ride with the two older kids."

"Okay, fine," I said. "I'll tell Hank when he comes out."

Rudy stopped suddenly. "Wait, did you say something about a Mafia guy?"

"No," I said. "That part was an exaggeration. The rest was all true."

"Oh, whew," he said.

We picked out a third horse and drove home. Rudy and I had spoken no apologies and made no obvious gestures of forgiveness to each other, but we didn't need to. It was out in the open, and we both knew it was over. By the time we got home, the kids were so excited that Rachel and Mary raced each other to the phone to see who could call her friends first and tell them about the horses. Mary beat Rachel to the phone, so Rachel went out the back door to go and tell Riley in person.

I sat down on the couch, and Matthew climbed up on my lap with his coloring book and crayons. I sat there half watching the television and half thinking about the new house and the horses and how I was actually getting excited about this move. Yes, the view of Old Man River would be gone, but I'd replace it with a view of hawks swooping in the pasture and the horses in the field. Besides, I was in New Kassel every day for work. I could see the river then. The river had been there long before me, before people, and it'd probably be there long after our reign on earth.

The police and CSU were finally gone from Bill's house. The tape was still up, though. Like that would stop anybody who really wanted to get into his house. I thought about the papers hidden in the fake bottom of the utility cabinet in his garage. I should tell Colin about it. I knew I should. To not tell him was keeping evidence from him. If I told him, though, chances were I'd never get to see what it was. Besides, even though I know that anger isn't a good enough reason to obstruct justice, I didn't want to tell him about the papers because of what had happened earlier today. Let him find the stupid things on his own.

The phone rang, and Rudy answered it. He brought the phone to me and headed for the kitchen. "Hello?" I said.

"It's Colin."

I hung up.

The phone rang instantly, and I knew it was him. I picked up the receiver. "I'm not talking to you," I said.

"Torie, I can explain," he said.

"You mean there's a justifiable, believable reason why you're a completely insensitive cad?"

"Torie, look," he said.

"Not interested in what you have to say, Colin. Not at all."

"I've got bad news," he said.

"What?" Instantly my scalp prickled.

"Fisherman found a piece of luggage with Bill's name on it," he said. "Washed up on the shores of the river. Found some shoes, too."

"Oh, God, no," I said. The hair stood up on my arms.

"I'm going to drag the river," he said.

"You can't drag the Mississippi!" I exclaimed. "The Mississippi is undraggable."

"I'm going to send down divers," he said, "and I've alerted the counties to the south in case somebody . . . washes up down there."

"Did you call Karri?"

"Yes."

I was speechless.

"Torie, is there anything I should know? Is there something you're not telling me that could help me here, with Bill?"

There was plenty that I wasn't telling him, but I didn't think any of it could help poor Bill. Anyway, that wasn't why I wasn't saying anything. It wasn't that I didn't want to answer him. It was more that I couldn't answer him. On the TV a news bulletin was running across the screen. *Body washes up in Ste. Genevieve.*

"Oh, my God, Colin. They found him."

"What? What are you talking about?"

"They found a body in Ste. Gen," I said. "I gotta go."

"Do not go down there!" he said, but I hung up on him. I took Matthew off my lap and set him on the couch. I handed the phone to Rudy, who was just now coming back from the kitchen.

"What? You look . . . worried," he said.

"Rudy, do you want me to tell you when I'm about to go off half-cocked and do something stupid, or do you want me to just leave you in the dark like I've done in the past?" I asked.

He straightened his spine and looked me

in the eyes. "I want you to tell me," he said bravely.

"Okay, look, I think they just found Bill's body down in Ste. Genevieve," I said. "I'm going down there now."

"What? Oh, no. That's terrible," he said, and sat down. "What can you do?"

"Identify the body, so Karri doesn't have to," I said.

"Wait, Torie!"

"You said you wanted to know these things, so there. Would you rather I told you that I was going to the grocery store or something?"

He shook his head, kissed me on the cheek, and said, "Be careful."

Twenty

The drive to Ste. Genevieve took me about forty minutes. I'd taken old 61-67 instead of Highway 55, mostly because I didn't want to have to mess with getting off the highway and driving through town when I got there. This way, I'd be almost at the river when I entered town. Of course, I had no idea where the body had washed ashore, so I spent at least ten minutes driving along the river until I saw all of the squad cars. They had the area roped off, and people had begun to gather along the zigzagged edge of the tape. News crews were parked haphazardly along the side of the road, and their camera lights punctuated the dark night with a halogen glare.

I pulled up, got out of the car, and ran up to the edge of the crime-scene tape. "Excuse me!" I called out. I waved my arms back and forth, but nobody paid much attention to me. Finally I just yelled as loudly as I could. "Hey!"

A young officer walked my way with that swagger that only comes with the cockiness of being an untried rookie. He had a white-blond crew cut and large blue eyes. His nameplate read KEN CALLYOT. "Yes, ma'am," he said.

"I think I know who that is," I said.

"What do you mean?"

"The body, I think I know who it is."

He raised the tape and motioned for me to follow him over to someone I assumed was his boss. The officer in charge was about sixty. Retirement age. His face showed the weariness that came from having had to clean up messes like this his entire adult life. His plate read T. C. ROUSSEAU.

"This woman thinks she might be able to identify the body," Calyott declared.

"Why?" Rousseau asked.

"I'm from New Kassel," I said. The man stiffened. Colin had called the surrounding counties to alert them to the possibility that there might be a body washing up on the shore. "Our mayor has been missing, and recently . . ."

Officer Rousseau held up a hand and said, "I know," he said. "We got the call. Are you the next of kin?"

"No," I said. "Next-door neighbor."

He exchanged a glance with Officer Callyot.

"Sir," I said, "I know his daughter really well. I just thought maybe I could do this for her, so that when she does view the body, it'll be at the funeral."

"Fine," he said and waved me over to the body lying on the ground, covered with a white sheet. "You said *his* daughter?"

"Yes," I said. "Why?"

"Because unless your mayor had a sex change operation, this ain't him," he said, and pulled back the sheet.

I gasped as I looked down into the lifeless blue face of Bill's wife. Mrs. Castlereagh. "Oh, no," I said and covered my mouth with my hand.

"You know her?" Rousseau asked.

"It's the mayor's wife," I said. "Mrs. Castlereagh." Her hair was plastered against her cheeks, and river foliage was stuck to her skin. Her clothes were torn and tattered. One arm was completely missing, and the lack of blood made me grotesquely aware that she had been dead when it had been severed. I took a step back and a deep breath and fought the bile that rose in my throat. "Oh, this is terrible."

"You don't know the half of it," he said

and pulled the sheet all the way back. Her feet were encased in cement blocks.

I fought back tears I looked to Officer Rousseau, searching his eyes for answers, but I could read nothing there except sadness. "I don't understand," I said. They covered Mrs. Castlereagh back up with the sheet, and I didn't care how much Colin yelled at me, I was glad I had done this so that Karri would not have to remember this her whole life. "If she . . . The cement. How did she wash ashore?"

"We're thinking her arm snagged on a tugboat or something. I think it might have dragged her a ways, until it reached shallow enough water that she couldn't sink again," he said. "I'm going to need to speak to your sheriff."

Just as I nodded my head, I heard Colin behind me. "I'm Sheriff Brooke from Granite County," he said.

"It's not Bill," I said to him, staring at the body. "It's his wife."

"Oh, no," he said.

I turned to leave, and Colin called out, "Stay put. I want to talk to you when I'm finished."

"Fine."

I went back to my car and sat there stunned, watching the newsman reporting on the death of a woman I had known almost my whole life. I don't think I could have left the crime scene if I'd wanted to. I couldn't seem to figure out where the ignition was in my car. Or the seat belt. I had no choice but to wait for Colin. The Castlereaghs had lived next door to me for thirteen years. I shook my head, wondering why it couldn't have been Bill instead. I suppose that wasn't very nice of me, but as far as I could tell, his wife was an innocent in all of this. This whole charade had been Bill's doing, whatever it was, and she was the one who ended up dead. With cement shoes.

Tears flowed down my face. I sobbed into my hands as I thought about the horror that had been her last minutes. Had she been alive when they threw her into the river? Or had they killed her first and then tossed her in, just to dispose of the body? A knock on the door made me jump nearly out of my skin. It was Colin, standing there with his hands on his hips. I wanted to hit him. I'm not saying that the impulse was logical, but I still wanted to hit him. I got out and wiped my tears on my sleeves. Crossing my arms, I leveled my gaze at him and dared him with a look to say one mean thing to me.

"Why'd you come down here? Because I

told you not to?" he asked.

"I came so Karri wouldn't have to see that," I said. "No child should have to see her mother like that."

"I could have identified the body. I know what the mayor and his wife look like," he said.

"Well, I wasn't sure if you were coming down or not," I said. "You said you were going to drag the river. How was I supposed to know what you were doing?"

"All right, all right," he said, and held his hands up in front of him. He made a motion as if he were going to hug me. I glared at him. After the things I had overheard him saying about me, how dare he try to comfort me? "You know, Bill is most likely at the bottom of the river, too," he said.

"I hope," I said.

"What?"

"If he escaped this" — I gestured to where Mrs. Castlereagh lay — "and she didn't . . ."

"I think this was over a gambling debt. I found a recent deposit of a lot of money in his account. It's a known fact that the Baietto and de Rosa families own casinos. With their presence in the town . . . I think it's a pretty logical conclusion."

"If he just made a large deposit, then why didn't he pay off his debt?" I asked.

"I think he was going to," he said, "but I guess whoever he owed the money to got tired of waiting. The deposit was in cash. A hundred thousand dollars."

"Where do you think he would get that kind of money?" I asked.

"Well, if he was gambling in dollar amounts that big, I'd say Bill had connections we know nothing about."

"You have proof he ever gambled? Or went to a casino? Do his kids say he ever went to a casino?"

"No, but it'll come. You remember how he was pushing the riverboat gambling in town a while back," he said, as if that explained everything.

"Whatever," I said and looked off into the distance. He was wrong, and I knew it. That money could have been for anything. For all we knew, Bill could have made yearly deposits of that size. Maybe it was a stipend from his mother. We knew nothing about her, other than she'd been arrested for murder and released. Who knew what happened to her after that? She could have become wealthy. Maybe the money was from somebody in his wife's family. Maybe they were having financial problems and borrowed money from a friend. To say automatically that it was a gambling windfall, when there was no evidence he'd even set foot in a casino, was ridiculous.

I wouldn't say any of that to Colin. I'd find out what this was all about on my own. Then I'd think about letting him in on it.

"What, you disagree?" he asked.

I stared into his eyes long and hard. He flinched at the intensity in my gaze. "What do you care what I think? You've got Lou Counts now to confer with. You two are doing a bang-up job on this case without me."

"You forget, I can haul you in and make you tell me what you know," he said.

"Then I guess you'll have to do that, won't you?"

"Torie, you're being silly," he said. "Not to mention hard-headed. You're interfering in an investigation."

"I'm going home now. Oh, by the way, who was the man at the Corner Bar that you were gossiping about me with?"

"Torie . . ."

"Just answer the question."

He said nothing.

"Fine, I can find out on my own," I said and opened the car door.

"Mort Joachim," he said.

"That's real nice, Colin. He doesn't even have the chance to form his own opinion of me. You have to give him one. What's the matter? Afraid he'll actually like me?" I said.

He hung his head, which was what he should have done.

"Oh, I will give you one tidbit of information," I said. "I think the cement used to anchor Mrs. Castlereagh was stolen off of my construction site. So if you haven't already been out there making casts of shoes and tires, you might want to."

"Torie," he said, "you can't be mad at me forever."

"Yes, I can," I said and got into my car.

"I'm married to your mother," he said.

"That's her problem."

Twenty-one

I cried all the way home. Just when I thought I was fine, I'd think about that poor woman, sitting at the bottom of the dark, cold river . . . then getting caught on something. And the tears would start all over again.

When I got home, Rachel was waiting up for me in the living room. Well, I'm not entirely sure she was waiting up for me specifically, but she was up watching television all the same. "Hey, kiddo," I said as I came through the door.

"Hi, Mom," she said.

"What's up?"

"Nothing," she said. She shrugged her shoulders. "You think I can go out and visit the horses before we actually get them?" she asked.

"I don't see why not," I said.

"Can Riley take me?" she asked.

I balked. Riley had just gotten his license.

Rachel, of course, did not have a license or a car. I was prepared for her to grow up and go to college and have a boyfriend. I was prepared for her to date. Just as long as she didn't have to get in a car to do it. Trusting my daughter in the car with a kid who'd only had his license for a few months and had uncontrollable hormones, as all teenagers do, was more than I was ready for. A car. Rachel in a car with a teenager driving.

"You don't really like Riley, do you?" she asked.

"No," I said. "I mean, yes. Yes, I do like Riley. He's a very thoughtful and conscientious young man, and he certainly seems to have your best interests at heart."

She was quiet a moment.

"Well, that is, as long as he's kept his hands where they belong. If he hasn't, then he's a slimeball and I take away everything good I just said about him." I took off my jacket and slipped off my shoes and sat down on the couch next to her.

"Is sex really all that bad?" she asked.

"Oh, wow," I said. I was not ready for a conversation about sex. Not to mention, I think all the blood ran to my feet just because she had used the word in a sentence so casually. As if she were asking about a new pair of jeans. "Um, you're too young, first of all. Sec-

297

ondly, no, it's not that it's bad, per se."

She crossed one flannel-clad leg over the other and gave me a look that I couldn't interpret. Whatever I was about to say was going to make or break what she thought of me as a parent and what she thought of sex. Don't you hate it when you're at one of those important crossroads with your kids and you feel completely inept? Or is it just me?

"It's just that parents want to make sure that their kids get all the chances that they can in the world. Babies are the pesky little side effect of sex," I said. "And then, there's those darn venereal diseases running about. And, oh, Jesus, Rachel, are you really considering having sex? I mean . . . you're too young!"

She burst into laughter then, and I felt a great pressure lift from my chest. "Nope. I just wanted to see what you'd have to say about it. It was pretty neat watching you sweat."

"You're evil," I said.

"No, that would be Mary," she said.

"You're feeling better, I see," I said.

"So, do you think Riley could drive me out to see the horses?"

I looked at her, imagining Riley taking the corners of the Outer Road at a hundred miles an hour. Being a parent was about surrendering your child to the rest of the world in stages. First was letting somebody else watch them. Then came sending them off to school. Then letting them stay all night with friends. Dating. Driving! This was one of those steps. And I had to take it.

"Sure," I said. "He can drive you over, but I want to talk to him first."

"Okay," she said. "He's out on the back porch with Dad."

"What?" I exclaimed. I sat there speechless as she ran out onto the back porch and dragged Riley into the living room. He had his hands shoved into his pockets and gave me a sheepish smile. I was fairly certain I had been set up. "Riley, hi."

"Hi," he said. "You wanted to see me?"

"Yes," I said. "I've got some questions for you. If you answer them correctly, then you are allowed to drive my daughter places."

"All right," he said. "Shoot."

"What does 'be home by nine' mean to you, exactly?"

"It means be home by nine," Riley said.

"By nine. Not five after," I said.

"Right."

"Get yourself a good watch," I said. "On your family tree, were your grandparents related to each other?"

"I . . . don't . . . think . . . so."

"That's always good," I said. "Who was last year's Playmate of the Year?"

"Mom!" Rachel squealed.

"I don't know," he said, blushing.

"Good answer!" I said and clapped. "What does the term 'pornography' mean to you?"

"Oh, my God, Mother," Rachel said. She hid her face.

"It means . . . not good?" he asked and glanced around as if the walls would help him.

"What does fifty-five mean to you?" I asked.

"Fifty-five."

"Not sixty. Speed limit, fifty-five. Not sixty," I said.

"Right," he said. "Is that it?"

"Nope," I said. "I've got a few more." I was having way too much fun with this.

"Do you own a van, a pickup truck, a motorcycle, or a Winnebago?"

"No to all of them," he said.

"Who's the monarch of England?"

"Elizabeth," he said. Hey, points for him that he didn't think a monarch was a butterfly.

"What is the most important subject in school?" I asked.

"Oh, Mom, can I help him with this one?" she asked.

"History," he said and smiled.

"And when a girl says no, what does she mean, exactly?" I asked.

"She means ask me again later," he said and smiled again.

I just glared at him.

"She means no," he said quickly. "Sorry."

I smiled. "All right, last question. Who loves Rachel more than anything?"

"You do," he said.

"Yes, I do. Don't give me any reason for my heart to be broken," I said a little too seriously. He nodded his head. We understood each other. "You passed the test, Riley. Now, I just hope that Rudy never gives you his list of questions. I guarantee you won't pass."

"Yes, ma'am," he said.

"All right," I said. "I'm going upstairs. Where are Mary and Matthew?"

"Backyard with Dad," Rachel said, staring into Riley's eyes. Oh, gag.

I headed upstairs and booted up my computer first thing. Just as I was putting on my jammies, the phone rang. I answered it. "Hello?"

"It's Collette," she said. "I've got a ton of info for you. Can you meet me somewhere?

301

Preferably outside of New Kassel. I need to get out."

"Sure," I said. "Name your place."

"Tucker's, up in South County," she said.

"On South Lindbergh and Union?"

"Yup," she said. "I'll be in the smoking section."

"All right," I said. "I'll be right there."

Tucker's has great food, but it isn't real kid friendly, so I rarely eat there. It sits across Lindbergh from the mall and across Union from the Best Buy. I walked in and was overcome by smoke, so I'm not sure there was a smoking section. It all seemed to be equally cloudy. I told the hostess that I was looking for somebody, and she pointed around the corner to where Collette was sitting at a small table, puffing away on a cigarette. "Thanks," I said to the hostess. The room was dark, with warm glowing yellow lights. I sat down across from Collette, and she smiled.

"Eat," she said.

"What? It's like nine thirty at night," I said.

"Eat anyway," she said. "I'm buying."

The waitress came over, and I ordered the grilled chicken breast with baked potato, salad with ranch dressing, and a glass of water. Collette cocked one eyebrow and stubbed her cigarette out in the ashtray.

"I got bad news," I said.

"What?"

"They just found Mrs. Castlereagh washed up on the riverbank down in Ste. Gen. Evidently something snagged the body and brought her to the bank, or she never would have been found," I said.

"Oh, no," she said.

"She was wearing concrete shoes," I said. "I don't know who got to her, Collette, but I know it was mob related. I just know it."

"What about Bill?"

"No trace yet, but I don't think his chances are very good," I said. "I just keep thinking about his kids. I mean, to lose both parents so suddenly. It's going to be really hard for them. But what did you get me up here to tell me?"

"I got information on the families. Tito de Rosa is not only the son of Victor de Rosa, he's the baby son, Victor's favorite. Word is he's grooming Tito to take over the family business when Victor retires," she said.

"And the family business is what, exactly?" I asked.

"Well, the business that we know about is exercise videos, believe it or not. They also own a few nightclubs along the lake," she said. "Authorities are almost certain that the video business is a front for smuggling. And it's a well-known fact that Victor was responsible for the murders of the three Baietto brothers. They just can't prove it. Victor will never serve time for it, but everybody in Chicago knows he did it."

"Wait," I said and held up a hand. "Did you say Baietto?"

"Yeah," she said. "Why?"

"The body that fell off of the paddle wheel during the parade was a Baietto," I said.

She swallowed hard. "Shit," she said. "I just swallowed my gum."

"Well, that's bad," I said.

"I know," she said. "Now I have to get a high colonic."

I made a peculiar face. I wasn't entirely sure what that was, but I knew it had something to do with a high-powered enema, and that didn't sound pleasant.

"Anyway, about two years ago there was a full-blown war going on between these two families," she said. "Supposedly it went back even further than that. It had something to do with the fact that Victor had eloped with Christian Baietto's granddaughter. Christian Baietto wasn't too happy about that, especially since they were Catholic. If you elope you don't get the sacrament, you know? So

Christian Baietto just knew for sure his granddaughter was going to hell for living in sin. Eventually they had a formal church ceremony, though. I found the announcement. However, Christian Baietto wasn't invited. That went over like a ton of bricks. He had Victor's accountant killed and then his brother."

"I guess they have large families so that they have family left over after everybody's done killing each other," I said.

"Or you have no family at all. That way, there's no weak spot. Family makes you vulnerable," she said.

"Oh," I said. "Right."

"At any rate," Collette said. "I think this feud has been going on for the better part of thirty years."

"All right," I said. "Well, what the heck are they doing in New Kassel and why have they brought their feud to my town?"

"That I don't know."

"Did you find out anything about Bill Castlereagh?" I asked. "I mean, have you found any connection between him and either of the families?"

"No," she said. She lit up another cigarette and pulled the smoke toward her as if that would keep it from assaulting me. Collette has smoked for a while, but I've spent a whole day with her before and not seen her light up. The fact that she was on her second cigarette in less than ten minutes told me that she was anxious.

"Why are you so nervous?" I asked, eyeing the cigarette.

"A person could die," she said. "Just from investigating these people. I cannot believe the son of Victor de Rosa was in your office!"

"I can't believe I made fun of him," I said.

She shook her head and laughed. "You got more balls than most men I know," Collette said.

"Thanks, I think." I was busy contemplating whether or not it was a good thing to be a woman and have that much testosterone when our dinner arrived. Actually, I wasn't very hungry. I'd already eaten, it was late, and . . . well, Mrs. Castlereagh's cadaver-blue face kept flashing in my mind. Still, Collette was buying, and if I didn't eat she'd get upset, so I made a good show of it.

"So, what do you think Bill's connection is to these people?" she asked as she cut into a medium-rare steak.

"I don't know. Colin seems to think it's a gambling debt," I said. "Does either family own casinos here? I mean, I can't even figure out when Bill would have been in Chicago long enough to get into that kind of debt. The last time he left for more than three days was when they took a cruise, back in '99."

Collette's face fell. "The fact that you know that about him is pathetic," she said. "You so need to get out of that town."

"He lives right next door. Of course I'm going to know when he's gone," I said.

"I don't know when my next-door neighbors are gone. Hell, the guy three doors down from me was dead for a week before anybody on my street noticed."

"See?" I said. "That's the sad thing about big cities. Nobody would ever be dead in his home for a week in New Kassel without somebody knowing about it."

She waved her fork at me and made a face.

"So, if I ask you something will you give me an honest answer?" I asked.

"Me? I'm incapable of giving anything other than the blatantly, scathingly honest truth," she said.

"Do you think I'm overbearing?" I asked.

"Of course," she said and took a bite of steak. "It's your God-given right as a woman and a wife to be so."

"I'm serious. I've overheard a few conversations . . . Lord only knows the ones I haven't heard," I said.

"About?"

"Well, me, and how people are happy that I'm moving out of town and how maybe Rudy can be in control of his marriage for once."

Collette gave me a serious look and stopped chewing. Then she burst into laughter and showed me the better portion of the chewed-up cow in her mouth. "Rudy will never be in control of his marriage, because he'll never be in control of you. No matter where the hell you live. You're a free spirit, Torie, old gal. No matter how much you try to hide it in that stupid little town."

"I don't hide it," I said. "Obviously."

"Look," she said, and grabbed my hand. "If Rudy was unhappy he woulda left a long time ago. I don't think he's unhappy. Honestly. Yes, I think you're overbearing and stubborn and nosy and you overreact and jump to conclusions all the time, but, God, Torie, that's why we all love you. Do you think Sylvia would have left her fortune to anybody less deserving? Honey, she hand-picked you."

"Thanks," I said. "I'm not sure I actually feel better, but since you seem to mean it as a compliment, then I'll take it as one."

"Good," she said. "Now, eat."

Twenty-two

The next morning, I was sitting in my office gazing longingly out the window that showed River Pointe Road and the lace shop. I couldn't stand it. I had to get out. I grabbed my purse and went shopping. A rarity for me, yes. It smelled like autumn outside. Woodsmoke drifted on the wind; a slight scent of hay was all around. I decided to do something special for dinner tonight. I stopped by the Grapes of Kath and got a bottle of wine. I really like sweet wines. They're harder to find than dry ones, but Kathy knows exactly what I like. She put a bottle of port on the counter just as I walked in. I paid for it and went down to the tearoom and bought some tea. I ended up at the tobacco shop. It was closed.

I had no idea whether Colin had spoken to Tiny Tim since the incident at the mayor's house. I was not in his circle of those who needed to know, and I'd forgotten to coerce it out of him. I wondered briefly if I should tell Tito that Tiny Tim had not opened his shop. I decided I would call Tito and let him know as soon as I got back to the office. I crossed the street and stopped at Debbie's Cookie Cutter. I picked up a dozen of her peanut butter cookies and then another assorted dozen. Debbie's cookies are so good that her store manages to thrive in a town with two other bakeries. As I was headed out the door, I noticed a sign in the window.

Don't forget your mother this holiday season. Give her a gift certificate from Debbie's Cookie Cutter.

It seemed a little early to be thinking about the holidays. Wait . . . *Don't forget your mother.* Something occurred to me then. Something I hadn't thought to check.

I all but ran back to the Gaheimer House. I skidded to a halt, opened the front door, and sprinted to my office. I pulled out the white pages for St. Louis and looked up the last name Castlereagh. I ran my finger down the page. Castlereagh, Lucy.

"Oh, shoot," I said and ran back and set the alarm. Then I ran back to the office. I picked up the phone and dialed the Murdoch. "Eleanore, it's Torie. Can I speak to Collette?"

"Room number, please?" she said.

"Eleanore, I don't know the room number, just give me her room."

"I can't do that. Against regulations," she said.

"Eleanore! It's me, Torie. I know Collette is there. Just connect me."

"Fine," she said.

A few seconds later, "Hello?"

"Collette, it's Torie. Are you busy?"

"Nope," she said.

"You want to go visit somebody with me?"

"Who?"

"Bill's mother," I said. "I don't know why I didn't think of this before. Bill put down that his mother died in 1968. It never even occurred to me that he could have been lying about her. She's in the phone book!"

"I'll meet you on the porch of the Murdoch," she said. "Five minutes."

Five minutes for Collette almost always means ten, so I had time to set my purchases down and walk over without running. First, though, I booted up the computer and went to Bill's Web site. I printed out the picture of him as a baby, then one of him with his whole family. They might come in handy.

A few minutes later we were on our way to

see Lucy Castlereagh. We drove in Collette's little red sports car, the windows down, our hair flipping all around in the cool morning.

"I can't believe I never thought to look before," I said.

"What made you think to look this time?" she said.

"A window sign at Debbie's Cookie Cutter," I said and laughed.

According to the white pages, Lucy Castlereagh lived in a house on Litzsinger. Parts of Litzsinger were really ritzy and expensive. However, her house number was not in that neighborhood. "Have you got a street guide?" I asked.

"Under the seat," she said.

I checked it and found the block number for the address in the white pages. Lucy lived just north of Manchester Road, east of Brentwood. Collette cranked the car radio, and we listened to music all the way up Highway 270 and then down 44. I was far too nervous to have a coherent conversation, and the music helped me calm down and focus. I had no idea what I was going to say to Lucy Castlereagh when she opened that door, provided she was home, but it was now or never. Hopefully, she would be able to tell me her son's secrets.

About a half hour later, we were parked on

her street, looking at a very cute and cozy brick house. We watched the house for a few minutes. There was no obvious activity going on, but that didn't mean she wasn't home. She was an older lady, after all.

"Well?" Collette said. "Did we drive all the way up here just to look at her house or what?"

"No," I said. "I'm going. Come on."

We stepped onto the porch. I knocked and looked around the neighborhood. A spider had made a huge web in the bush next to the porch. I studied the spider as he worked, waiting for Lucy Castlereagh to answer the door. Just as I was about to give up, the latch on the door quietly turned.

A very small blue-haired woman answered the door. "Mrs. Castlereagh?" I asked.

"Yes," she said. "You're not Jehovah's Witnesses, are you?"

"No," I said, smiling.

"Good, 'cause I ran them off not three days ago."

"No," I said. "I'm not from any church. I'm actually from a small town south of here. I wanted to ask you some questions about your son."

"You reporters?"

"I am," Collette said, "but this isn't for a piece. This is personal."

"Personal?" she asked. "Which son is this about?"

"Bill," I said.

"Bill's dead," she said.

I glanced at Collette. Had they found the mayor's body overnight? I hadn't even thought to turn on the news, and I felt fairly certain that Colin would not have called me to tell me. "Ma'am," I said, "can we please come in and talk to you about him? This is my friend Collette. My name is Torie."

"Well, all right. Not sure what good it'll do. Been through all this already. Seems every few years somebody finds out and they all come around and ask me a bunch of questions again." I had no idea what she was talking about, but I let her talk. She opened the door and let us into a spotless and sparsely decorated home, with hardwood floors and a dozen or so gorgeous plants. They were the healthiest houseplants I'd ever seen. That was one more domestic mystery that I had never cracked. I killed everything. If it was green, it'd be brown within a week in my house.

"Would you like something to drink?" she asked.

"No, thank you. We'll make this quick," I said.

She sat down, cautiously at first. Then she stared out the window.

"Mrs. Castlereagh, we're very sorry for your loss," I said.

She shrugged her shoulders together and suddenly looked about sixteen. With wrinkles, of course, but the motion was so childlike, it instantly made me think of youth. "It's not like I really knew him."

I sighed. "Well, first of all, I want to know if you've ever lived in New Kassel, Missouri, or Granite County."

"Heavens, no," she said. "So what is all of this about?"

"Well, your son went missing about a week back, and there's been a lot of unusual activity in our town, and I was wondering if you could maybe help us shed some light on the situation . . ." Lucy Castlereagh's face had grown white with horror. She stood abruptly and headed toward the door.

"You can leave now," she said.

"I'm sorry," I said. "I . . ."

"Did we say something wrong?" Collette asked.

"I don't know what game you're playing at," she said, "but my son has been dead for fifty-six years."

I shivered. "The baby that died," I whispered. "Mrs. Castlereagh, I am so sorry. I

315

think there's been a terrible mistake. Your son Bill — William Jarvis Castlereagh — is the mayor of New Kassel, where I live."

"My son William Jarvis Castlereagh died when he wasn't but two days old," she said. "I don't understand."

Collette looked at me, confused, then said to Lucy, "Please, come back and sit down."

Lucy did, but she sat with such trepidation that I couldn't help but feel sorry for her. "I had Bill at home. No trouble. I was up walking around after a few hours. I was in the kitchen," she said. "Looking at a picture that my other son had drawn for me. I'd left Bill lying on the bed, with pillows propped around him. The doorbell rang, and I went and answered it. It was my mother-in-law. She came in and talked for a while and then asked if she could see Bill. I told her he was back in the bedroom. When she went back there . . ." Her voice trailed off, and for a moment I wasn't sure she was going to finish the story.

"Somehow he'd gotten one of the pillows over his face. He'd stopped breathing."

"I'm so sorry," I said.

"When my mother-in-law gave her statement to the police, they thought I had done it. They arrested me, but they couldn't prove anything."

Collette and I were deathly quiet.

"I did not kill my son," she said.

I reached into my purse and pulled out the two photographs that I had printed from Bill's Web site. I handed her the one of Bill as a baby, sitting in his front yard, with the Mississippi in the distance. "Are you trying to tell me that this isn't your son?" I asked.

"No, I already told you. He lived just under two days."

"Do you recognize this man?" I asked, and handed her the picture of Bill and his family.

She shook her head in the negative.

I leaned back on the couch and sighed.

"I don't get it," Collette said. "What's going on?"

"I knew I was going to feel stupid once I figured this out. It's identity theft. You find an infant that died at birth, or close to it, and you take his birth certificate and get a Social Security number, and you take on his identity. It's a lot harder nowadays, but back in the fifties or sixties it was a lot easier. I'm assuming Bill did this in the sixties, since he showed up in New Kassel in 1969 as Bill Castlereagh." I ran my fingers through my hair and let out an exasperated sigh. "I can't believe I didn't see it."

"I don't understand," Lucy said.

"Mrs. Castlereagh, I am so sorry to have

bothered you today. I think the man who is the mayor of our town has stolen your son's identity," I said.

"Why?" she asked.

"I'm not sure," I said, "but I think he might have gotten into some trouble. At any rate, I am so sorry."

"Well," she said, "I guess your mayor must have needed it. And since my boy never got to use it, guess it doesn't hurt none."

Her attitude surprised me. Some people would have been really upset if somebody had stolen their child's identity. I thought about Bill's wife and her cement shoes. I wouldn't say nobody was hurt by his actions. Collette and I said good-bye to Lucy Castlereagh. I must have apologized another ten times for bothering her before I made it out the front door.

As we stepped out into the late October sun, I glanced over at Collette, who was speechless. I shook my head as we made our way down the stairs to the car. We got in and drove away, and it must have been a good two or three minutes before I finally exploded.

"It was all a lie!" I said.

"What do you mean?" she asked.

"All of it. The whole damn family tree was a lie."

"After all of that, you're upset because Bill faked his family tree?" she asked.

"No, Collette," I said. "I'm just saying that his whole life was a lie. Not only is he not Bill Castlereagh, but he couldn't just stop the lie with Bill Castlereagh's family tree. No, he had to go in and connect the real William Jarvis Castlereagh's family tree to a bunch of prestigious family trees. He wasn't satisfied with the identity he'd stolen. He had to make it better," I said. "I can't believe this. Do his children know? Did his wife know?"

"I don't know," she said. "But you know what I'm wondering?"

"What?"

"Not who he isn't. Who he really is," she said.

"I betcha I can tell you within the hour," I said.

"Really?" she asked.

"Yup. But you're going to have to do some breaking and entering with me," I said. I had a feeling if I could just get to that metal cabinet in Bill's garage, we would get answers.

"I've got my nail set," she said and laughed.

Twenty-three

I felt vaguely like Collette and I were Thelma and Louise as we stooped on the mayor's front porch with a flashlight and her nail file set. Of course, I realized with some trepidation that things didn't end well for Thelma and Louise. At any rate, we had decided to wait until dark to break into the mayor's house, basically because we didn't want to get caught. The fact that we didn't want to get caught was a sure-fire giveaway that we knew that what we were doing was wrong. I'd deal with that later. I should probably make an extra-long appointment with Father Bingham.

Right now, I was just grateful that only one neighbor could see the front of Bill's house, and that was me. On one side of Bill's house were the woods, across the street was the river, and behind his house was a neighbor whose house faced the other direction. So I figured we were pretty safe. Still, we waited until dark.

Collette said a few cuss words, and finally the lock gave a *chunk* sound and the door opened. "I don't want to know how you knew how to do that," I said.

"Oh, please," she said. "Are you trying to tell me you've never broken into anything?"

I was silent. Not only had I entered premises I shouldn't have in the past, but even Mary had done so on a few occasions. I thought about that for a second, and the implications were too scary for me to confront on the mayor's doorstep.

"That's what I thought," she said. "Try being Saint Torie with somebody else. Won't fly with me, sugar."

"All right, all right," I said. "You don't have to be snotty."

She opened the door and held her hand out, gesturing for me to enter. "Oh, I get to go first, eh?" I asked.

"This is your case," she said.

I stepped inside the dark house and stopped — sooner than Collette expected me to, I guess. She crashed into me, which pitched me forward. I landed spread-eagle on the floor, the wind gushing out of me. "God," I said. "Will you watch where you're going?"

"I'd be happy to watch, if I could see," she whispered.

We both managed to get to our feet. I headed straight for the garage door with the help of a flashlight. Dark smudges all over the doorknob showed where the CSU had taken fingerprints. Mine were among them, I reminded myself. Collette flashed the light on, and we stepped into the garage. We glanced around to make sure nobody was going to jump out at us.

The coast was clear, so I went over to the metal cabinet. I yanked on the door and knelt at the same time, and when I did a stray cat jumped out of a corner and squealed. Collette nearly died right then and there. "Oh, Jesus Christ!" she called out.

"Take it easy," I said, heart hammering in my throat.

"Take it easy? I think I peed in my pants," she said. "Does urine stain?"

"Not if you wash it out," I said. I yanked on the shelf in the bottom of the cabinet and it came up easier than the first time I'd discovered it. "Give me the flashlight."

I grabbed the light from Collette and flashed it into the hiding space of the cabinet. I reached in and pulled the papers out and sat down on the floor of the garage. "Get up off the floor," she said to me.

"Shh!" I said. I held the flashlight in my mouth and gazed at the papers I held in my hand. There was what I assumed to be the mayor's real birth certificate. "Carmine Antonio de Luca."

"All this time the mayor was a wop?" she asked.

"Collette, that's not nice."

"Hey, my grandmother was from Sicily. I'm allowed to say that. What else did you find?"

"He was born in Chicago. Uh, here are his graduation papers. Some banking records. A few deeds to property," I said.

"What? Like his house?" she asked.

"I'm assuming, since these were hidden, that no, these aren't to this house." I looked at them closer. One was for a piece of land in Nevada. A house in Boston. A house in St. Louis.

"What's he doing with all that real estate?" she asked.

"I don't know."

"Wait," she said. "Did you say de Luca was his name?"

"Yes," I said. "Why?"

"I can't remember exactly, but I know the de Luca family had something to do with the Baiettos. They were allies," she said.

"Okay, that's making more sense," I said.

"All right, can we get out of here now? Our life of crime is creeping me out," she said.

Suddenly a voice came from the door leading into the living room. "Freeze! Put your hands on your head!"

I looked up just as Lou Counts flipped on the garage light.

"Oh, great," I said, standing slowly. I shoved the papers behind me onto a shelf, and raised my hands.

"Who is that?" Collette said.

"New deputy."

"She needs a manicure something fierce. God, and who does her hair?"

"I knew you couldn't stay away," Lou said to me. She was so proud of herself. "You think you're such hot stuff. I knew if I just waited around here, you'd be back."

"Congratulations," I said. "You're smarter than the sheriff."

"That's not saying much," Collette said out of the corner of her mouth. "Can we put our hands down now?"

"Your prints were all over that cabinet," Lou said. "How stupid do you think we are?"

"Did you bother to look in the bottom of the cabinet?" I asked.

"No," she said, gripping her gun tighter.

"Then you're pretty stupid."

"Torie, the woman is holding a gun on us, could you not insult her?" Collette asked.

"Right," I said. Forgot about that.

"Come on," Lou waved. "You're under arrest."

"Fine, Lou, but first you need to call Colin and tell him that I've figured out the whole thing with Bill. They haven't found him dead yet, right? So he could still be out there alive. And I might know where he is." Nevada, maybe. Or Boston. Or St. Louis.

Lou never got a chance to spout whatever sassy thing she wanted to say to me, because at that point she was hit over the head with something heavy. She slumped to the floor. Standing behind her was Tito de Rosa.

"Now what were you saying about knowing where to find Carmine?" Tito asked.

Twenty-four

"I take it back, Torie," Collette said. "How I ever could have thought that New Kassel was boring is beyond me. How do you get yourself into so much trouble?"

"I think it's safe to say that it's an art form," I said.

"Shut up!" Tito said. He motioned a gun at us. "Out to the car. Put your hands down, though. I don't want any attention."

Collette and I walked out to his car through the mayor's living room with our hands down. I glanced over at my house. *Come on, Rudy, just once be nosy and look out the window!* Of course, I knew that wouldn't happen. Tito made Collette get in the backseat and me in the front. He held a gun up to my head and glanced back at Collette. I've never in my life felt anything colder than the barrel of that gun.

"One false move and your friend will have a new hat size, okay?"

Collette gulped. "Okay," she said.

We drove away. I looked out the window as my house faded from sight. I was overwhelmed with the fact that I might never see it again. Or the people inside. Tears welled in my eyes, and for one second I thought I was going to be one of those crazed women in the movies who start begging for their lives and promising things that they don't have. I took a deep breath and fought back the tears. *Think, dammit!*

I was fairly certain Collette had her cell phone in her jacket pocket. She could probably get to it without Tito noticing. If only I could let her know what I was thinking. God, being without super powers really sucked.

Tito took the Outer Road, and we drove right by the very place where the motorcycle assassins had struck the night of the hayride. "So, were the motorcycle guys yours?" I asked.

"Shut up," he said.

"You're going to kill us anyway," I said. "Why not tell me?"

"Torie, could you please not use sentences with words like 'kill' in them?" Collette asked.

327

"What? You think he won't think of killing us unless I remind him?" I said.

"You're always so negative," she said. "Think positive. Think like he's a generous, God-fearing man and then maybe he will be."

Right, that's why I keep thinking about having you use your damn cell phone and you don't!

"Both of you shut up," Tito said.

Within a few minutes I understood where we were going. The construction site of my new home. He pulled the car into the makeshift gravel driveway and cut the engine. "Get out," he said.

"Oh, Jesus," Collette said. "Torie, I love you."

"I love you, too," I said.

"Oh, please shut up," Tito said. "Now get out of the car."

"Look," I said, "I'm not dying until you tell me what the hell is going on."

Tito laughed. It was a genuine laugh, and for just a split second I understood how he functioned in the real world. If I hadn't known that he was a Mafia man, a hit man, the son of the Godfather, I would have thought him to be a very charming Italian guy with expensive taste in shoes.

"All right, Torie," he said. "Here's a little bedtime story for you."

I loved this part. Because while the bad guy was busy telling me what he did or didn't do, it bought me time either to think of a way out of this mess or to have somebody show up on a white horse and rescue us.

"Carmine was the golden boy of the de Luca family. The de Luca family were a neutral family in the early sixties," he said. "Then they aligned themselves with our enemies."

"The Baiettos," I said.

"Very good," he said. He waved a gun at us and made us start walking behind the pile of wood and cement that would someday be my house. A house I might never get the chance to actually live in. Only the moonlight illuminated our path. "But Carmine had fallen in love with my aunt, my father's sister, Lily. It was impossible for them to be together, but Carmine wouldn't listen."

I found it hard to imagine Carmine — "Bill" — in any romantic entanglement whatsoever, but I'd go with the moment. What choice did I have? But I still didn't understand why anybody would want him.

"He got my aunt pregnant," Tito said. "My grandfather went nuts. Here his daughter was not only pregnant without being married, but she was pregnant by a man who was now our sworn enemy."

I could see where this was going, but I'd just let him keep talking because we were running out of time and I still hadn't figured out a way to get us out of this whole mess. I glanced into the darkness of the woods. There was nothing there but owls and hawks and deer. Maybe a coyote. The only out I could find was to run. The terrain was unfamiliar, and Tito would most likely start shooting, but being shot while running away seemed better than being shot while looking at the barrel of the gun. I think my logic may have been flawed there, but I was fairly hysterical.

"My grandfather sent my aunt back to the old country to have her baby, because he wasn't about to let them get married. The baby was put up for adoption somewhere in Florence. Where I'm assuming it is still living."

"Okay," Collette said. "So how did all of that end up with Carmine becoming our mayor?"

"Well, as you might expect, the Baietto family told Carmine to get out of town and never come back," Tito said. "But Carmine couldn't just leave. He couldn't let my grandfather win. So he managed to steal four million dollars from my grandfather. In the process, there was an accident and several of my father's top men were killed. My grandfather swore revenge and put a warrant out for Carmine's death. Warrants don't expire when the head of the family dies or retires."

"So all of this time you've been looking for Bill?"

"Not actively looking, but we all knew what had to be done if we ever did find him," he said. "I know four million doesn't seem like that much money nowadays, but back then it was significant. It was the death of my grandfather's men and the . . . deflowering of his daughter that signed Carmine's death warrant."

"I don't understand," I said. "Where does Tiny Tim fit into this?"

"Yeah," Collette said. "What about Tiny Tim?"

Apparently she was aware of the fact that I was trying to buy us time. Little did she know that I actually was just that nosy and couldn't die without knowing the truth. Because I was fairly certain that there wasn't a way out.

"Tiny Tim works for the Baiettos. Evidently there was some sort of sworn allegiance to Carmine. In other words, if Carmine got in trouble, they'd send somebody to help. Tiny Tim was sent to help."

"And the dead guy on the paddle wheel?" I asked.

"He was sent to help Carmine as well. I took him out."

"So who did I see Bill arguing with that night?" I asked, confused.

Tito shrugged. "It might have been Tiny Tim trying to talk Carmine into leaving town." He raised his gun. "All right, Torie. You got your answers. Tell me where Carmine is."

"I can't believe you can just kill a person," Collette spewed at him.

"It's nothing personal," he said.

"It is personal!" Collette said. "Only God has the right to give and take life."

Tito hesitated for a moment. "A little late for that, I'm afraid," he said.

"No, wait!" I said. "You still haven't answered one thing."

"What's that?"

"How did you guys find out that Bill was in New Kassel?" I asked.

"Oh, good question, Torie," Collette said.

"That stupid Web site," Tito said and laughed.

"Huh?" I asked.

"My mother wanted to take a little vacation," he said. "She was surfing the Net looking at places to visit. The Chamber of Commerce Web site for New Kassel has a picture and a link to Carmine's site. My mother saw the picture of Carmine and recognized him."

"Oh," I said. Bill's arrogance wouldn't let him become completely invisible. Guess that just proved that the Internet really did make the world a smaller place. Twenty years ago, probably nobody would have ever found Bill hiding out in this tiny town.

"So all of this was about a thirty-year-old grudge?" I asked.

"Most things are about old grudges, Torie," he said. He waved the gun at me, and Collette started crying. My breath caught in my throat. "Now, where's Carmine?"

"If I tell you, you'll kill us."

"I'm going to anyway," he said. "This will just make my job easier."

"Well, then," I said, sobbing, "you can go straight to hell and look for him yourself."

Out of nowhere Eg Hanshaw came running from around the edge of my new house. He had a big old rifle in his hands. He never even hesitated. He took the rifle, aimed, and shot the gun right out of Tito's hand. Immediately Tito fell to the ground, screaming. Collette collapsed onto her knees, and all I remember about the next ten seconds is wondering if my heart was ever going to beat again.

Eg ran over and put one leg onto Tito's abdomen. He lay writhing in pain on the freshly turned dirt. "Don't move," Eg said to Tito. Then he took his cell phone off of his hip holster, flipped it open, and called the sheriff's department.

"Tell him to send an ambulance to Bill's house. Lou Counts is there unconscious," I said.

Eg nodded and repeated what I said to whoever had answered the sheriff's department phone. I also heard him tell the dispatcher to send an ambulance to the construction site. Finally I could stand no longer. All of the energy seemed to flow out of my fingertips, leaving me feeling like I was near death. I fell to the ground and landed on my back, staring up at the stars. Sobs came in waves, and my heart did little flip-flops. From off to my right, I felt Collette's hand reach over and squeeze mine. I squeezed back and just cried, turning the stars into twinkling lights that fused together.

Twenty-five

I stood in my attic office staring out the window at the snow. Several months had passed since I had almost died in my new backyard. We'd moved into the new house. It was wonderful, but it hadn't started to feel like home yet. I took solace in the horses in the backyard and the family of hawks that seemed to hunt perpetually in my back field. There was no more river out of my window. No more neighbors for me to spy on.

And no more Colin as sheriff.

The phone rang, and I picked it up. It was my mother. "Torie," she said, "I want you to come out to the house, if you can."

"Sure," I said. "I have a few errands to run in town first." Town, of course, meant New Kassel, not Wisteria, where she lived. I was already dressed. I'd been ready to go to town for a while. I'm not sure why I had stood in my office staring out at the snow-covered pasture for a half hour. I suppose part of it was the fact that I love snow. Part of it, I knew, was that I wasn't quite sure what to do with myself. I felt like a stranger in my own house.

I got in the car and drove toward New Kassel. It was a Saturday. Rudy had taken the kids to the movies in Wisteria and left me alone to try to get some work done. I arrived in town, and just the sight of the skyline and the river behind the town seemed to soothe me. I parked at the Gaheimer House and walked down to Debbie's Cookie Cutter and stocked up on chocolate chip cookies. Comfort food.

I was in desperate need of comforting. Collette had taken the job in Tucson, so who knew when I'd see her again? It's not as though she's sentimental and would come home for holidays. No, Collette would just pop into town when I least expected it. I missed her already.

I nearly ran into Sam Hill as I was leaving the Cookie Cutter. "Torie," he said.

"Hi, Sam," I said.

"You ready to give me that interview yet?"

"No," I said.

"Lotsa rumors swirling around," he said. "You could help end that."

"Talk to the new mayor," I said.

"He won't talk to me."

"Sorry."

"Are you coming to the grand opening?" he asked.

"Of what?"

"The microbrewery," he said.

"Oh." I had forgotten that he'd gone ahead with his plans. "When it is?"

"February twentieth," he said. "So you've got a few weeks to clear your calendar. I'll buy you a beer."

"Thanks. I'll be there" I said. I moved past him and out into the snow-covered street. Big, fat, heavy flakes seemed to fall to the ground with a purpose. I love the snow. I looked up the street to where the Murdoch Inn stood at the bend of the creek that shoots off the Mississippi. It was postcard perfect in the snow. Then I glanced back down the street in the other direction. The direction of my old house.

I walked up the road, staying close to the railroad tracks. When I reached the spot, I stopped and turned to look at my old home. There was a new family in there now. There was also a new family in Bill's old house. I stood there long enough to see a little girl run out of what had been the Castlereagh house and meet a little girl from my old house in the front yard. They started building a snowman, and a lump rose in my throat. These neighbors, at least, would be friends.

I swiped at a tear and looked out at Old Man River. The snow dissolved into the gray of the water, floating southward.

Rudy had been right. Bill, or Carmine de Luca, had hated me for a good reason. He knew he was living right next door to the very person who could have destroyed him. I could have discovered his secret at any time if I'd studied his charts long enough, and he knew it. If only he'd let me help him! I knew I could have helped him. If his wife had heeded my warning that very first day, she'd still be alive. Bill would most likely still be sitting in his jail cell, but at least his wife would be alive.

I couldn't believe Bill was in jail, but I guess you can't just steal somebody's identity and get away with it. Not to mention there were things Carmine de Luca had done that Bill would be paying the price for. Some things the statute of limitations did not run out on. Of course, most of that hadn't even gone to trial yet.

The sheriff's car pulled up just as I swiped at the last tear. Mort Joachim got out of the car and walked up next to me. "Mrs. O'Shea," he said and tipped his hat. Mort is

338

younger than I am. It's unsettling when your doctors and law enforcement officers were born when Nixon was in office. In fact, the sheriff standing in front of me was born after man walked on the moon, and somehow that just didn't seem right. He has blond hair and piercing violet eyes. I'd never seen violet eyes on a man before. He looked so wet behind the ears I felt compelled to offer him a towel.

"Call me Torie," I said.

"Look," he said, "I'll get straight to the point."

"What's that?"

"I've got a missing person down in Meyersville," he said. "I think you might be able to help me on this one."

I was stunned. "What?"

"I'm at a loss. Mayor Brooke told me to ask you for help," he said.

"H-he did?" I asked.

"He said it sounded like something you'd be able to solve."

"Oh," I said.

"I can make you a special consultant to my office," the new sheriff said.

"You'd do that?" I asked.

"Your track record is pretty impressive."

"How is Lou?" I asked.

"She came back to work last week," he

said, and glanced out at the river.

"Do you think that might be a problem?" I asked.

"I'll keep you two separated," he said and smiled.

"Well, I don't know what to say . . ."

"Think it over. In the meantime, remember that I've got an eighty-year-old woman who just vanished into the night," he said.

"No," I said. "I don't need to think it over. I'll help."

"Good," he said. "Come by my office and I'll fill you in."

"I will," I said.

He left, and I went back to staring out at the giant body of water. I could barely see to the Illinois side now, the snow was so heavy. I must have stood there for fifteen more minutes when I heard shoes behind me. I turned to find Colin standing there.

"Thought I'd find you here," he said.

I said nothing.

"I wanted to let you know that I visited with Bill in jail. Or Carmine, whichever you want to call him. He said to tell you that Sylvia had helped him with his five-generation charts," Colin said.

I closed my eyes. The woman had been dead for a year now, and yet her presence was still felt throughout the entire town. "Why?"

"He said he threatened her. She believed him, evidently, and helped to create a fake pedigree for him," he said.

"Yeah," I said. "I sort of expected that was the case. Now I even wonder if Sylvia made it too perfect so I would notice."

"Which you did," he said.

I said nothing.

"Torie, look, I'm sorry," he said. "About . . . You know, what I said about you to Mort. And for the things I said about you to other people that you don't even know about. You're my wife's daughter, and it was inappropriate, regardless."

"You're damn right," I said and smiled.

"The deeds that you found led us right to Bill. Once again, you found what I should have found."

I said nothing, because what did a person say to something like that? That was a pretty hefty concession.

"So, are things okay between us?" he asked.

"Things will never be all right between us," I said and laughed. "I hate you, remember?"

"And I think you're a nosy know-it-all."

We laughed together for a moment. "Seriously, Colin. You and Rudy ganging up on me like that. I can't tell you how badly that hurt me."

"I know," he said. "Why do you think I dropped the charges for breaking and entering? Figured I owed you that much." He turned to go, then stopped. "You gonna stare at that river all day?"

"Maybe," I said. He took about ten steps back toward the main part of town. "Colin."

"What?"

"Things are okay."

He smiled and kept walking, and I kept staring out at the river. I went by the Gaheimer House a little while later and talked with my sister for a bit. She was supposed to be giving tours, but with all of the snow, there was no business. She was pregnant again and confused as to how it had happened. I seem to recall feeling that same way when I got pregnant with Matthew.

I ran by my mother's house and visited with her. It seemed as though I was just whiling away the time because I was unsure with what to do with myself. Mom sent me home with lasagna pesto roll-ups and a chocolate cake with peanut butter icing. More comfort food. I love the fact that my mother knows me so well that I don't even have to tell her when something's wrong. She just knows when comfort food is required and delivers.

I pulled my car into the driveway of our new house. It's a beautiful house. A large oak tree stands in the front yard, its tiny top branches stretching into the cotton-stuffed sky. When we'd picked the spot for the house, I had told Eg that I wanted the tree to remain in the front yard. They'd managed not to destroy it during the construction. I sat in the car for a minute, staring up at my new world. Moonstone, the butter-colored horse, came galloping along the fence. He knew I was home.

Somebody tapped on my window, and I jumped. It was Riley. I shut off the car and got out. "Hey, Riley," I said.

"Hi, Mrs. O'Shea," he said. "Can I talk to you?"

"Sure," I said. We started walking toward the house. He seemed nervous.

"I wanted to ask you . . . Well, I sort of bought Rachel a promise ring."

I stopped. "You did what?"

"It's nothing, really. It's not like we're engaged."

"You can't be engaged. I think you have to be of legal age and be able to vote to be engaged. I'm pretty sure that's a requirement somewhere," I said.

"Calm down, Mrs. O'Shea," he said. "It's nothing serious. I . . . I'm just promising to get her an engagement ring . . . someday. That's all it means."

"Oh," I said.

"Like, years down the road. After college," he said.

"Oh," I said, feeling better. College was still in the plans. That was good. "You like her that much?"

"She is the greatest girl I've ever met. I swear, her smile fuels the sun," he said.

I stopped and stared at him. Wow. If he had felt one ounce less for her, he wouldn't have been worthy. But he was worthy. I draped my arm around his shoulder. "You're all right, kid."

We opened the front door, and Matthew came running toward me. "Mommy!"

Rachel met us at the door, and Mary came through the living room carrying a big basket of eggs that she'd just gotten from the chickens. They all dispersed, and I stepped into the kitchen, where Rudy had made a salad and bread to go with the lasagna roll-ups that my mother had sent home. "I hear you got a new job," he said, smiling.

"Huh?" I asked.

"Special consultant to the sheriff's department," he said.

"Yeah," I said and smiled. "You all right with that?"

He glanced around the room and finally stepped over and hugged me. "Yeah," he said. "I think I am. Are you?"

"Yes," I said.

"Come and eat!" Rudy called out to the house at large.

Moonstone wasn't the only one who knew I was home. Suddenly I was filled with a satisfied feeling, and I knew it, too.

About the Author

Rett MacPherson is the author of eight previous Torie O'Shea novels. She lives with her husband and three children in a suburb of St. Louis, Missouri.